SCATTERLINGS

Isobelle Carmody

SCHOLASTIC

For Nanny and Pop Carmody,
who gave refuge to this scatterling

Scholastic Children's Books,
Scholastic Publications Ltd,
7–9 Pratt Street, London NW1 0AE, UK

Scholastic Inc.,
555 Broadway, New York, NY 10012–3999, USA

Scholastic Canada Ltd,
123 Newkirk Road, Richmond Hill,
Ontario, Canada L4C 3G5

Ashton Scholastic Pty Ltd,
PO Box 579, Gosford, New South Wales,
Australia

Ashton Scholastic Ltd,
Private Bag 92801, Penrose, Auckland,
New Zealand

First published in Australia by Penguin Books, Australia Ltd, 1991
First published in the UK by Scholastic Publications Ltd, 1995

ISBN 0 590 55905 2

Typeset by DP Photosetting, Aylesbury, Bucks
Printed by Cox & Wyman Ltd, Reading, Berks

10 9 8 7 6 5 4 3 2 1

For a long time there was silence and endless sleep.

Then came a grinding sound – a metallic scream and a dazzling flash of whiteness.

A voice screamed in fierce celebration: "*Hallelujah!*" as if from inside the dream. It was such a peculiar sensation that she came closer to waking, too close to retreat back into the quiet shadows of unconsciousness.

Something was covering her face, pressing against her lips.

Feeling half suffocated, she clawed her way free.

She was in the back of a van surrounded by blankets, pieces of broken glass and unfamiliar implements. Through a dark tinted window under her, running the length of the cabin, she could see foliage pressed against the glass. A matching window above showed the sky. Clearly she had been in an accident and the van had overturned.

She sat up, fighting a dizzy sickness, wondering if this meant she had been hurt. Her throat felt raw and bruised.

Trying to remember what had caused the accident, she became aware of a fierce hissing noise in the cabin. Gas!

Her heart juddered into a faster, uneven rhythm. Get out, she told her sluggish limbs. Move!

Disorientated by the angle of the vehicle, she was unable to find the door, but the thick window glass was broken at one end. Pulling herself nearer, she gagged at the acrid smell of mashed foliage which flowed through the opening. She smashed at the glass, making the hole bigger. The glass was surprisingly tough.

Fortunately the van was not flush with the ground and there was enough of a gap to allow her to slide out.

She went head first; a faint, hot breeze blowing against her face. It was a tight squeeze and the effort made her head ache. Absently she noticed the van was white.

"Ambulances are vehicles which are painted white and carry sick people to hospital buildings where

they can be treated ..." said a queer staccato voice inside her mind.

Ambulance, she thought dazedly. I was in the back of an ambulance so there must have been something wrong with me before the accident.

The metal above her creaked alarmingly, and she made a last violent effort to free herself from under the vehicle before whatever was holding it up gave way.

Once out, she laid her head on the ground, waiting for the waves of sickness to recede.

Something crawled down her neck. Irritated she batted at it. Her face felt wet. She brought her fingers up to her eyes and stared at their red tips. My blood, she thought, sickened. Maybe she had head injuries and that was why she had been in an ambulance. She couldn't remember the moments leading up to the accident, and that meant she must have been unconscious when it happened. She swallowed convulsively, wondering how badly she was hurt. She did not feel any really serious pain, only weakness and bruising.

"*Serious injuries are often completely painless ...*" the clipped internal voice offered.

She blinked, startled.

The van creaked again and the hissing intensified. She dragged herself away, driven by an instinct of danger that bypassed the fog and the queer voices in her mind. Her thoughts moved sluggishly, as if her head were full of wadded cotton.

Maybe I'm drugged, she thought.

A loud groan stopped her and a realisation struggling through the mental soup broke through to the surface. If she had been the passenger, there must have been someone driving. Someone was still inside the ambulance!

Grimly, she worked her knees up under her body. She paused, gathered her strength and pushed herself back onto her knees. She was nightmarishly weak.

She did not know how she could help the driver. She stared at the overturned wreck, struck by its unusual shape. It had seemed odd from the inside, but she had attributed that to the vehicle being upside down. But even crumpled and overturned, it looked like no ambulance she had ever seen. Where were the wheels?

Someone groaned again. "Help . . . me." She could not tell if the driver were male or female.

She reached out and took hold of a low-growing branch of one of the huge twisted trees growing all around, using it to pull herself to her feet. The tree grew aslant out from the hillside and she guessed the road the ambulance had left was higher up the hill.

She swayed groggily. Her lips moved but her voice came out as a breathless croak. She calculated five steps to the edge of the ambulance. It seemed a thousand.

She took one drunken step forward.

The hissing noise rose to a sudden crescendo, ending in a loud, dull thump. The force of the explosion lifted her off her feet and threw her back against the tree. A gout of flame rose, forming an umbrella over the ambulance, then falling to engulf it.

The driver started to scream.

"Maya! Maya! Help me! There's fire ..."

The words disintegrated into shrieks, then into a horrible animal gurgle of agony.

Then there was no noise but the crackle of fire leaping into the trees and brush around the van.

"Death is a thing all humans fear, because it is a mystery each must face alone ..." whispered a new voice, a boy's voice.

Dazed with horror, she stared at the burning wreckage.

A smell wafted on the breeze. Her stomach rumbled hungrily at the scent of roasting meat to be replaced abruptly by a curling revulsion at the realization that the smell came from the burning driver.

Her stomach lurched and she leaned forward, vomiting with savage force on the ground at her feet. Little was ejected but a thin bile, but she continued to heave and retch until she was nearly suffocated. The smell of burning flesh filled the air and disgust gave her the strength to stagger away from the sight and smell of the ravaged vehicle.

Tears streamed down her face at the memory of the voice, begging for help. She shuddered, knowing she might easily have shared the driver's gruesome fate. She wondered how long before help would come.

Pressing her hands to her head, she tried to remember why she had been in the ambulance. What was the last thing she remembered? A blur of images filled her mind, tilting and swirling like pieces of glass in a kaleidoscope.

"*Your name is Merlin,*" said the boy's voice in her mind, whispery and edged with inexplicable sadness.

The name felt like it belonged to a stranger. Aloud, it sounded like something she was saying for the first time.

She pressed her fingers into the eye sockets hard enough to make her eyeballs ache. She breathed slowly and deeply, deliberately thinking of nothing; of the lovely deep blackness from which the accident had wrenched her. Gradually her heartbeat slowed. She opened her eyes.

All around were the immense trees. If she wandered away from the wreckage, no one would ever find her. They might even think she had been burnt. She guessed she was on an experimental government farm by the size of the trees.

"*The government has begun to look at new ways of increasing timber yields. Genetic manipulation of certain varieties has produced giant trees whose timber yield is extraordinarily high,*" offered the mechanical inner voice.

The sound of footsteps cut through her confusion.

"*Movement alerts the hunter to the whereabouts of the hunted, when stillness would have made them all but invisible,*" advised the dry inner voice.

"Come in, Sedgewick," said a voice distorted by a loud burst of static.

"Sedgewick here," a youthful masculine voice responded.

The first voice answered over what sounded like a two-way radio: "Have you seen anything of her yet?" The speaker was an older man with a smooth, peremptory way of speaking. Someone used to ordering other people around, Merlin thought. Obviously both man and boy belonged to a rescue team. She opened her mouth to call out.

"Do you think I am a savage to track footprints in the dirt?" Sedgewick asked resentfully.

There was a slight pause. Merlin waited for the older man to respond, puzzled by the antagonism between the pair.

Another burst of static, then the man answered in measured tones. "You are certain she was not burned?"

"It looks like she got out through a broken window. We'll need heatseekers to find her. We should have brought them with us."

"No one expected that she would need to be

searched for," the man said coldly. "She could not have the wit nor the desire to hide."

Merlin was very still. She did not like the way the older man talked about her. What did he mean she didn't have the wit and why should she want to hide from a rescue party? She felt curiously unwilling to alert the pair to her presence. If they were a rescue party, there was something very odd about them.

The youth was speaking again. She could not see him, but judged him to be less than a few metres away. "Well, she has gone. The flier is a burnt-out mess and there is no signal on the tracer."

She frowned. Flier? That explained why the ambulance had looked so queer, and why she had been unable to see the road. But even for a light plane or helicopter, it had a strange shape.

A sophisticated sounding woman cut in on the transmission. "Andrew, her instinct for self-protection may have been aroused by the nearness of danger. She is functioning in some form; that is obvious. The question is, how far is she restored? I believe we would have found her by now if she were simply wandering aimlessly."

"Unless she is hurt, Sacha," the man answered smoothly. "I seriously doubt that she is fully functioning, whatever the stimulus. Just the same, we will return for the heatseekers, if only to ensure finding her before she makes contact. She must not be allowed to communicate with any of the outsiders. That would be disastrous. She would be contaminated."

The woman called Sacha interrupted. "You heard the flight recording. It was sabotage. The scatterlings may have her."

"I see no reason to believe this was any more than random sabotage by the scatterlings. They couldn't even know she existed. Oren should have been more careful."

"Well, what are we to do now?" Sedgewick asked impatiently.

"I have said already we will return for the heatseekers. Come back to the flier," Andrew ordered. "Out."

Sedgewick swore softly to himself. Merlin held her breath and closed her eyes as the footsteps came towards her. She was filled with fear at the thought of being discovered.

The footsteps stopped. She opened her eyes a slit, imagining him staring down at her.

She stifled a gasp of astonishment.

He was standing only inches from her on the other side of a bush, wearing a smooth, seamless, plastic suit, white boots, gloves of the same shiny-looking material, and a dark-tinted bubble helmet that completely concealed his features. He looked like a spaceman from a science-fiction movie.

As she watched, the bubble tilted this way and then that in a vaguely dissatisfied manner.

"He's looking for me," she thought, with cold horror.

She held her breath as the gleaming helmet turned in her direction. For one terrible instant it was still, and she thought he had spotted her, but after a long moment, he turned right around and looked the other way.

Sweating with fright, she closed her eyes and listened.

At long last, she heard footsteps; this time receding purposefully. He had given up. She opened her eyes, trembling from head to toe.

She watched the white suit growing progressively smaller through the trees. It reminded her of the clothes laboratory technicians wore when they were handling contagious diseases. Or radioactive substances.

A terrible suspicion filled Merlin's mind. The grotesquely large trees; the memory of experimental government farms; the white suits – was it possible there had been some kind of scientific accident? She remembered something else. One of the searchers, she thought it was the woman, Sacha, had said something about contamination. But if something had gone wrong, where did she fit in? Was she a survivor? A witness? A subject?

It sounded as if she had been drugged. That would explain why Andrew had called her witless. But the talk of her hiding made her think she had been a prisoner. If only she could remember. Maybe being drugged had affected her memory. But why would the government drug her?

"What the people know of the activities of their own elected government is ludicrously minimal," said the inner speaker with complete disregard for the relevance of the information it offered. Maybe there had been some kind of government cover-up. Merlin bit her lip.

A song fluttered into her mind like a torn scrap of paper: *"It ain't no use to sit an' wonder why, babe . . . it don' matter anyhow . . ."* The voice was raspy, bitter and oddly compelling.

She stood shakily, deciding the singer was right. There was no point in sitting and wondering. She had better get away from the wreck before the searchers returned. She would have to get to the nearest city. Maybe the police could help her. Or better still, a newspaper because if it were a government cover-up, maybe the police were in on it too. She began to walk in the opposite direction to that taken by Sedgewick. The words of the song echoed in her thoughts.

"Some things, some songs, some words, live longer than men and women . . ." said the boy's voice, secretive, confiding.

Merlin frowned. The voice was hauntingly familiar, yet she was unable to remember a name or even a face to go with it. She wondered if hearing voices inside her head meant she was mad. She felt perfectly sane, if confused.

If she could just remember what had happened before the accident.

Even her name seemed strange. If not for the voice in her mind, she doubted she would even have remembered it. Her steps slowed. She stopped.

She realized she could remember nothing about herself.

The discovery took her breath away. It was not just that she had forgotten the accident. She had forgotten everything but impersonal bits of information and even those came to her through the insistent inner voices. Her head began to throb painfully, resisting her attempts to force a memory. Her heart was beating very quickly.

She found she could remember things – streets, cities, cars, even television programmes and voices, news broadcasts, but nothing that had anything to do with her as an individual. And the memories were oddly generalized. She tried to focus in on a day and a sense of panic welled up in her at the realization that she had no idea *when* it was – not the day nor time of year. Not even the year!

"*Amnesia: loss of memory,*" pronounced the tinny voice, smothering the rush of terror. She was struck again by the extraordinary fact of the voices in her mind, as incredible in their own way as her loss of personal memories. The passionless mechanical voice appeared to be dominant, stating facts as if they were being read from a dictionary or a computer memory bank.

The thought of computers seemed to touch a hidden well of knowledge and she was swamped by detailed memories of the working of computers.

I must be something to do with computers, she thought, grasping at the meagre clue. She concentrated on amnesia but her mental dictionary seemed unable to elaborate its laconic interpretation. She could not decide if a selective loss of memory were possible. It was not that her mind had been wiped clean, a total forgetting; she appeared only to have forgotten things connected with her own existence. All except for the two internal voices. Would an accident do that? Or was it something that had happened before the accident?

She rubbed her eyes tiredly, then stared at her hand, looking beyond the blood and dirt to the dark gold skin.

My skin, she thought. This led to the discovery that she had no idea what she looked like. Her hand looked alien to her, as strange as the hand of another person.

Her name was Merlin. She remembered her name, but not her face. Was that possible?

All at once it seemed vital that she see her face. She felt certain she would recognize it, and her memories would return. Lacking a mirror, water would be the next best thing.

"Water catchments are best located in depressions in the ground ..." suggested her mental mentor helpfully. Merlin nodded. Ignoring aching limbs, she plunged straight down the incline at a run. It did not occur to her to question the information offered by the mysterious voice.

The incline was unexpectedly slippery, and she was forced to slow down. The trees were thicker and older, cutting off all direct sunlight. The ground flattened out, and amidst the whispering of wind through the leaves, she heard the unmistakable sound of running water. The noise led her to a small waterfall, dropping a few metres into a shallow depression in the ground.

She knelt beside a still runoff pool, and pushed away a crust of dead brown leaves.

A face looked up at her from the water, dark-complexioned as the skin on her hand. The girl in the pool was about fifteen. The hair around the face was shoulder-length, coarse and copper-coloured. The water was stained an ochre hue, and this made the skin and hair even darker; the eyes a peculiar yellow shade.

It was the face of a stranger.

She lifted a shaking hand to the side of the face where the blood dripped, watched the surly-faced stranger mimic her, touching fingers to a dark, jagged

14

gash running all the way down the hairline and onto her neck. The stranger traced the cut. Her fingers encountered something hard under the bloodstiff collar of the tunic. She squinted into the bleary water, trying to make out what it was. Some sort of neck jewellery, a collar. It looked like a featureless circlet. It was tight in one place on her throat, as if it had been bent. Maybe that was why her throat hurt.

She ran her fingers around it, searching for the clasp. She turned the circlet, feeling something long and thick attached to the collar sliding up her back.

She turned the collar right round, and reached underneath the tunic. Her fingers found a series of attached loops. Puzzled and curious, she pulled it out.

It was a length of chain.

I n the distance, Merlin saw a city.
She had toiled to the top of an uneven spine of rock rising steeply above the other hills, determined to get her bearings. She was shocked to find that dark, foreign trees blanketed hills and valleys in all directions as far as she could see.

A faint smudge of smoke on the horizon behind was the sole sign of the wreck she had left. Otherwise she might be the only inhabitant of the endless wilderness. There was no sign of the searchers, though once, moving away from the crash-site, she had heard the sound of movement in the trees. The scuffling was random and clearly the sound of some kind of animal rushing away. Whatever creatures lived in the forest, they were quick and shy, and

Merlin saw nothing but the occasional bird fly up, startled by her approach.

Where on earth am I? she wondered, amazed at the size of the wilderness region.

That was when she spotted it.

Almost hidden behind a ridge were the unmistakable angular shapes of skyscrapers. She was flooded with relief. All she had to do was get to the city. Then she could do something about finding out who she was.

"*Cities,*" the mechanical informant said suddenly, "*contain all the comforts and wonders that humankind can devise, and all their vices . . .*"

In the open, the sun was painfully bright. Merlin went back into the thick shade with relief. Though she had no way of knowing exactly what time it was, she guessed from the sun's height it was late morning. That meant she should be able to reach the city by nightfall. It did not look too far. She did not like the idea of being forced to sleep in the brooding forest, ignorant of the dangers of its resident wildlife.

She was unnerved by the trackless wilderness, finding it easier to conjure up visions of cities: bustling streets, people hurrying along pavements, newspaper stands with sellers shouting to attract customers – than to envisage the less populated parts of the world. This made her certain she had been a city dweller, and most likely, an inhabitant of the city she had seen from the ridge.

The air was cool in the shade, and a faint breeze blew constantly, ruffling the leaves and setting up a rattling whisper. Everything grew close together and appeared to vary little in type. Apart from the enormous trees, there were only sharp, wiry grasses and a low spreading bush. Wherever the sun was able to penetrate the foliage, the ground was hard and bare.

Merlin turned her mind resolutely to the conversation she had overheard between the searchers, sifting their words for clues about herself.

The woman had been called Sacha.

Merlin had not liked her clever, cultured voice any more than she had liked Andrew's supercilious tone. Andrew was clearly the leader of the trio while Sedgewick appeared to be least important in the hierarchy. She had thought him young, but he must be older than he sounded to be working with other scientists. It occurred to her that he might have worn the white suit to protect himself not from the environment, but from her. The idea that she was the victim of some mad experiment was farfetched, yet she could think of no other alternative that fitted all the facts.

"*When you have excluded the impossible, whatever remains, however improbable, must be the truth . . .*" offered her memory with the air of quoting some irrefutable authority.

That's all very well, Merlin thought ironically. But what happened when what fitted all the facts made no sense? She imagined herself trying to explain to a policeman what had happened. She would sound mad.

She chewed her lip. Perhaps that was what Andrew would tell people. She would have to be careful. It might be better to telephone a newspaper office from a public phone, just to see how they responded. They might already know what it was all about. Maybe she was even registered as missing.

She forced her mind back to the conversation between the searchers.

At some stage she had certainly been their prisoner. Why else would she be chained? Her fingers tugged automatically at the collar. It chafed but she had been unable to get it off. It seemed to be completely seamless.

She drew a sharp, startled breath, remembering something else.

One of the searchers had spoken of sabotage. Bits of the conversation floated back into her memory. Andrew had said the destruction of the flier was random sabotage. He had blamed a group called the scatterlings.

But who or what were scatterlings and why would they want to destroy the flier?

Again she wondered where she was. The weather was tropical, but the vegetation was not. She could remember quite a lot about world weather patterns, and she remembered a television programme during which the announcer claimed weather patterns were changing because of the heating up of the earth's atmosphere. She could see the television announcer's face and neat short hair quite clearly, and that made her lack of personal memory all the more incomprehensible.

Merlin wished she had looked more closely at the city but she consoled herself with the hope that its familiarity would bring back her memory.

She had ripped up much of the tunic she wore to make bandage sandals. The soles of her feet were very soft and even the little walking she had done had made them sore. Her legs had been stiff, too, at the start, as if she were not accustomed to physical exercise. But she was growing used to the movement, her muscles more willing.

Her stomach growled and she pressed her hands to her flat belly. When she had vomited after the accident, her stomach had been empty of solid food. Yet she was not gaunt and undernourished. Whatever else had been happening to her, she had not been starved. Once she reached the city, Merlin knew she would have to find somewhere to eat, bathe and get some clean clothes. Without money, her only option was to find a Salvation Army refuge or a charity soup kitchen before she was arrested for vagrancy.

She was startled when a vivid mental picture of a cake stall run by charity to raise money dropped into her mind like an image in a slide show.

"Charitable organizations try in vain to stem the growing number of street children in the cities who die of exposure and hunger ..." the mechanical voice said.

The names of the charitable institutions and the cake stall sat oddly alongside the gaps in Merlin's memory. How was it possible to remember things like that and yet forget her own face?

Weary and preoccupied, she almost missed the road.

What made her look down was the sound of something crunching under her feet. A black material lay in biscuit-thin slabs half concealed by the grass. Merlin stopped completely when she realised she was walking on the remains of a very old road: a fragile crust of tar which cracked like eggshells under the slightest pressure.

She was filled with excitement. The disused road must lead to other, used roads. She walked along the edge rather than along the centre of the road, not liking the sound of it crunching underfoot.

The nearness of safety made her suddenly nervous that Andrew and his searchers would catch up at the last minute. She looked over her shoulder anxiously but the dense foliage prevented her seeing more than a few metres.

Listening for signs that she was being followed, Merlin noted again the absence of human noises. Surely a city so big would be audible a long way off.

She had the sudden awful thought that the accident, whether nuclear or biological, had killed all the people. That would explain the silence and the white suits. Maybe Andrew and his people had been trying to help her before she was dangerously contaminated. The city might be silent because it had been evacuated.

"Primary death figures from a nuclear holocaust would produce a misleading impression since final figures must include not only immediate deaths, but deaths relating to radiation spawned diseases, and hereditary dysfunctions leading to death. It would take several lifetimes to gain a true statistical picture ..." reported the mechanical voice.

Merlin shivered. She appeared to have a morbid character which was not helped by the mechanical doom-mongering of her memory. There was no point in worrying about death and disaster until she was in a position to do something about it. Besides, if there had been an accident that killed the people, there would be no animals either, and the furtive rustlings in the bushes assured her the creatures living in the wilderness were alive, if wary.

As for Andrew's people, none of the three had sounded like they were worried about her coming to harm. She had done the right thing, and the road told her she was getting close to the city.

At length the road she was following intersected with another disused road. Further along, yet another road intersected, ending in a mess of rubble formed by the collapse of an immense bridge which had once supported an overhead bypass.

Merlin was amazed that such major roads had been allowed to fall into disrepair. She had been listening unconsciously for city noises. She could imagine them vividly – car horns, brakes screeching, engines humming.

The absence of these sounds gave the impression that she was still some distance from the outskirts of the city. This made the first sight of it, moments later, staggeringly unexpected.

She came out of a thick copse of trees, and there before her lay the city. The old road she had been following led directly into the centre. The forest grew right up to the edge of buildings and through wide cracks in the road's surface.

All the roads running into the city were ancient; brittle as pieces of burnt toast. The city itself was a ruin. Skyscrapers were skeletal hulks of rotting stone and weathered steel. Glass was gone from the windows, and outside, steps were crumbled and overgrown with shaggy yellow grasses.

Trees once confined to circular grills had grown to a monstrous size, their serpentine roots twisting and writhing in all directions, cracking open what remained of pavements.

There were cars too, still parked in the street, though they were little more than rusting, gutted hulks, lacking all finish and interior materials. Leather and padding had rotted to a dry, black lace.

Water ran freely along widening fissures in the street, and water plants grew along the edges, pushing up through manmade surfaces to dangle tendrils in the water. Leaves formed great, brown, soggy banks along the bottom edges of skyscrapers, where the wind had blown them.

Merlin walked forward slowly, numbly.

The wind rattled a piece of corrugated metal high up on a roof and the monotonous grinding noise made a fitting desolate accompaniment to her footsteps.

She had been afraid she might find people dead or dying. She had even envisaged a city abandoned by its citizens. But not a ruin of such magnitude.

The puzzling thing was the completeness of the decay. A decade of neglect would not cause so much corrosion. Such slow inexorable destruction would only occur over a very long period: hundreds of years.

All the signs that might have offered clues to her whereabouts were long since eroded. The city was a faceless, featureless skeleton.

A few more years and the encroaching forest would eradicate all traces of the crumbling buildings. There was no clue as to what had made people leave. There was no sign that the city had been bombed or physically damaged, no skeletons to say that people had died there.

Merlin felt oppressed by the age of the ruin, the enigma of its emptiness, the silence, the echoing lifelessness.

She noticed the remains of a large sculpture overlooking one street corner and frowned. Odd that she should be so certain it had been a sculpture since the fretted stone looked like nothing more than a lump of marble toppled from the surrounding buildings.

The humped shape gave her a shivery feeling, drew her nearer.

Her skin puckered into gooseflesh.

"In this sculpture, the artist has made of the stone something soft and pliable ..." the whispering boy's voice said, and Merlin saw the sculpture in her mind's eye. It had been a nude woman with flowing hair. There was still the shape of the head, bowed, and part of one arm left. But this was barely enough to discern a human shape, let alone that of a woman. Yet Merlin remembered it clearly as a complete piece of art.

She shuddered and backed away, frightened.

Around her, the city seemed to reshape and reform before her eyes, assuming a ghostly familiarity. A corner, the outline of a tall building, the knowledge of other streets, all offered themselves as vivid memories of a big, bustling city. She had once seen those streets and watched cars hurry along them, street lights flicking on and off, bright, frivolous shop façades. But her memory was of a vigorous, busy, populated city, not an ancient ruin.

She might have stood that way for hours, silent and perplexed, if it had not begun to rain. She had failed to notice the ominous banking of clouds over-shadowing the sun.

The rain, when it fell, was no light spittle, but a hard forceful downpour that hammered on all surfaces and flattened smaller plants to the ground.

Merlin stared up into the sky, astonished at the suddenness of the downpour. She yelped in pain when one of the drops stung her face and bolted for the nearest doorway, praying the rain would not send the building above down on her head. If it often rained so hard, she doubted the city would last another year.

The rain increased in force until it was visibly eroding what remained of the street surface; black rafts of tar were wrenched away and whirled violently down fissure rivers. The sound was deafening.

Eventually the rain fell so heavily that, like a grey curtain, it cut her off from the street.

There was no door to the building and Merlin moved inside, too tired to worry about the roof collapsing. There were no seats or carpets or furniture left, just black damp rotting remnants of the past and a dangerously sagging floor.

She sat on the edge of an old stairwell disconsolately, wondering what to do. If only there were someone to talk to.

"It is a vast, lonely world," the inner voice confided. *"It is a hard thing to have no friend to share it."*

Merlin determinedly ignored the voice in her mind.

Andrew had been worried she would be found or would communicate with whoever sabotaged the flier. That meant there was help to be found. All she had to do was find the people who had destroyed the flier – the scatterlings – before Andrew and his searchers found her.

The trouble was she had no idea how or where to look for them.

Her stomach rumbled, and the brief flare of hope drained abruptly, leaving her aching with hunger and tiredness.

She shivered. She had no desire to stay in the dead city, but at least it offered shelter.

The building above creaked dramatically, as if reminding her it was an unsafe refuge at best. She shivered again and wished she had not been so enthusiastic about ripping up the tunic for footwear.

It was dusk before the rain stopped. Merlin emerged from the doorway timidly. The wind was much stronger and fairly howled along the street.

Chilled to the bone by an icy gust, she looked around at the darkening city uncertainly, deciding she was less concerned with hunger than with finding a way to keep warm.

The mechanical voice of her memory comfortingly assured her that human beings were capable of surviving long periods without food, but could die overnight of exposure.

Quite suddenly, she felt a different kind of chill.

Someone or something was watching her.

Merlin stared around with dread. She felt eyes boring into her and knew she was not alone in the crumbling city. The thousand gaping windows stared down at her.

She swallowed and took a step backwards, her legs stiff with terror.

Shelter or no shelter, exposure or not, night in the terrible dead city no longer seemed any sort of solution. She turned and walked quickly back the way she had come, conscious of the wet crunching noises her feet made in the quiet.

The faint dusk sunlight had almost faded as she reached the treeline again but she sighed with relief.

Only then did she look back, but the city was no more than a dark shape in the night.

3

She was being followed.

As if triggered by her unease, the inner whisperer spoke again. *"They watch me. I wonder if they suspect the truth ..."*

"Shut up," Merlin hissed, unnerved.

Ever since leaving the deserted city, she had been hearing things – the rustle of leaves, the sound of a small branch falling to the ground, something other than the scurrying departure of little animals. She knew she would be defenceless if whoever or whatever had watched her in the city decided to follow and attack. Now that it was night, she felt even more vulnerable.

She remembered seeing wild deer in an enclosure at the zoo. The animals had been unafraid of the people filing past their enclosure because experience told them they would not be attacked. But the small animals she had not managed to catch a glimpse of in the wilderness behaved as if they were accustomed to being hunted. And perhaps whatever hunted them, was now after her.

Merlin walked carefully trying not to make any noise, but the forest was now unnaturally quiet. This made her more afraid than ever. She tried stopping unexpectedly to see if she could detect footsteps behind her, but there was nothing except the endless, mocking gibber of the wind in the branches.

Yet she could not rid herself of the certainty that she was being followed.

It was very dark when the sun first set, but at length a full moon rose, shedding a clear silvery light. Merlin was little cheered by this. Exhausted, she knew she would have to stop soon to rest, if nothing else. Then she would be easy prey.

Her eyelids were drooping heavily and she was almost stumbling, asleep on her feet, when she heard the distinct sound of twigs snapping behind her.

She froze, suddenly as wide awake as if someone had thrown ice water over her. Her heart thundered in her throat, nearly suffocating her. Sick with fright, she knelt and took up a lump of stone from the ground to defend herself.

She stood facing in the direction she had heard the

footstep, willing herself to stop shaking, schooling her expression.

There was nothing for a long, eerie moment, then the faint sound of leaves being brushed aside. Merlin swallowed, trying to will saliva into her parched mouth. The hairs on the back of her neck stood up on end and she stared into the shadows challengingly, fighting off paralysing terror.

"Who ... who's there?" she called. There was no answer but the subtle commentary of the wind's passage.

Merlin relaxed slowly, her terror ebbing away. She looked at the stone wryly, cursing her imagination.

"You'd be easy prey even with that rock," said a voice directly behind.

Merlin stumbled sideways in her haste to turn around, her heart leaping in her chest so violently she thought she would have a heart attack.

A youth of about sixteen was standing less than a metre away, leaning in the inky shadow of a thick-waisted tree, watching her.

Shock gave way to a rush of fury. "Why did you sneak up behind me!" she shouted, hurting her raw throat.

The youth straightened up with casual grace and came closer.

Merlin gaped as she saw him in the full moonlight.

He was tall and lean, wearing nothing more than a loin cloth and a leather belt. In one hand he held what looked like a crude crossbow. Slung over one shoulder was a pouch containing arrows and two long furry-looking animal carcasses.

With his dark, dirty skin, bare feet and coarse brown hair falling over broad, thickly muscled shoulders to his waist in unkempt coils, he resembled a dirty young Tarzan.

Merlin repressed an hysterical giggle and resisted the urge to retreat as he peered into her face. His own face close up was heavily marked and one ragged scar ran right over his left eye giving him a permanent lopsided wink.

"Who are you?" she asked, her voice a rusty whisper.

"*My name is William,*" whispered the voice inside her mind shyly, and for a second, she thought the youth had spoken.

"Not so fast," he answered softly. "Names are not things to be bandied around like chunks of burnt meat. You are the stranger here." He tilted his head, staring at her out of one gleaming eye, the rest of his face in shadow.

"I followed you from the old place. What did you go there for?" he asked, resting his bowless hand on the hilt of a small axe stuck through his belt. Merlin licked her lips nervously, as her inner adviser reminded her that humans were as dangerous, if not more so, than wild animals. And the youth looked half wild anyway.

"Old place?" she stammered.

He lifted his hand to point and Merlin flinched, thinking he meant to strike her. His teeth flashed white in a smile at her involuntary movement. A slow burning anger licked at the edges of fear.

"Back there. The place of Babel where the wind lives," he said.

The mechanical voice said: *"The tower of Babel was a mythical tower whose construction was interfered with by the gods."*

Merlin realised the youth meant the deserted city. She could not help wondering at the way he talked. Perhaps he was part of an isolated religious sect that lived in the wilderness.

Her mind obligingly offered a variety of religious orders, but the youth seemed not to fit into any of them.

"Why did you go there?" she asked, reluctant to display her ignorance.

Again his teeth flashed whitely. "You are a tricksy one. Question for question is it, then? Is this the new way clanfolk meet?"

Merlin said nothing. Inside her mind, the voice she now called the William voice said: *"I do not believe the clanfolk are stupid or dull or even savages. They are simply a primitive culture, and they will mature ... if they are allowed ..."*

"All right. Question for question," the youth announced, taking her silence for an answer. "And answer for answer. I went there for knowledge. You do not believe me?" he asked quickly, defensive. "The wind hears all the secrets men and women whisper. I go there to listen to the voices on the wind." He lifted his brows interrogatingly.

Merlin swallowed, still unwilling to mention her memory loss. But some answer was required. "I was curious," she said at last.

He nodded. "I, too, the first time. But once you go there, you will always go back. The Babel place takes a piece of you as barter for your intrusion. That stolen piece draws you back." He sighed. "Sometimes I think I am bewitched."

Suddenly he leaned near again, staring at her head. "Your hair! What happened to it?" He sounded shocked. Merlin lifted a self-conscious hand to her head.

"What's the matter with it?"

"What's wrong? It's cut," he said.

Merlin wondered when it had become a crime to cut hair. Some instinct of privacy made her glad the collar of her tunic concealed the chain and collar she wore.

"Only the Citizen gods cut hair," the youth went on. His voice was suspicious and an alarm bell clanged in Merlin's head.

"It was burned," she said quickly.

The youth tilted his head and stared at her critically. "Makes you look like one of them," he said darkly.

"*It is us against them,*" the William voice whispered urgently. "*I must take care they don't guess what I am doing . . .*"

"Them . . ." Merlin echoed. She could not think of a way to ask who "they" were without having to first explain her amnesia.

"Ford," he said shortly.

Merlin stared wildly. Did he mean he had a car nearby?

"What are you called?" he asked pointedly.

"*Your name is Merlin . . .*" the William voice husked.

She realised Ford was the youth's name. "Merlin," she said hastily, glad there was at least one easy answer.

"Funny sort of name," he observed.

What about yours? Merlin thought indignantly.

"So where do you come from, then?" he asked.

Merlin searched for a noncomittal answer. "Near the sea," she said at last.

Ford looked interested. "Really? But I suppose you did not come so far alone. Conclave is only two days away. A good time to join us, eh?" he asked ironically, as if she had made a sly joke.

Merlin nodded, wondering what he was talking about, and who she was meant to be joining, and what a Conclave was.

Where am I? she wondered desperately. This was something more than an experiment gone wrong. What had happened to the world?

"I haven't quite made up my mind about joining," she said into the lengthening silence.

Ford burst out laughing. "What else will you do? You can't go back. Too late for regrets now."

"We'd better find a sleeping place," he added purposefully. He yawned widely, then bent to retrieve his bow. "Too far to go to the Hide tonight." He turned his back and set off at a brisk pace. He had gone a few steps before he looked over his shoulder at Merlin, who had not moved. "Come on, then!" he called.

Merlin hurried after him, not sure whether to be relieved that she was no longer alone. Nothing Ford said had made the slightest sense to her. Either he was retarded – but he did not sound half-witted – or she really was in some other country. But it was a country with customs she had never heard of.

"Pity you didn't come sooner," Ford said absently. "One of Sear's old traps netted a Citizen gods' flier. I wish I had seen it," he added regretfully.

Merlin was glad he had not looked at her as he spoke. She realized incredulously that Ford and someone called Sear were the saboteurs the searchers had mentioned. That meant she was on her way to the camp of the scatterlings. This seemed a less promising development than she had imagined in the face of Ford's primitive appearance. What sort of help could a group of savages offer her? She decided again to say nothing of her amnesia, or of her presence in the wrecked flier, until she was able to judge what help Ford's people were capable of giving her. And how they would react to her story.

Her unease stemmed partly from fear of appearing ignorant and partly from the odd mixture of naivety and savagery in Ford. He had sounded proud of the accident, careless that it had caused the dreadful death of the driver. He was so sure she was some sort of runaway come to join his gang. What would he do if he found he had made a mistake? The vast difference between Ford and Andrew's technologically advanced people confused her. She wondered why Ford called the searchers "Citizen gods".

"Does the cut pain you?" Ford asked, seeming to sense her mental turmoil.

Merlin shook her head hastily, wondering what medication he would offer. "I ... fell," she said lamely, touching her forehead.

He made no comment. To her heartfelt relief, they did not walk far. The ground began to undulate gently and Ford called a halt in a deepish depression with a flat grassy bottom. Hooking his bow and arrow pouch from a tree branch extended over the crevice, he pulled the axe from his belt and tested its sharpness with a deft thumb.

Merlin stared at him apprehensively until he took

up one of the carcasses. Seeing that he was about to gut them, she backed away hastily.

"I'll get some wood for the fire," she offered.

Ford looked at her quizzically. "You're bold enough or maybe stupid. A fire away from the Hide is a deathbond," he said with the air of quoting a proverb. "But maybe you're right. The Citizen gods will be too busy collecting their dead to be out hunting tonight, and a fire would be a fine thing."

Hunt? Merlin thought. Did the Citizen gods hunt the scatterlings?

Ford bent to his grisly task and Merlin hurried off into the trees, wondering if he had intended them to eat the meat raw. Revolted at the notion, she took her time collecting twigs and dead wood, feeling for the driest wood automatically. When her arms were full and she was certain the skinning and gutting process would be over, she went back.

"You took your time," Ford said mildly. He took the wood from her and set it up for a fire before taking two stones carefully from a small pouch hanging at his waist. He struck them together sharply, letting the resultant sparks fall onto a feathery curl of grass which began to smoke. Setting down the flint stones, he bent close to the ground and blew until the spark became a minute flame which was transferred swiftly to the pile of sticks.

Merlin wondered why he did not use a match.

In a short time, a small fire crackled between them,

flinging orange sparks into the starry sky. The meat was lain across the fire in strips and a delicious smell filled the air. Merlin forced away the memory of the other roasting flesh, and her belly rumbled loudly.

Looking wilder than ever in the leaping glow of the flames, Ford grinned at her engagingly. "Hungry, eh? How come none of you runaways ever think to bring food?"

The meat was burned on the outside and almost raw in the middle, but Merlin ate every piece that was offered to her, amazed at how good it tasted. There was no talk while they ate.

She was replete first and sat back with a sigh. She studied Ford curiously across the fire thinking it was impossible to tell his racial background from his features – a slight upward slant to his eyes made him look Spanish or Portuguese. Thick long black lashes and slashing dark brows; high, sharp cheekbones and a full lower lip completed the picture of someone with mixed ancestry. His skin was darker than hers, and the firelight tinted his eyes an unusual shade of yellow. She wondered what colour they were in the daylight. He was dirty, and clearly expert at living off the land, but off what land? She debated asking him what country they were in, but decided against it. The thing that really puzzled her was his speech and accent which were exactly the same as hers, and as the Citizen gods'.

Her thoughts struck a chord in her patchwork

memory and the William voice spoke: *"You are strange, yet you are no monster. You are not grotesque, only different..."*

Different how? Merlin wondered. Then she pushed the question away, refusing to let it distract her.

She was becoming adept at ignoring the constant interruptions from the inner voices. Yet she felt more confused than ever at her own state. Each time she learned something new, it seemed to increase her overall lack of comprehension. She had clung grimly to the notion that there was an explanation for all the strangeness.

But now, that belief was fading.

She was staring into the flames when she felt herself watched. Glancing up, she found Ford staring at her. Unperturbed, he went on staring until she shifted uncomfortably.

"All right, we'll talk then," he said. "Is it true that the people from the Seaside Regions ride on the waves on boards?"

Surfing, Merlin thought incredulously. He's asking me about surfing!

"Surfing is a sport..." the mechanical voice began pedantically, but Merlin repressed it, aware Ford would go on questioning her unless she forestalled him.

"The Citizens will be angry about the flier," she said carefully.

Diverted, Ford burst into uninhibited laughter.

"Yes, yes! They will know who did it. And they will search for us, but they will not find us." He grinned wolfishly into the flames. "They will learn not to think of us as easy prey. Then let them fear for their forbidden city."

"City?" Merlin echoed.

Ford nodded eagerly, his half-closed eye giving him a mocking air. "Few have seen it, but I will take you there when it is safe. The scatterlings do not fear the wrath or rules of the Citizen gods." He shook his head. "The monstrous bubble which covers the forbidden city is a strange, splendid sight. I have dared to go close and press my face against it, and it is hard like a rock and cold as a stone from the bottom of a stream. Only this close it is possible to see the forbidden city within, which is a sister to the Babel place. But it is dark and cold and no sun shines on it. I do not like it as much."

Merlin said nothing, completely confounded. A city under a bubble – a dome? A bizarre notion occurred to her. Perhaps she had been put into suspended animation. It seemed ludicrous to think of being preserved like a pickle or a frozen pea, but trying to find rational explanations had only led her deeper into a labyrinth of confusion. Maybe she had been used as a subject and had woken years and years later. That might explain why she did not remember anything about the world. Perhaps Andrew and his people had resurrected her and had chained her in case she reacted violently. That would explain why a long-dead city was familiar and why nothing Ford said made any sense.

Common sense rebelled at the outlandish idea, yet it was oddly persuasive because it seemed to explain so many things: the domed city, radiation suits and fliers, all of which sounded like the ingredients of a futuristic science-fiction novel.

"You might even see one of them," Ford said, breaking into her speculations.

Merlin blinked at him stupidly.

"The Citizen gods," he said impatiently. "We caught one of them once. Stripped of those shiny skins they wear, he was white as the cooked flesh of a chooken." He shook his head, apparently disappointed in her lack of reaction. Merlin was trying to work out whether he meant chicken, rather than chooken.

"But the eyes were the strangest thing of all – blue like the sky had been dripped into them. And Sear says the Citizen gods have different coloured eyes: some green like grass or brown like wet bark, but none yellow like ours."

Merlin licked her lips, remembering how her eyes had looked yellow in the puddle of water. And she had assumed the firelight had turned Ford's eyes yellow. She had never heard of people having yellow eyes. If a lot of time had passed, it was possible eye colour had altered. But why were her eyes that colour?

The voices were silent on the subject.

"I talked to him, too," Ford said, still caught up in his memories of the captured Citizen. "I wanted to ask him why they had come out of the forbidden city after so long. He was half-mad, screaming and cursing. Said he'd die without the shiny skin. He died the next day." Ford shrugged.

Merlin nodded, understanding from this that the radiation suits protected the Citizens from something in the atmosphere to which Ford and presumably she too were immune. She made no attempt to fit that into her theory of suspended animation. It was easier not to try to fit anything she had encountered into her memory of the world.

"Have ... have you been inside the dome ... bubble?" Merlin asked. She realized she had made a mistake when Ford stared at her narrow-eyed.

"What do you mean? If I had been inside, I wouldn't be sitting here talking to you, would I? Are you trying to be funny?"

Merlin let him make of her silence what he would. Finally he spat disgustedly into the fire. "I suppose it's because of you coming from so far off. You wouldn't joke if you came from an Inland clan."

Merlin took up a twig and poked at the ashes, avoiding his eyes. The silence lengthened and she racked her brains for something to say.

"I know more than most about the Citizen gods and what I know does not make me want to laugh." Ford sounded subdued. Merlin looked up warily, but he was staring fixedly into the flames. "It is not a good thing to want to know so many things. I've been told that all my life. Curiosity killed the clansman." He laughed bitterly. "Yet not all children are made for obedience. Even as a child, I always asked too many questions. Yet, sometimes, the hunger to know is like the green mushroom – it claws at your belly from the inside."

Fascinated, Merlin waited, but Ford said nothing more, preoccupied with his queer alien thoughts. But, alien or not, she understood what he meant. Her own insatiable need to understand what had happened to her was a kind of hunger too. It startled her to find this similarity between them, and for a moment she forgot her loneliness.

"I know what you mean," she murmured.

Ford looked at her sharply, as if he suspected her of mocking him. Seeing her expression, he sighed. "I don't meet many people who think that knowing and wanting to know are worthwhile things. Even the wardens who are supposed to be so wise, only care about being well fed and safe. Wanting to know is sometimes dangerous." Ford smiled suddenly. "But not among the scatterlings. You will like Sear. He is hungry for knowing too, though he wants only to know the secret of the Citizen gods' magic."

He fell silent, as if this depressed him.

Merlin was surprised at his willingness to talk so freely to a stranger. But perhaps he already saw her as a member of the scatterlings.

She started when Ford jumped to his feet without warning, stiff with tension. She opened her mouth to speak but he shook his head urgently, motioning her to silence. Like an animal scenting danger, his nostrils quivered.

"Quick. The fire," he hissed.

Merlin responded to the urgency in his tone, shovelling dirt over the flames and smothering them. Ford reached over and dragged her roughly to her feet and into the trees. "Eyeball," he whispered, apparently in explanation. A few metres back in the trees, he pushed her down and sank to his knees beside her. She stared back through the trees, trying to fathom the danger.

"See . . ." Ford breathed in her ear, pointing.

Merlin squinted in the darkness. She heard a slight metallic whine and then she saw a small oval-shaped metallic object glide through the air and hover directly over the remains of the fire.

"It will think it started itself," Ford whispered. "It's too stupid to work out that people lit it, and might still be around. It would be a different story if it were Citizen gods inside a flier."

"Can it hear us?" Merlin whispered.

"We don't think so. If they can, it doesn't seem to

help them find us." The floating oval rotated slowly, then glided away.

"I guess we'd better not light the fire again," Ford said. "We might as well get some sleep. We'll start early in the morning. It's safest to travel before the middle hours. That's when the Citizen gods come out in force." Ford rose and they both went back to the clearing.

"They won't come back, will they?" Merlin asked anxiously.

Ford shook his head, yawned loudly, then stretched himself out on the ground where the fire had been. "They can't find us on body heat of less than three. The fire made three. Haven't you heard the saying two's company, three's dead?"

"*Two's company, three's a crowd*," the mechanical voice corrected.

"Come on, while it's still warm," Ford said exasperatedly. Merlin swallowed, before lying down beside him. She jumped when he pulled her roughly nearer, her back curving against his stomach.

"What's the matter?" he asked a moment later. "You're shaking. Are you sick?"

Unable to trust her voice, Merlin shook her head and wished she had kept the rock. She was suddenly frightened of what the primitive youth might do to her. Ford yawned again and sighed heavily. Moments later, he was snoring softly into her hair.

Merlin lay awake beside him, slowly relaxing. It

was cold but shared body heat kept her warm. Shamed by her suspicions, Merlin knew she had been a fool to imagine that Ford intended to molest her.

Drifting to sleep at last, she dreamed she was peering through thick black smoke, which suddenly became dark glass. She tried to break though the glass. For some reason it was vital she reach the other side, but the glass was impregnable. Faintly she could hear a voice calling to her, muffled by the wall of glass.

Gradually, she recognized the whispering William voice. *"Merlin, do you hear me?"* She struggled to answer, but could not utter a sound.

When she woke, it was still night. The moon was very bright and she looked up at it wondering about the voices in her mind. The words she kept hearing were memories, she was certain of that, but they were strangely clear and seemed to rise in response to her own thoughts. She was able to repress them with an effort, especially the mechanical instructing voice, but it was easier to ignore them. Besides, it was possible they might be the beginning of her memory coming back.

She wondered who William was or had been. Odd that his voice was so clear in her mind, yet she had no idea what he looked like. He was no more than a voice whispering to her, and sometimes, she felt, to himself. Strangely, she never remembered her own responses to his words.

With a sigh, she rolled over to find herself face to face with Ford. He seemed younger than he had awake, and she studied his sleeping expression, remembering the wistfulness in his voice when he had spoken of his hunger for knowledge.

Suddenly he opened his eyes.

"Are you afraid of me?" he asked softly, his lips close to her forehead.

Merlin was too startled to answer.

Ford smiled. "I don't know how things are done among the Sea Region clans, but among the Inland clans, the mating heat is not a thing to unleash lightly."

Merlin felt her face burn.

"You will find us unlike traditional clans. Our lives are harder, but we have more freedom. We choose our own mates and our own tasks without the advice or interference of the wardens. We are not bound by traditions. It is a good life, or would be, if the Citizen gods had not come out. But, without them, there would be no scatterlings," he added philosophically.

He was silent for a long while, and Merlin thought he had gone back to sleep, but presently he said drowsily: "There are enough things to be afraid of without imagining dangers. I am not someone you will ever need to fear."

Merlin was vastly relieved when he began to snore again.

Her face felt hot, but one thing was clear to her. Going to Ford's camp was the best course of action for the present. It was definitely safer to travel with him than without, and she could always slip away before they got to the scatterlings' camp.

She slept again, and woke near dawn to Ford shaking her. "Come on, get up. Can't you hear them calling?"

Merlin could hear nothing.

"Get up!" he urged. "We'll be able to travel back to the Hide with them. They must have been out to hunt!"

She scrambled to her feet, heart thumping jerkily. It seemed she was not to have any choice about going to the camp. It was some minutes before Merlin heard shouts in the distance. She reflected that Ford must have unusually fine hearing.

Moments later a girl hurtled into the open with a blood-curdling yell of greeting. Like Ford, she wore nothing but a loin cloth, and her small breasts bounced as she threw herself into his arms. Her hair was longer than Ford's, a dark straw colour. Merlin felt herself blush. No wonder Ford had been amused at her fears in the night. The girl was covered in black, dried mud, but, in spite of the dirt, she was very beautiful. Instead of a bow, she carried a thin spear.

Oddly, neither of the pair spoke, but only stared

intently at one another. The girl then turned to face her, and Merlin noticed her eyes were the same searing yellow as Ford's.

"My sisterblood, Era," Ford said. "Era, Merlin is to join us."

The tall girl sneered openly: "An Offering runaway."

Ford scowled and pushed his sister away from him. "Without the Offering, no one would choose to leave clan and family."

Era tossed her head, unmoved by her brother's rebuke. "What happened to her hair?" she demanded.

"It was burnt," Ford answered repressively. "Where are the others?"

"Coming," Era said, still eyeing Merlin. Her expression softened and she swung round to face Ford. "Did you get my Sending about the flier?"

He grinned broadly. "Did I! Have they found it yet?"

Era nodded. "Of course. They are taking this very seriously. It is worse than when we have killed them on foot. I think they will now regard the scatterlings as dangerous enemies. The skies will be full of them hunting us. We have stirred up a stingers' nest."

Ford nodded. "But they will not find the Hide unless they comb the forest on foot. I doubt they will have the courage for that, especially now. If only the clans would fight them as well."

"Where does she come from?" Era asked sharply, as if Merlin were not there.

Irritation flickered across Ford's features. "She comes from the Seaside Region."

Before Era could speak again, there were more whooping shouts and three more ran into the clearing. Two were boys younger than Ford, and one was older, almost a man, his stocky body savagely scarred. All wore brief loin cloths and carried either spear or bow and full cloth pouches. After greeting Ford, they turned to stare at Merlin who felt unexpectedly nervous at their combined scrutiny.

"She is Merlin – from the Seaside Region, she says," Era announced.

The bushes behind them rustled and another girl came out. Unlike Era, she wore a full loose shift like Merlin's. Her black hair was combed into a long plait that brushed the ground when she walked. She moved more sedately than her companions. And though her eyes were the same colour as theirs, they had an unfathomable quality that made them unique.

"Ford," she greeted in a guttural voice. "You have come back. What wisdoms do you bring us this time from the winds?"

To Merlin's surprise, Ford coloured slightly and grinned. His single good eye flicked as from its own volition to Merlin and back to the other girl.

"So," the dark-haired girl said, after a long pause. She turned to Merlin. "So, you are Merlin?"

Merlin frowned, certain no one had spoken her name in the girl's presence, unless she had been listening before she showed herself.

"And this?" She pointed to Merlin's shoulder-length hair.

"It was burnt," Ford said.

"Ah. Merlin is ... an unusual name."

"As good a name as Marthe," Ford said in a hard voice.

Merlin was surprised at his aggressively defensive tone, since he had said as much to her himself. And why was he defending her anyway?

"You trust her, then? Before mindbond?" the dark-haired girl asked insistently. "You will rely on the wordbond of a stranger?"

"No!" Era said.

"Yes," Ford said defiantly. Brother and sister exchanged a long look, and again Merlin sensed a silent interchange. Era looked away first, angrily.

"If she is not what she seems ..." began Era, then she shrugged dismissively.

"We will see," Marthe said, her eyes slanting through the grey early morning light with an ambiguous expression.

M erlin walked between Ford and the older youth called Sear, the leader of the scatterlings. He had been first to rebel against the Offering, Ford told her.

She dared not ask what an Offering was, since it was assumed she had come to join them having rejected it too. They took her arrival casually, as if runaways were commonplace, and the scatterlings' Hide a well-known refuge.

"*The population of street dwellers increases daily* ..." the mechanical voice began. Merlin repressed it feeling she needed all her wits to deal with the scatterlings.

Marthe walked slightly apart from the others, and

Merlin often felt the girl's eyes boring into her as they walked.

In retrospect, it seemed to Merlin that the confrontation in the clearing had been stamped with a ritualistic air, all except for Ford's defence of her. That still puzzled her, particularly since Ford had not said a word to her since, and even seemed to be avoiding her.

She wondered what they had meant by mindbond. Some sort of pledge of faith, she guessed. Ford's sister, Era, had seemed dismayed. Merlin felt uncomfortable and guilty that Ford had staked his word on her truthfulness. She had not intended that to happen, any more than she had set out to deceive them about herself. It had just seemed less complicated to make up an acceptable lie than to try and explain an incomprehensible truth.

"Ours is a race of liars . . ." the William voice said sadly.

Merlin refused to feel guilty. She had decided to slip away without a fuss the first chance she got. When she reached the camp she would be questioned thoroughly, Marthe's eyes told her that. It would not take much to reveal she was neither from the Seaside Region nor a runaway from the Offering.

Unfortunately, no chance of escape had so far presented itself. Flanked on all sides by the scatterlings, she could do no more than hope fervently for a diversion.

54

She had considered telling them the truth, but she was too frightened they would regard her as one of the Citizen gods they had murdered. She sensed Ford would be sympathetic, but Era and Marthe were too hostile, and there was the problem of Ford vouching for her. They were a primitive people and might even kill her for lying. She had no plan beyond getting away from the rebels and did not waste her time planning future courses until she had managed that.

To pass the time, she tried to look at everything that had happened since waking in the wreck from another angle. Instead of trying to fit it all into a theory that would explain her own situation, she simply looked at the facts, regardless of how strange they were.

There were two distinct groups of people: the technologically advanced and physically frail Citizens, who dwelt in a domed city and wore clothing to protect them from the environment which was violently poisonous to them, and the primitive yellow-eyed clanpeople, of which Ford and the scatterlings were a rebel faction.

There was conflict between the Citizens and the rebel exiles, and between the clanpeople and the rebels, all apparently over the Offering, which seemed to have been begun by the Citizen gods. The Offering sounded like some sort of slavery.

Merlin did not belong to either group, yet she seemed to contain elements of both. Physically, except for her cut hair, she was a clanperson – sharing their physical characteristics of golden skin, yellow eyes and immunity to the poisons in the atmosphere which affected the Citizen gods. But she had no memory of herself as a clan member, or of any sort of people in the world who possessed their odd physical characteristics. The world as she remembered it had more in common with the advanced culture of the Citizen gods. But the world she had seen since wakening in the wrecked flier was completely alien to her.

Except for the strangely familiar ruined city.

And none of that told her why the Citizens had held her captive and chained her, or why she had been travelling in a Citizen flier when it crashed.

This last thought disturbed her most of all. What if the scatterlings found out the truth and decided she was a spy? Merlin thought sickly of the driver screaming as he burned, and of Ford's callous pleasure in the death of a hated Citizen god.

Catching the enigmatic Marthe watching her speculatively, Merlin tried to outstare her, but was defeated by the flat expression in the other girl's eyes.

It was further than she had expected to the scatterlings' Hide, and they were still walking in the late afternoon. Merlin flopped down with weary gratitude when Sear announced they would rest and eat. She forced herself to remain alert, recognizing this might be her sole opportunity to get away without being noticed. But Era watched her constantly.

Sear shared out tough, stale strips of dried meat from his pouch. Merlin managed to conceal two strips under her tunic, reckoning that she would not find it easy to come by food if she did manage to get away.

Listening to the talk, she guessed they were approaching the region surrounding the domed city Ford had mentioned. By the sound of it, Sear planned for them to give the dome a wide berth.

Merlin found herself wondering if she had done the wrong thing in evading the Citizens. Perhaps it would be better to simply head for the dome and give herself up.

"I am a fool to hope, I know, but that is one of the few saving graces of human beings," the William voice whispered inside her mind.

Sear had begun to talk, and Merlin drifted nearer, curious.

"I will get inside the dome. I will find out what happens to our people, and what I learn will help me free the clans from the lies and tyranny of the Offering," Sear was telling a group of scatterlings.

"And if the clans prefer the security of immortality in the forbidden city to the uncertainty of death?" Marthe asked with heavy irony. "You will force your freedom on them?"

"What immortality?" Sear demanded. "This

immortality they offer the clans is a lie. Only a fool chooses to live by lies. And the Lord wardens are worse than fools. They betray our people for dreams.''

"What of the wardens? They do not drink the visiondraught given by the Citizen gods," said one of the others.

Standing beside Sear, Ford answered: "True. They sell their souls for the power the Offering gives them over the people, and discredit the mindbond so they will not have to bare their own deception to one they would judge.''

Era lifted her chin angrily and turned to face Ford. "It began when the Lord wardens decreed they would accept wordbond from the Citizen gods, rather than demand mindbond.''

"The Lord warden of our clan said we had no right to demand mindbond of a god; that a god is truth," said another.

Sear laughed harshly. "No one is beyond the truth. If I did not think so, I would not have turned my back on clan and Conclave. I would now be a Blessed Walker. Instead, I have killed three of the Citizen gods!" He spat the final words out with real hatred.

Marthe smiled her strange bitter smile. "If what you say is true, then the wardens will not hear the truth when you bring it to them. The Lord wardens will have you executed.''

Sear shook his head, looking abruptly tired. "What

do you want me to say, Marthe? I am no warden with a sweet and convenient tongue. I see that this Offering is evil. I cannot accept that the clans must live by lies. I have to make them see the truth. If force is needed, then so be it."

"Can anyone be made to see the truth?" Marthe asked, unexpectedly gentle.

Sear frowned savagely. "The world has changed since the Citizen gods came with their Offering and their visiondraught. It has become uglier. Words alone will not heal this wound. I will find out the truth and I will bring it to the clans. Then I will deal with the wardens."

"Are you so sure the freeing of our people is the only reason you hunger to enter the forbidden city?" Marthe asked Sear. "It seems to me you hunger too much for the Citizen gods' power."

Sear gave her a hot look. "Our people would benefit from the skills and powers of the Citizen gods."

"Are you sure of that? And it will be a simple matter? To master the power before they find you and kill you?"

Sear ignored this. "We must capture a Citizen god and demand mindbond so that we will know how to enter the dome."

"We have tried that. Their minds are closed and they always die too soon to tell us anything," Ford said.

Sear nodded eagerly. "They die because we tear their white skins. We must capture one without breaking the skin. We can force them to speak."

"And if you do manage to get into the city? What then?"

Sear looked at Marthe challengingly. "I told you. I will find proof and weapons. When the clans know the truth, they will fight the Offering."

"And what then? If you gobble up the power of the Citizen gods, will you become another Citizen god to dominate the clans?" Marthe asked.

"I have no hunger for such powers," Sear said wearily. "But I will rule my own life. The clans must return to the honour of mindbond."

"Perhaps the wardens drove us out so that we might discover the truth without fear of retaliation from the Citizen gods or from the Lord wardens," Marthe said.

Sear gave her a startled look. "You think that?"

Marthe shrugged. "I say only that many things are possible. Would all the wardens be power-hungry traitors? Perhaps there is no other way for them to oppose the Lord wardens."

"It is a thing I had not thought," Sear said. He glanced at Ford. "We must explore this possibility with Bramble."

Ford nodded.

"Whatever their reasons, the Offering is an abomination," Era said. "Those who supported it will resist the truth because it must mean the end of their domination. When we have won, we must force the wardens to mindbond, and those who hide their eyes from the truth will die. Their blood will be barter for the Blessed Walkers.''

Merlin looked at Era, shocked at her easy acceptance of killing. She was bewildered by all she had heard. It seemed the leaders of the clanpeople had permitted the Offering. Again Merlin wished she could simply ask what the Offering was. But she dared not expose her lies. Sear had sounded a little mad when he cursed the Citizen gods for lying. He seemed to have a violent hatred of lies. What if he discovered she had lied? She looked around and found herself staring into Ford's troubled face across the clearing.

"*Merlin?*"

She gaped. She had distinctly heard Ford say her name, but his lips had not moved.

Why do you refuse to Accept me? How do you close your mind like the Citizen gods?' she heard him ask.

Again his lips did not move and Merlin realized, amazed, that he was reproaching her telepathically.

"*Merlin?*"

"Merlin?" Sear repeated aloud, coming up behind her. She started violently.

"I suppose all of this is a shock to you? When I first left, I did not fully understand how it was. We have learned much about the Citizen gods and the Offering. But we do not have proof that the Offering is a lie and so we remain outcasts. But we will not be outcasts forever.''

Merlin nodded faintly, wishing someone else would call Sear's attention before she betrayed herself in ignorance. She was still reeling mentally from Ford's use of telepathy.

Sear smiled. ''Ford Sent to me that you were an asker of questions, like him. It is not an easy thing to be. But perhaps this time it has saved your life. Life among the scatterlings is not soft, but it is better to live hard with honour than to bask in soft lies. After mindbonding, you will truly be one of us. There is pain, but the rumours that say mindbonding is harmful were begun by the Lord wardens to end the practice. You need not fear it.'' He smiled, patted her shoulder and announced the break was over.

Merlin hoped she did not look as frightened as she felt. Sear's words underlined her danger and increased her desire to get away from the scatterlings. Ford's telepathy terrified her, for it was clear the mindbond meant some sort of telepathic communication. What would they do when they discovered she was not telepathic?

''It is possible in the future that human beings will make better use of their large brains, and that such abilities as telepathy and telekinesis will become as

commonplace as ordinary speech," offered her inner voice.

Merlin wondered if all the scatterlings were telepathic. That would explain the long silences she had noticed between them. The Citizens were not telepathic. Ford had said their minds were closed. Merlin shivered with fear at the thought that the scatterlings might think she was a Citizen. She felt sick with fright realizing Ford must have tried before to reach her. He had been puzzled by her lack of response, but he had not told anyone else yet.

Merlin felt the now familiar prickling feeling that warned she was being watched. Ford had come up behind her.

He looked at her questioningly. "How do you close your mind to me? I feel your thoughts drawing away. Is this something the Seaside Region clans can do?"

"I'm tired," Merlin stammered idiotically.

He frowned. "I have never heard of such an ability. Do you hide your mind because I did not ask aloud for mindbonding? I know it is the traditional way."

Merlin bit her lip, searching for words. She realized Ford thought she chose not to communicate telepathically with him. It had not occurred to him she was unable to respond. He seemed to find an answer in her silence.

"Perhaps it's me you reject, rather than my Sendings."

Merlin blinked at the hurt in his voice. She bit her lip, unable to tell him the truth. "I hardly know you," she said weakly.

"I thought our hunger for knowing made us kindred spirits," Ford said. "Perhaps you are afraid of mindbond. There is little pain, and is is not like ordinary pain. I would offer to make the mindbond at the Hide, if you will it."

Merlin licked her lips. "If we are friends ..." she began, intending to ask him for help, but he would not let her finish.

"I speak of the mating heat, and you speak of friendship?" He sounded affronted.

Merlin gaped. Mating heat? She had thought they were talking about telepathy.

"Ware," Marthe said loudly in a dull voice. She held up her hand and Merlin heard the trees rustle nearby.

A girl in a grubby white shift stepped out from the trees and glided towards them. She passed within a hair's width of Sear, but did not glance at him. The others moved aside quickly, giving her a clear passage through their midst. She looked at no one. Her mouth hung slackly open. A dribble of saliva ran down her chin and onto her grubby bodice. Her eyes were small dusty pebbles, completely expressionless.

"The Citizen gods fly. We must split up. Two's company, three's dead," Marthe said, when the girl had gone.

"Two's company . . ." began the internal voice, but Merlin repressed it savagely, her thoughts full of the blank-faced girl. The scatterlings seemed more saddened than surprised at her extraordinary appearance and disappearance, so Merlin dared not ask who she was.

Ford moved towards Merlin, but Marthe stepped between them. "She will travel with me," she told him firmly.

Ford looked mutinous, but then his face cleared. Merlin guessed Marthe had said something to him telepathically. They all left in pairs a few minutes apart. Merlin and Marthe were last to go.

When they were alone, the dark-haired girl turned to Merlin. "You had better go now, while you have the chance."

"I knew at once that you were not a refugee from the Seaside Region," Marthe said. "It was obvious you were hiding something. The others might have seen it too, except they were too full of excitement about the crash of the flier. I saw the truth only because I Remembered your coming from my dream: a stranger – strange to us and to herself – with no knowledge of our ways, who would come among us."

"Remembered? You mean, you knew I was going to come? You could see the future?" Merlin asked, astounded.

"I wish I could see into the future," the William voice confided wistfully.

"Precognition has never been proven conclusively . . ." the metallic voice said caustically.

Merlin clamped down her thoughts, silencing the voices.

Marthe's face was impassive and ascetic. "I have the gift of Remembering what has passed and what will come to pass."

"Then you knew I lied to Ford and the others. Why didn't you expose me?"

"It is not the way of Rememberers to act without reason. I have considered your coming, and having considered, it came to me that you must leave us."

Merlin hardly heard her words. "If you can see the past and you knew I was coming, then you must know who I am and where I come from!"

Marthe gave her a cold look. "Remembering is not a certain art, and there is much I fail to Remember, or to understand clearly, and much that may not be told. I say only that you are the stranger who was to come among us. I have seen that should you reach the Hide, you will fail the truth-testing of mindbond, and you will be killed, as will Ford, who chooses to bind his fate to yours with his acceptance of wordbond." She frowned. "That was something I did not foresee, but he has a touch of Remembering too, though it is usually a feminine gift. He is fascinated with you, because he senses you are different, and his heart

66

draws him always to the unknown. He mistakes his hunger for knowledge for the mating hunger. He does not, or will not, see that you represent darkness and despair for him and for us. Great danger and chaos follow with you like a stealthy shadow. And so I tell you: Go! Take your burden of strife away from us!''

Merlin swallowed a lump in her throat. ''You ... you must have me muddled up with someone else. Sure I lied about who I am, but only because I don't know who I am. You make me sound like a monster.''

Marthe held up her hands. ''Weave your web of words in other ears than mine. I have seen that you are the great liar. You wanted to leave so strongly – I heard you – so now go.''

''Where can I go?'' Merlin asked, frightened by the queer ominous predictions of the swarthy Rememberer. To her mortification, she burst into tears.

After a long moment, she scrubbed the tears from her eyes and cheeks, humiliated that Marthe might think she had cried deliberately. But Marthe's expression had softened fractionally.

''I have seen you enter the Valley of Conclave. Perhaps you are meant to find your answers there,'' she said.

''A meeting?'' Merlin asked, trying to sound calm.

''Much more than a meeting,'' Marthe said. ''There will be many hundreds of clanfolk there, from all over the land. They travel across the Region of Sands to take part in or to watch the ceremonies, to seek wisdom, to barter goods and services. Some will have gathered in the Valley of Conclave already, and others will be travelling there still. Conclave will convene in three days."

"Won't they know I'm not one of them?" Merlin asked uncertainly.

Marthe shook her head. "If you are careful, no one will recognize that you are a stranger, for customs differ greatly between clans and each clan will think you belong to another. But you must not call attention to yourself. If you are revealed to be clanless, you will be executed as an exile who made the mistake of trying to rejoin the clans, or worse. Stay away from anyone wearing black robes, for they are Rememberers, and may know." Marthe drew her ragged shawl around scrawny shoulders. Fleetingly she looked more like an old woman than a girl. Merlin realised the Rememberer was about to depart and was suddenly terrified of being left alone.

"What will you tell Sear?" she asked.

Marthe looked over her shoulder austerely. "That does not concern you. A Rememberer is a sacred adviser and is not questioned. Know that if you are found by Sear or any of the scatterlings, they will probably kill you."

"Kill me?" Merlin said aghast. "Why didn't you just tell them to kill me straight away and save all the bother?"

"I considered it, but the course was ill-fated,"

Marthe said calmly. "You must not die by clan hands. You should leave now. It may be that you will reach the Valley before nightfall."

"Of course," Merlin said angrily. "And where is this Valley of Conclave?"

Marthe lifted her brows. "Travel towards the setting sun until you see in the distance the shape of a great hill. Go towards that hill and you will come to the place where the Region of Great Trees meets the Region of Sands. You will see that the hill hides a smaller twin. The Valley of Conclave lies between these two. It can be entered only through a narrow pass from the right side as you face the hills. All travellers will use the great highway across the Treeless Plain, which runs close by the Region of Great Trees. You must join the road unseen and enter the Valley as just another traveller. Do you understand?"

Merlin nodded bleakly. "Thank you," she said ironically.

The Rememberer inclined her head regally.

"One last thing. Your course will founder, though I cannot say how, if you are exposed in the Valley. Therefore ask few questions lest you call attention to yourself. Listen and learn what you may that way. Seek out those on the Mound of Wisdom and let them speak." She drew her shawl over her head and departed without a backward glance.

Merlin stared after the Rememberer until she was

swallowed up by the dense forest. Then she began to
walk towards the setting sun.

$\mathbf{M}$erlin fingered the iron band around her neck, half wishing she had shown it to Marthe.

Regrets warred with unease when she thought about her strange conversation with the sombre Rememberer. There were so many questions Marthe might have answered, yet the few words she had spoken had been vague and frightening. What more might she have said, had she chosen?

Merlin tried to tell herself Marthe was primitive and superstitious, except the Rememberer did not strike her as a fool or a witless visionary. Underneath her cold manner, she had been genuinely dismayed at Merlin's appearance and grimly determined to drive her away from the scatterlings. Her determination forced Merlin to take her warnings seriously. But she could not honestly believe she represented some sort of evil omen for Marthe and the exiled scatterlings. She, who seemed to have so little control of her own life and fate, could hardly be a danger to anyone else. Marthe had called her a liar but surely the lies she had told were not so terrible.

"Once upon a time, there was a great and powerful sorceress called Merlin . . ." the William voice began softly. Merlin wondered suddenly why she always remembered William whispering. The voice offered no answers to his ghostly presence in her mind.

She sighed resolutely. There was enough to contend with without worrying about Marthe, or the mysterious William. What was it Ford had said? That there were enough real worries in the world without imagining new ones?

Merlin was surprised to find she missed the scatterling youth.

He had treated her well, though she had hardly been appreciative at the time. He was the only one since she had wakened to have offered her unconditional friendship. She had not spoken to a friend since . . . she couldn't remember when. She laughed bleakly at her own joke.

She had failed to see Ford's value because she had been too preoccupied with her own problems. The truth was, she thought sadly, she had been more than slightly frightened by his savage appearance – his scarred eye and his near nakedness. She was ashamed of her prejudices, but in honesty, she had to admit that she had been even more unnerved by his sudden interest in her. Remembering the hungry way he had looked at her, she shivered.

She missed Ford's company, but she did not miss his gaze or the alien quality of his appearance. She did not miss his telepathic questioning. She was sorry he had decided to be attracted to her. When he had talked about his hunger for knowledge, she had actually forgotten the differences between them. Of course, she couldn't possibly love him. He was too strange and different for that, but she thought they might have been friends.

"I speak of the mating heat, and you answer me with friendship?"

The memory of his scathing tone made Merlin redden. Maybe friendship between them wouldn't have worked anyway. She was getting sentimental and stupid because she felt lonely.

Merlin had spent the previous night curled in a hollow tree-trunk in a barren clearing, too tired to search for anything safer. Her last waking thought had been that the only dangerous animals in the Region of Great Trees seemed to be two-legged ones.

She did not wake until a beam of sunlight stabbed like a knife onto her cheek. Extricating herself from the tree, Merlin was stiff and sore all over, the muscles in the backs of her legs knotted and tight. Hobbling back into the shade cast by the giant trees with their tough, pungent leaves, Merlin came to the conclusion that she must have led a very lazy life to be so unfit.

"Exercise should be moderate and consistent, and supported by a nutritionally balanced diet for the fullest effect," the mechanical voice advised.

"Sure!" Merlin snarled. The shadowed ground was soft underfoot, and moist, as if fed from a subterranean water source. Thirsty, she had only to gouge a hole in the ground and wait for it to fill. The water was cold and slightly brackish.

She then massaged her muscles gingerly until they felt less rigid, relieved herself and set off, chewing the final tough strips of meat.

She felt euphoric at having survived the night alone. She was not starving, even if the remaining meat had smelled spoiled; she had quenched her thirst and was well rested. And for the first time, she woke with a purpose.

Perhaps that explained her surprising calmness. She wondered if Marthe really could see the future. Remember, she had called it. It had been unnerving to be told that she would go to the Conclave because the Rememberer *saw* it. On the other hand, Marthe had seemed to imply that she saw a combination of possible futures, rather than a single, certain future so perhaps she was not as positive as she made out. The thought of being able to see the future was a fantastic if confusing notion. Of course most of what had happened since the accident would fall into the realm of impossible fiction in the world of her memory.

Where am I? Merlin wondered again. The question had less force than on the previous night. She was beginning to accept her new life, simply because she had no memory of another to regret. As well, there was the pressing need to come to terms with the changed world, and to understand it, which left little energy for curiosity about the past.

She was not sure the Conclave would yield anything useful, but it was better to be travelling there with a purpose than blundering around aimlessly among the trees. If she stayed in the forest, she would be found by the Citizen gods or the scatterlings; either way, it would be dangerous.

She decided not to think beyond the Conclave. If that answered no questions, she would worry then about what to do next.

Midway through the morning, Merlin climbed a steep ridge. At the crest she saw Marthe's distant jagged hill. She felt a rush of relief and realized she had secretly feared that the Rememberer's directions were calculated to get her lost, despite their apparent clarity. She sent a silent apology to the Rememberer and set off at a brisk pace down the other side of the ridge. Before long, she was walking up again. The ground became increasingly corrugated. One minute she was carefully picking her way down a steep descent, the next she was panting her way up a sharp incline.

Each time she reached the top of a ridge, she took fresh bearings from the hill. She was gradually moving away from the sunset and closer to the hill and calculated that she would reach the end of the Region of Great Trees by late afternoon.

In fact, she reached the edge of the Region of Sands shortly before midday.

The Region of Great Trees ended with perfect and impossible symmetry, as if someone had cut along the edge with a pair of shears, and lain it in the middle of a desert of pale yellow sand. This reminded Merlin of her original notion that the trees were part of an immense plantation. Through the gaps between trees, the Region of Sand stretched unchangingly to the horizon, and a wall of solid wavering heat lay up against the cool, dark shade offered by the trees. The hill she had followed was not in the Region of Great Trees as she had supposed.

A road ran straight from beyond the flat horizon towards the trees, breaking off abruptly a few metres from the treeline, and curving back on itself towards the side of the hill which now revealed its shy twin.

Between them must lie the Valley of Conclave. Merlin could see no telltale gap, but Marthe had said the way into the Valley was narrow. The Rememberer had warned her to get onto the road unseen. This would be more difficult than it had sounded. There was an unbroken line of traffic right from the horizon, and few gaps between groups. And even when there were gaps, the road was so straight and the terrain so flat, she would be seen from miles away.

Stupidly, she had not asked Marthe why it was important that no one see her come out of the trees. The road curved within a few metres of the treeline at one point, and Merlin decided she would make her break from there. Working her way through the trees, she was careful not to expose herself to the travellers, though they seemed to ignore the trees altogether. Merlin wondered why they kept so carefully to the road. No one even looked at the trees or took advantage of the shelter they offered from the searing sunlight.

She sat down using a bush right at the edge of the treeline to screen her in case someone did happen to glance her way. Breaking off strategic branches, Merlin was able then to see the road right in front of her and in both directions.

Settling down to wait for a break in the traffic, she was in no hurry to join the road. She was glad of the opportunity to study the other travellers.

There was no uniform dress code among them. She had half expected all the people travelling to the Conclave to be dressed similarly but there was a dizzying variety in the clothing they wore. This confused her until she remembered Marthe had told her the clans were very different.

The strangest thing though, was that despite different clothes and dramatic variations in body shape and facial race features, all of the pilgrims had darkish skin. No one's skin was white as she remembered white skin. The skin tones ranged from her own pale golden shade and progressed to a dense chocolate brown. Uptilted Japanese eyes and thick Negroid lips went equally with all colours. There was not a single definite race type among the travellers.

She puzzled over this for a bit, before accepting she had no more likelihood of understanding this than her own dilemma.

Gradually, she noticed there were variations in dress that seemed to mark one clan from another. Idly, she began to try categorizing clans by their clothing.

There were those she named camel clanfolk, clad in flowing robes bound with thongs of leather. The men and women were hard to differentiate in this group, but they all rode on shaggy, camel-like creatures.

These were the first animals Merlin had set eyes on, apart from the dead ferret things Ford had caught and killed. Again she wondered at these animals that were not quite like those she remembered. Her memory was filled with pictures of wild creatures in cages and roaming free in a natural state.

Abruptly, she forced the questions away and went on studying the bypassers.

Some travellers wore rich, fluttering layers of vividly dyed cloth. Even from a distance, their ankles and arms sparkled with gems. She called these the jewelled clan. It appeared the wealth of clans varied too. Some of the jewelled clanfolk rode in small, ornately finished sedan chairs, carried by men who looked like they came from another poorer clan.

"Unequal distribution of wealth is the basis of the world's wars and poverty," the mechanical voice said. Whatever else had changed, Merlin thought this had not.

She found herself remembering thin, huge-eyed Cambodian children from a culture starved and victimized by wealthy nations for whom their tiny country was no more than a warground. The children were as clear as all the other memories, and she wondered at this. Was it possible she had met those children?

If so, why did she remember the children but not meeting them? She thrust the unanswerable questions away, recognizing composure lay in not constantly staring into the gaping holes in her mind.

There were two clans who wore scant dress, and Merlin was unsure if they were one clan or two. The second group also wore loin cloths but they were so heavily painted that at a distance they seemed to be wearing patterned body suits.

All the travellers, regardless of dress, carried baggage. The poorer clans carried their own, while others used servants or the camel beasts. She guessed these bundles represented the products Marthe said would be sold and traded at the Conclave.

This reminded Merlin that she possessed neither money nor goods to barter. She wondered if this would cause her any difficulty and experienced a sudden suspicion that Marthe had known she would need money, but had not bothered to tell her. The Rememberer had been very anxious to get rid of her.

Merlin chewed her lip uncertainly. So far, everything Marthe had told her had been proven true. There was no real reason to suspect her now.

Just the same, Merlin knew she was at the mercy of the other, and without warning a wave of loneliness and despair washed over her at the knowledge that she had no choice but to trust someone who had disliked and feared her. She realized her composure was a fragile wall.

"*True friends are rare, and should be treasured above all things,*" the William voice said.

Oddly, this made Merlin think of Ford. She had spoken of friendship to him, but in reality, that was not what she had offered. And now she was alone. Merlin's eyes filled with tears. The questions that had tormented her since she had woken flew at her, savage as magpies protecting their nests. Merlin cried without restraint, and tears rained down her face with alarming ease.

"*Your name is Merlin,*" the William voice said.

"Great. That helps a lot," Merlin snapped, then grinned, struck by the idiocy of getting angry at the disembodied voice. This gave her the strength to throw off the moment of despair.

The truth was that the only one who could help her was herself, so she might as well get used to it. She must rely on her instincts and trust them; she thought Marthe had not lied when she said there might be answers for her in the Valley of Conclave, so she must find a way to enter the Valley.

She wiped her face dry with what remained of her tunic, determined not to cry again.

She jumped at the sound of a voice, then realized the wind had changed direction and was carrying snatches of conversation from the road towards the trees.

With a feeling of excitement, she inched forward on her belly to the very edge of the shade, listening.

No one even looked at the treeline, but Merlin was not brave enough to show herself in case someone did. She thought they might be afraid of the trees. Why else would they refuse so rigidly even to look at them? Perhaps there was a taboo associated with them. That might explain why Marthe had stressed the importance of joining the road unnoticed.

There was a lot of laughter, Merlin thought. This boded well. It was the laughter of people who expected to enjoy themselves. Merlin frowned at the sudden clear memory of a vivid and intricate painting of a country fair.

"*This picture is very old*," the William voice whispered reverently.

Merlin thrust the words and the painting from her mind and forced herself to concentrate on the travellers.

To begin with what she could hear was too disjointed to make sense, but at last a group of serious-faced men in rough, sweat-stained clothes passed by, walking slowly. Merlin strained her ears.

"Baltic clan have silk for barter this year ..."

"... odd since they have no knowledge of the secrets of ..."

"... one of the men married a silkmaker from Fallon and he learned the way of silkmaking in mindbond. She had no choice as his mate. There could be no secrets between them ..."

"This will change the fortunes of Baltic."

The words faded. Merlin frowned, wishing she dared to go nearer to the road. The snatches of conversation were tantalizing.

Behind the men came another group of men wearing elaborately embroidered kaftans and vests. The jewelled clan, Merlin guessed, though there were few jewels in evidence. Like their clothes, their manners were elaborate and ornate.

"... he tried to bribe the warden not to Choose the boy, but the warden denounced him to the Lord warden. He was executed, of course, and the boy taken anyway."

"What about the woman? Surely she was not blameless ..."

"I have heard the mindbond is more dangerous than was known. Nallar no longer practises it so commonly ..."

The group passed on and Merlin wondered about the function of the wardens. They sounded powerful – judge, jury and lawmakers all in one.

A harried-looking older man passed, holding the slender elbow of a pretty, petulant girl with intricately braided hair. The pair were surrounded by servants laden with bundles.

"... I cannot offer grain directly to Fallon, my doveling. They have no need for grainfoods. I will have to offer our grain at low cost to Gawlor for coloured dyes, which I will then have to offer to Fallon at prices less than Gawlor ..." the man said pleadingly.

The girl looked bored and unimpressed and Merlin grinned. If she were not mistaken, the older man was husband to the pretty sulking girl. She began to see that Conclave was, as Marthe had said, much more than a meeting of clan groups. The talk among travellers was all of trade and barter advantages and gossip concerning different clan yields and prosperity. There was no mention of money and this made Merlin wonder if the clans used money at all. It sounded as if they relied solely on barter. That would explain the wealth of the clans with desirable produce or abilities – Fallon clan's silkmaking, for instance.

As time dragged on, Merlin began to fear she would never get onto the road, let alone into the Valley.

It was hunger in the end that made her take the chance.

Traffic along the road eased fractionally towards late afternoon, while the numbers of travellers in groups increased, making it harder for them to stay within the borders of the road. Some way off, Merlin noticed a large group from the jewelled clan. They seemed to be playing a complicated running game. There was a lot of laughter – Merlin could hear them despite the distance. Every few minutes, someone would rush at someone else; there would be a brief chase and a scuffle before the pair resumed the path. The runners often ran very close to the trees.

Merlin's heart began to beat swiftly when she saw there was a gap between this group and the next. She stood up, and found her legs rubbery with fright. She had to try it, she told herself sternly. It might be her only chance. If she waited until the noisy jewel people had drawn just past her, then walked down quickly to join the road, there was a good chance she would not be noticed.

Once she had reached the road, she would drop

back, lengthening the distance between her and the other group. Merlin hardly noticed the people passing in front of her, so intent was she on the game-players.

If she could just break away from the trees at the moment one of the runners was close to the treeline, she doubted she would be noticed by either the game-players, intent on the antics of their friends, or by the group coming up behind, who would take her for a game-player.

The group before the game-players passed. Merlin gathered herself. Her heart beat out a jerky tattoo and she felt sick and breathless.

What would happen if she were seen?

As the group drew level, there was a feeling of inevitability in her breast; a now or never ultimatum forcing her to go on regardless of the risk.

"Some things are worth a risk," the William voice said urgently.

"Now or never," she whispered, taking a deep breath.

She stepped out into the blazing sunlight, and walked on stiff legs towards the road. It seemed a very long way. She felt terribly vulnerable. Her back hunched as she walked. She could almost hear the words: "Hey, what do you think you're doing?"

But no one called out.

Merlin stepped on the road, suppressing the urge to be sick. It was dreadfully hot and her back and hands were already damp with perspiration. She had not expected the blazing wall of heat beyond the shade.

Slowly, and with great apprehension, she forced herself to look behind. The other group had drawn near enough for Merlin to see they were painted people, but they took no notice of her.

With a thrill of elation, Merlin realized she had done it.

Relieved and utterly drained of energy, it was all she could do to keep walking. There was a loud burst of laughter from the group in front of her.

"Ha! Got you."

"My win this time. Serves you right ..."

Merlin heard the words from a long way off, as if she were under water. She forced herself to walk steadily, opening the distance between herself and the jewelled people. She judged it to be less than a kilometre to the hill. From the trees it had seemed closer. The sun beat down savagely on her naked head. She thought longingly of the water in the Region of Great Trees.

Sand lay over the road like a fine powder, shifting and drifting under the passing feet. The road itself was a proper paved highway crumbling away at the edges. Merlin wondered who had made it.

Her head was throbbing from the intensity of the sun long before she reached the narrow path leading into the Valley. Sweat dripped steadily from her chin and fingertips and she gasped with relief when the path curved into heavy cool shade.

The sudden cold restored her scattered wits.

The narrow path was bordered by solid, natural walls of stone on either side, and led steeply down and under a stone arch. From the top, there was a clear, if restricted, view of the Valley.

Directly in front was a virtual city of tents divided into sections – clan groups, Merlin guessed. Minute puffs of bluish smoke suggested cooking fires and her stomach creaked loudly.

On the far side of the Valley, the two hills were still yoked together by a wall of stone, making the slender path the only way in and out of the Valley. Near this wall was a great, still mirror-like pool of water. Beside this, at the back of the first mountain, a rough temple was carved into the stone cliff.

Everywhere there were crowds of people, numerous and active as ants.

At the very end of the path, just beyond the arch, the pass became so narrow only one could enter at a time. With a note of alarm, Merlin realized there were two people flanking the end of the pass like guards.

Frightened, she looked behind her. No one seemed disturbed by the guards, if that was what they were, but it looked as if they were questioning each arrival. With a sinking heart, she knew that the press of people behind gave her no option but to go on.

Her heart began to race.

The two gate people stared silently at a painted man, then nodded after a moment and he passed through. Merlin was close enough to hear them speak – except they were silent.

Another man came to the end of the path and the same thing happened.

This warned her the two gate people were using telepathy. What would happen when they came to her? Her mind whirled. Ford had said he sensed her thoughts. Was it possible for her to project them? She looked like the clanpeople and she shared their immunities. Could it be that she also had telepathy? She had never tried. Trembling with fright, she tried to make her mind receptive. Marthe had said nothing of the gate-guards, but she had made it very clear that exposure meant danger.

Merlin's heart thundered as the last of the richly dressed jewel people went through. Then it was her turn.

"*Clan*?" asked the gate-man telepathically. Merlin almost wept with relief. But how was she to answer? She dared not say Fallon clan because of her rags. She savaged her memory for another name, and prayed it would suit, then she thought it as loudly as she could at the guard. If she did not have telepathy, she was about to find out.

The gate-man winced visibly. "No need to scream it at me," he said aloud wryly. "I can take a mindprint without that. Nallar clan it is. Now pass and peace to you."

Merlin stumbled forward into the Valley on legs that felt curiously detached from her body, wondering if a mindprint was something like a voice or fingerprint. Whatever they had been looking for, Merlin's mindprint had passed muster. She was in!

"Did he say you belonged to Nallar clan?" asked a masculine voice politely. Merlin froze. The speaker was one of the wealthy looking game-players who had gone in before her.

"Nallar?" drawled a slightly malicious masculine voice. "She is no more of Nallar than I."

There was an appalled hush from the rest of the group.

"What are you saying, Delpha?" asked one of his companions. "Are you calling her a liar?"

"Since when did Nallar dress in rags?"

Merlin looked at her accuser. He was tall and dressed in a black, tight-fitting body suit that accentuated his extreme thinness. A brilliant scarlet silk coat fluttered from his shoulders and a jewel-encrusted belt hung low on his hips. His eyes glittered gold through heavily painted drooping eyelids.

The red-faced man who had first spoken looked from Merlin to the man he had called Delpha. "Do you charge her with lying?"

Delpha twisted his thin lips into an ambiguous smile. He moved continually as he spoke: sinuous, graceful movements of hand and hip. "I said nothing about lies," he answered after a deliberate pause.

"But what do *you* say to her appearance, and her claim to be of Nallar?"

The other frowned heavily. "Such an accusation is not a matter for humour, even your peculiar brand of humour, Delpha."

"Poverty is no matter for laughter. It is unfortunate that some clans are less well endowed than Fallon. Perhaps Nallar has fallen on hard times." The new speaker was a rather effeminately handsome golden-haired man with long, beautifully smooth curls.

"I do not concern myself with the poverty of other clans," Delpha said langourously.

A dazzlingly lovely young woman reached up and stroked his cheek. "Don't take any notice of Delpha, Aran. He doesn't care what he says, so long as it causes a fuss," she said.

"I don't see that I am expressing any outrageous ideas to upset your lady's delicate mentality, Aran. My position is well known," Delpha said. "I ask only why we should trouble ourselves with clans stupid enough to settle themselves in inhospitable and barren terrain, yet sly enough in hindsight to come to Conclave and beg for charity? If Nallar has fallen, I will not offer aid," Delpha announced.

He turned abruptly to stare at Merlin, who had been trying to edge away. "And, Lady Meer, perhaps you can tell me when Nallar began to cut hair."

"It was burnt." Merlin spoke quickly, cursing

herself for not remembering how Ford and Era had reacted to her short hair.

Delpha raised dark saturnine eyebrows. "Burnt? How?"

Merlin blinked rapidly.

"But I don't understand how Nallar can have become a poor clan," said a girl with protruding eyes and a plaintive voice.

"Your lack of understanding is no surprise, Mya," Aran said caustically, sounding suddenly anything but effeminate. "Or have you begun to study the clans in your spare hours?"

The girl flushed unbecomingly and Delpha turned to watch her, seeming to lose interest in tormenting Merlin without an audience.

"I see no reason to bother myself with studying other clans, since their business is not mine," Mya said loftily.

Delpha laughed sharply, seeing a new target for his spite. "Unless the wardens decide to oathbind you outside Fallon ..."

Mya looked at him, her lower lip trembling. "But we ..."

"Mya. He's teasing you," Aran said. "You should not be so ready to believe all that is said to you. Ignorance is a thing study would repair."

"A good trait for an oathmate, I should have thought," said Delpha.

Mya burst into tears and ran off.

"Delpha, it is cruel of you to treat her that way when you have led her to believe you offer suit," said the lovely young woman who seemed to be paired with Aran. "You know she is terrified of being sent away from Fallon. And I do not like your allusion to the requirements of a bondmate."

Delpha shrugged. "Then it is fortunate that you continue to reject my suit." Merlin tried not to cringe as his sardonic gaze fell on her again. "And what are we to make of this one? Is Nallar fallen on hard times?"

"That's enough, Delpha," Aran said with cool finality. "The gate-guardians would have exposed an exile mindprint. If you have some other accusation to make, then demand mindbond of her and be done with it. But I somehow doubt you will make such a demand whatever your suspicions, because then she would know the truth of you also."

Delpha gave him a look of dislike. "I would not call for mindbond so freely here, Aran. The practice is out of favour." Before Aran could respond, he turned to face Merlin. "Well, girl, do not think yourself too fortunate. Aran merely defends you as one of the pawns in our game." He looked significantly at the Lady Meer.

Aran flushed angrily, but his lady spoke before he could react to Delpha's implication that the Lady Meer was another such pawn.

"Perhaps we could barter her services as a maid,"

said the Lady Meer kindly. She alone of the group seemed to see Merlin as a human being.

Aran smiled at her. "Why not? Bors?"

A big man in peasant clothes stepped forward.

"Bors, take her to the stalls," Aran ordered. "Arrange for her to be cleaned and dressed appropriately. And feed her. My lady will have no use for her until night falls."

Bors waited while Aran and the others departed, before turning to Merlin. "You are lucky, girl. If Aran had not intervened, Delpha would have sharpened his claws on you. Instead, you are to be taken to the stalls at Fallon's expense. Come, I will take you to the bathing tents."

Merlin followed the big man beyond the clan tents to a separate area for trade and barter which had not been visible from the path. She was amazed at the way Aran and his lady had never bothered asking her if she wanted a job. They obviously meant it kindly, but they had behaved as if she had no choice.

There were dozens of tents fronted by trestle tables laden with every kind of ware from cloth and rugs to jars of fruit and spices, and even sculptures and paintings. There was a large corral to one side, where a herd of the camel creatures milled in endless spirals. Merlin wondered if the animals were the only ones able to tolerate the long, hot journey across the Region of Sands. The smell of the pens flowed over the stalls to mingle with the odours of sweat and the perfumes of buyers.

But above all these Merlin detected the enticing odours of cooking food. Her mouth watered at the smell of meat roasting, sweet apples dipped in brown sticky toffee, and fresh loaves of dark bread.

"Could I eat first?" she asked. Bors grinned down at her. "Why not?"

After filling the gaping hole in her belly with bread and meat and sweet baked potatoes, Merlin tried some of the more exotic fare – purple crusted pies with a strong berry smell, a greenish donut with a very bitter filling, and a number of unusual fruits.

Licking her fingers sleepily, she sighed, unable to fit in another morsel. All she wanted to do was sleep and rest her distended belly.

Bors roared with laughter. "You are a person after my own heart, though your legs must be hollow. What is your name?"

"Merlin," she answered, and her languid air vanished as Bors frowned.

"That is not a name I have heard before ..." he said. "And you say you are of Nallar?"

Merlin felt all the food she had eaten revolve uneasily in her stomach.

"A word of warning," Bors went on. "Beware of Delpha. He will blame you because Aran bested him in front of the Lady Meer on your behalf. He is the sort who seeks revenge for the smallest slight, and there is bad blood between Delpha and Aran's line." He did not seem to expect a response. He led her to a large white tent. "These are the public bathing tents." He looked down at her. "This is your first time at Conclave?"

Merlin nodded uncomfortably. "I have not been here before ..." she said vaguely, wondering how she had exposed her ignorance. Bors nodded noncommittally and turned to a thin, pinch-mouthed woman swathed in white robes who had come out of the tent.

"This girl needs a bath and ... all the rest of it. And then she must be sent along to Fallon's stall for clothing," Bors instructed in a new imperious voice that told Merlin the bathing woman was lower on the clan social scale.

The woman appeared to recognize the big man and ushered Merlin into the tent with a servile smile.

"Make sure you reach Fallon's tents by nightfall," Bors called after them. "Someone will show you the way."

Merlin followed the woman through a long narrow section of the billowing tent. Flaps set all along one side led to separate enclosed areas, each containing towels and a round, flat pan. A vision of chrome taps and bath racks disappeared. Some of the sections were curtained, indicating they were occupied. A glimpse of a woman bathing guided Merlin's behaviour when she was left in one of the rooms.

The length of chain hanging from the collar looked incongruous against her naked body when she shed her rags. She draped a towel around her hair, taking up the chain at the same time. If she kept her head down, it was unlikely the collar would be noticed.

Before long, a young boy appeared carrying an enormous jug of steaming water on his head. Fortunately, he did not notice her reaction to his casual invasion. Without speaking, he poured warm water from the jug into the pan. Setting down the empty jug, he solemnly handed her a small phial of what looked like oil, and departed.

Merlin sniffed the bottle. She did not recognise the scent, but it smelled delicious. She poured it gingerly into her palm. It lathered up. Looking around to make sure no one was watching through the tent flap, she whipped off the towel, wet her hair and washed it. Massaging her scalp vigorously, she let the froth fall onto the water and slid under to her chin hiding both collar and chain with a sigh of relief. She had no idea what would be made of the collar, if anything, but Marthe had said to avoid drawing attention to herself and she had a strong feeling the collar would do exactly that, were it noticed. She had not anticipated so many minor pitfalls in passing herself off as a clanperson.

Of course, neither had she imagined being challenged within moments of entering the Valley. Still, things had worked out well enough as long as she could manage to stay away from the Fallon clan.

Her eyelids drooped. It was nice to be clean. And to be content. She patted her tight stomach and stifled a giggle.

Then she sobered. She would have to be careful of the malicious Delpha. Marthe had been very explicit about the dangers of being caught in a lie. But Merlin refused to worry in advance. It would not be too difficult to disappear among the hundreds in the Valley.

In the meantime – she stretched out luxuriously – she might as well enjoy the unexpected pampering.

Her heart jumped when the jug boy returned. The water was very hot but she dared not sit up until he was gone.

She wondered fleetingly if the bathing pans and all the other paraphernalia had been transported across the desert to the Valley, and what the permanent clan settlements were like if they treated themselves so lavishly during Conclave.

The boy returned with another jug of water. This time he set the jug on the ground beside the bath. When he left, she sat up and poured the jug over herself, gasping in shock as freezing water cascaded over her.

Shivering, she used the towels provided to dry, then donned a calico robe hanging on a stand, relieved to have the collar and chain hidden again.

She was just in time because the boy returned carrying a small bowl of something that looked like milk jelly.

She noticed the boy's eyes linger on her hair and decided it was time to go.

"You are ready for the rub?" he enquired.

Merlin pointed to the robe. "And ... my clothes."

"Your other clothing was burnt," the boy answered. "It was not thought you would wish to keep it."

Merlin shrugged, feigning boredom, and wondered what was to happen next. She had not wanted to go to Fallon's stall, but it seemed she had no choice unless she meant to walk round in a bath robe.

The jelly proved to be a smooth, stinging substance which was rubbed into the bare skin. The boy was deft and impersonal as he smoothed it over her flesh, but Merlin only let him rub her arms and legs and even then she felt embarrassed and selfconscious. When he was finished, he produced a comb and tidied her hair.

"It was burned," Merlin said casually. "The ends were trimmed for neatness."

"Your hair is a rare colour, and it will grow," he said commiseratingly.

Merlin was escorted by the boy to the Fallon silk tent, where she chose a pale-golden silk tunic with a high collar, slit from knee to waist on either side, a green shawl, loose trousers and flat sandals. The man in charge of this stall had been visited by Bors and expected her.

"Very nice, though it is a pity about the hair," he said when she was dressed. "Are you to join Fallon's pleasure tents?"

Merlin shook her head firmly, having some notion what they might be.

The man shook his head regretfully. "Perhaps when your hair grows. It is an unusual colour, like unwoven red silk." He reached out and stroked a curl. Merlin moved away fractionally.

"I am to serve the ... Lady Meer," she said.

The man nodded and sighed. "Well, you had better go to her now. It grows near to dusk and she will want you to help her prepare for tonight's feasting."

He led Merlin out of the silk tent and pointed out the fluttering purple banner of Fallon's dwelling tents in the fading daylight.

Merlin headed off briskly in the direction he had indicated. When she was safely surrounded by people, she changed direction, walking hastily back the way she had come, but skirting the silk tent. She caressed the lovely silk between finger and thumb, wondering how wealthy Fallon was to be capable of dressing casual hirelings so magnificently. Or perhaps the clothing and food were to be paid for by her services.

This meant she was stealing, since she had no

intention of presenting herself to Bors' master. She shrugged. If she were caught, she would have more to worry about than a few stolen clothes.

She noticed a man staring covertly at her hair and hurried away, thinking she must cover or somehow disguise it. If the Fallon clan were looking for her, they would be bound to mention her hair. She might have pulled the shawl over her head, but since no one else wore a shawl that way, she would stand out again. As well, Fallon's silk marked her. From what she had overheard, the silk appeared to be valued highly. She wondered if it would be possible to exchange the silks for more practical and anonymous clothing.

Crossing right to the other side of the trade area, she removed the green fringed shawl and folded it neatly. Before long she came upon a stall selling rough textured cloaks with hoods. The stall holder was lighting a torch. She stood back for a while and watched a man barter a beautifully carved jug for a coat. When this transaction was concluded, Merlin stepped up confidently, imitating her forerunner by pointing aggressively at a long cloak with a cowled hood.

"This for two of those."

The man stared at her, his eyes noting her hair. He hawked and spat on the ground. Merlin was not disheartened by this blunt show of disinterest. He had done the same to the man with the carving. He reached out and fingered the shawl disparagingly, shaking his head.

"What then?"

The man shrugged as if she were forcing him to deal with her. He eyed the shawl with dislike, but Merlin noticed he could not resist touching the silk. She smiled and he scowled, seeing that she had noticed.

"Two cloaks is too much."

"For Fallon silk?" Merlin asked archly.

The man grunted, shifted on his feet and shook his head minutely.

"Well, if you are not interested . . ." She took up the shawl. The man's hand snaked out, grasping her wrist.

"Wait a bit. What about a full cloak and a smaller one?" he offered. Merlin was certain the shawl was worth more than that, but she was growing uneasy about staying in the trade area in case Bors came looking for her. Yet she did not want to seem too eager to sell in case the buyer became suspicious.

She pointed to a square scarf. "The big cloak, the small one and that."

The man hesitated, then shrugged. "All right."

The exchange made, Merlin hurried off. On her way through the stalls she exchanged the small cloak for a knife and a loaf of bread, and the scarf for a jug of cordial. Cloth was clearly valuable.

Pleased with her purchases, Merlin flung the cloak

around her shoulders, hiding the silken tunic and trousers. Pulling up the cowl, her hair was also hidden and at last she felt as if she were invisible in the milling crowds.

It was growing dark, and rather than stay near the trade area, she tailed along behind a group of people making their way towards the temple she had seen from the path. She had a feeling the Mound of Wisdom Marthe had mentioned would be somewhere near the temple.

Two small girls were lighting torches marking the walkway in front of the temple, throwing its façade into sharp relief. The pool glinted darkly, offering a perfectly reversed image of the temple.

Most of the people walking along the path went to the temple, but the path continued. Merlin followed it, hoping it would bring her to the Mound. She had little expectation that she would learn anything about herself, but even the bath tent had shown her how much she had to learn about clan society.

The path ended at the edge of a square of raised ground planted with bushes and small trees. There were torches at the edges of the Mound and the light dimly revealed people walking or sitting on benches on the Mound.

Taking a deep breath, Merlin stepped up and walked towards an old woman seated alone in a shadowy arbour of trees. Uncertain how to open a conversation, she hesitated.

The woman had not noticed her standing in the shadows. She smiled at someone coming up behind her. Merlin turned to see an elderly man approaching, his long grey hair bound in a loose plait. Unconsciously, she stepped back into the trees so that she could not be seen.

"Greetings, Helf," the old woman said.

"Sheula, it is good to see you," the old man grunted painfully, sitting down next to the woman on the bench. "It is a weary journey to the Valley these days."

"Yet you come when you need not," Sheula responded.

Helf nodded. "I come to speak of my idea for the clans to exchange-foster the children of other clans. Ora believes you will rule against me."

The old woman nodded decisively. "Warden Ora is correct. I do not favour the clans becoming too close. Yours is a dangerous idea and unpopular among the other wardens."

Merlin's heart jumped at the sudden realization that the two old people were wardens. She stood very still.

"Dangerous?" Helf snorted. "Sheula, you sound as if I propose some dark and potent blending of bloods."

"Isn't that it?" Sheula asked.

He looked taken aback. "I do not know what it is you fear, Sheula, you and the others. Once it was considered healthy for clanfolk to move from clan to clan and for mindbond to take place from one clan to another. I propose this plan to promote harmony and better understanding between the clans. This selfish isolationism must end."

Sheula looked unmoved. "Surely Conclave meetings are enough to show you what can come of bringing the clans together. Each year, little more is done than squabble."

"That is my point. One Conclave a year is not enough. If there were more traffic between clans, there would be more ease of discussion, more harmony. Before the Citizen gods came, there was talk of more frequent meetings. Now we meet only to make the Offering."

"You are a dreamer and a fool, Helf, to believe there can ever be harmony between clans. No wonder Sadik does badly this year if this is a sample of your wisdom," Sheula said coldly.

Helf looked indignant. "You are clanbound. You oppose this idea only because it is new."

Sheula snorted. "It is you who are clanbound, Helf. You speak of mindbonding, yet you know as well as I do that it is a barbaric throwback. Wordbond is enough."

"I do not share that view. Wordbonding permits lies. Mindbonding went from fashion only when the Citizen gods came out," Helf added.

"Perhaps it is time you stepped down from wardenship. Better still, if you are so dissatisfied, become an exile. Join the scatterlings."

"At least they honour the mindbond," Helf snapped. "Or so I have heard."

The old woman's expression was sour. "Sometimes you come perilously close to heresy."

"I am too old to be afraid of breaking rules, Sheula, and too old to fight with anything but words."

"Your words almost saw you slain last Conclave."

Helf inclined his head. "I only advocated that we request mindbond with the Citizen gods that we might better understand the process of separating the soul from the Blessed Walker."

"You did not want understanding! The Lord wardens saw that. You would have had us insult the Citizen gods by demanding proof of their word?" Sheula hissed.

"There was a time when the mindbond was considered an honour, not an insult," Helf sighed. "But that was voted down. It is past."

"Your attitude is dangerous, Helf. I am your friend, but do not walk too far out onto a thin branch. I would not speak of mindbonding or the scatterling exiles."

"So now wardens must guard their words. Would you report me?" Helf asked gently.

Merlin wondered that the wardens did not guard their words more carefully. But perhaps they were so elevated in clan society, no one would dare denounce them but another warden.

Sheula shook her head. "No. But you must be more orthodox in your attitudes. Accept what must be. Sadik is an isolated clan holding, but you must keep up with the times. The clans tithe children to the Citizen gods, just as they tithe to Conclave. This is for the good of the many. You know that. Before this, our people were hunted down and herded like cattle. Many died. It is for the best."

Helf shook his head, and Merlin saw despair in his eyes. "I thought this too, until my boy was Offered, and suddenly it seemed too high a price to pay for peace. Sometimes, it seems to me the visiondraught is payment for the Offering."

"The visiondraught is a gift from the Citizen gods, and increases the wisdom of the Lord wardens. You gave the boy up because it was the law, and because it was for the boy's good as well. Before, he was your servant, no matter that you had come to love him. Once Chosen, he had the chance to become a Blessed Walker," Sheula said.

Helf nodded sadly and stared down at his hands. Merlin was filled with pity for the sad old man. The conversation told her the Offering was indeed some sort of slavery. But why were the children given to the Citizen Gods called Blessed Walkers? It seemed no one knew what the Citizen gods did with those taken. Sear had been determined to get inside the Citizen gods' domed city to find out what happened to the clanfolk. But he had also talked of immortality, and the old woman on the Mound spoke as if being taken to the forbidden city was something wonderful.

With a gasp, Merlin realized this might be the answer to her loss of memory. Perhaps she had been Offered!

"Is someone there?" the woman called. Merlin's heart began to race as she realized she had given herself away – to two wardens! She had no choice but to try bluffing her way out of it. Reluctantly she approached the bench where the elderly couple were seated.

"What clan?" the woman demanded.

"Nallar," Merlin said, hoping the old couple were not of or well acquainted with the Nallar clan. At least she was no longer wearing rags.

Sheula nodded. "A good safe clan in these troubled times, though there is a rumour Nallar falls on hard times."

Merlin shrugged. The old woman looked at her expectantly, and Merlin had a flash of inspiration. "I come to the Mound to seek wisdom. My brother is to be Offered," she said, hoping she had phrased it correctly.

Helf looked up at her compassionately. "Accept the grief, child, for it is a sharp blade that will not blunt with time."

Sheula gave him a quelling glance. "Your brotherblood will return as a Blessed Walker, therefore give praise to the Citizen gods that his soul has been Chosen to dwell forever in happiness inside the forbidden city."

Helf reached out and drew Merlin closer. "Child, you have lost your brother firstblood, for he must be so for you to grieve. You must believe him dead for the one that returns will neither laugh nor weep nor speak to you."

Sheula rose and stared down at the old man. "Helf, you put this matter badly. Girl, in the early days, when the Citizen gods came from the forbidden city, our people did not understand, and many died. Then the Citizen gods revealed to the wardens their wish to grant eternal life to some few chosen clanpeople. And so began the Offering. Do not grieve for your brother, since he is one of the fortunate. The Blessed Walkers grace us as shadows of our loved ones and reminders that their souls are now sacred."

Merlin nodded slowly. It seemed those taken were returned. She had assumed they were kept or killed. She wondered why those who returned did not simply tell the rest what had happened to them. Or perhaps they were forbidden to speak.

"What is your blood name?" Sheula asked abruptly.

Merlin's heart missed a beat. She coughed, casting about for a name.

"Mou ... Mount," she said at last.

Sheula frowned. "An uncommon name."

Merlin stepped back. "I . . . I will have to go back. I am expected to wait on my Lady M . . . Meryl."

"Meryl?" Sheula said. "I do not know that name . . ."

"Goodbye," Merlin stammered, hurrying into the darkness. She stumbled along the path, glad it was now all but deserted, fearing she would hear the sharp-voiced Sheula cry out after her.

Passing the temple, her heartbeat slowed to normal.

Glancing at the pool of water, Merlin noticed a boy walking through the crowd standing beside the water. People bowed their heads as he passed, but the boy neither acknowledged them nor showed any expression. Like the girl in the Region of Great Trees, his mouth was loose and his eyes blank.

A terrible realization struck Merlin. The old man on the Mound had said those who came back from the forbidden city would neither laugh nor smile nor speak. And then she knew!

This boy was a Blessed Walker. *Blessed*!

With a flash of horror, Merlin remembered the mindless girl in the white shift who had appeared suddenly in the Region of Great Trees. But what could have been done to reduce these children to mindless automations? Sickened, Merlin, for the first time, sympathized with the scatterlings' hatred of the Citizen gods. She could understand why the scatterlings had turned their backs on the clans and wardens who preached that the walking catatonics were Blessed Walkers.

She walked on more slowly, remembering the misery in the eyes of the old man called Helf.

It was worse than murder, Merlin thought, horrified at the idea of children delivered up by their families to such a dreadful fate. It was now clear that the Citizen gods hunted clanfolk before the Offering was established. Then it had been decided to give clanpeople to the Citizen gods in exchange for peace and something called visiondraught. The whole business about immortality was just a way for the clanpeople to quiet their consciences about those sacrificed.

But Helf's doubts and regrets showed that not even all wardens accepted the myths fed to them by the Citizen gods. It seemed Marthe was right when she said some wardens did not welcome the Offering and the Citizen gods.

And why did the Citizen gods take the clanpeople, only to return them mindless?

Merlin shook her head wearily. It seemed she had travelled to the Conclave not to answer questions, but to gather them! She had no idea what to do next.

"Girl!"

She stopped dead, recognizing the voice of Bors. Turning slowly, she searched for words to explain her failure to appear at Fallon's tents at dusk. But the grimly accusatory look on Bors' face froze the excuses on her lips.

"You are not of Nallar, Merlin, if that is your true name. Who are you, and what are you up to? I demand mindbond."

7

"Why bring her here?" Aran asked.

He had been astounded to walk into the tent and find Bors alone with Merlin. She had the distinct impression Bors had been just as startled at Aran's appearance, though he claimed to have been searching for him.

A look of decision came over Bors' roughly hewn features. "I spoke with someone from Nallar in trade. He had never heard of a girl whose hair was burned. But when I accused her of lying, she did not deny it. She claims to have lost her memory. She said she has never mindbonded."

"You are a fool, Bors. All children learn how to mindbond. She is probably part of one of Delpha's complicated plots to discredit me and you have helped by bringing her here," Aran said.

"There is more. She claims to have been with the scatterlings."

Aran and his lady paled visibly in the flickering lantern light. Aran turned to face Merlin. "Who are you?" he asked grimly.

Merlin said wearily. "I told him: I don't remember. I stumbled on to the scatterlings in the Region of Great Trees. They would have known me if I were one of them. They thought me a runaway from the Seaside Region."

Aran shook his head. "This is impossible, Bors. You have put us in an intolerable position by bringing her here."

"You ... you think she lies then?" the Lady Meer said wistfully.

Aran looked at her sharply. "Of course she lies. It is an incredible story. If she had been an exile, the gate-guardians would have known it. They mindprint all of those Chosen, so they have mindprints of all runaways. What else could she be but a runaway if she was in the Region of Great Trees? If the gate-guardians let her through, she was no runaway. What else can she be but a spy?"

"Perhaps there is some other explanation. It is possible she *has* lost her memory. She spoke of Ford and Era," Bors said softly.

"Anyone might know the name of rebels," Aran murmured.

Merlin said: "The one called Ford had light-coloured hair and a scar – here." She pointed to her own face. Aran's lady moaned.

"Meer, please!" Aran said warningly to her. "Ford is an exile and dead to the clans. I will call the gate-guardians."

The Lady Meer put her fingers on Aran's rigid arm. "Aran, I must know. You would give your life for Bors and he for you, though you are called servant and master. Why shouldn't we speak freely before him? I thought Ford dead when the Rememberer said I would not see him again in this life. I must be sure this girl does not speak true."

Aran gave a defeated sigh. Meer turned eagerly to Merlin. "Tell me something about him that no spy would be told."

Merlin thought of Ford. "He ... he told me he asks a lot of questions. All the time. He says that has got him into trouble, but that he can't help himself."

"Not good enough," Aran snapped. "Delpha, more than anyone, would know that of Ford."

Meer looked at Merlin beseechingly.

She remembered something else. "There ... there is one other thing I remember him telling me. But I just don't remember when ..."

"Please," Meer whispered.

Merlin bit her lip. "He told me, when he was small,

a warden stuck a stick into a stingers' nest and gave him honey. He ... he said he was happy at that moment," Merlin added lamely.

Meer turned triumphantly to Aran. "I was there that day. And so were you. There was no one else but that old warden, and he is dead. Ford shouted out his happiness." She smiled tearfully. "Do you remember?"

Aran nodded and his face was sad. "I remember."

Meer swung back to face Merlin. "Ford lives, then? He is well? And Era?"

"They survive," Merlin said in a hard voice, knowing these people must have condoned the Offering of Ford and many others.

Meer flinched from the coldness in her voice. "You blame me, us. It is no more than I deserve. Era supported him, and when that failed, she fled with him." She began to weep softly.

Aran gave her an agonised look. "Meer, my love, don't. What could we have done? Opposed the clan wardens and be exiled?"

"Yes! Yes!" Meer sobbed wildly. "Why not? Isn't brotherblood worth more than fine silks and comfort?"

"Meer, we believed in the wordbond made between the Conclave of Lord wardens and the Citizen gods. We thought of him as a traitor," Aran said, falling on his knees beside her.

She shook her head, refusing to take comfort from

his words. "We did not believe. We *chose* to believe. It was easier to do that than to question the Lord wardens' decision to co-operate with the Citizen gods. I thought only of myself. I was afraid the hunting would begin again. I told myself the Blessed Walkers were fortunate, when in truth those we sent were a blood sacrifice ..." Her voice broke and she wept.

Aran stared at Bors helplessly. "Our lives are in your hands."

"Who would believe one soon to be elevated to warden status had denounced the Offering on the word of a humble servant?" Bors asked, an odd note in his voice. "What made you believe the Offering was a farce?"

Aran shook his head. "As Meer said, it was easier not to face the truth. Then one night I was praying in the clanshrine. It was dark and two Lord wardens came in, not seeing me. One of them spoke of exchanging one child for another in the Choosing. The Lord warden who asked for the exchange said he preferred a good servant to a mindless dolt. It sounds like a small thing, but he spoke with such disgust of the Blessed Walkers. I could no longer close my eyes ..."

Bors put his hand on Aran's shoulder. "You will not be permitted to speak of this. Some wardens guess the truth and accept the Offering; some do not. But those who accept have the power of the Lord wardens and the Citizen gods' deathweapons behind them. And you will not be permitted to demand mindbond to expose them. At the least, you would be exiled. You might survive, but she ..." He looked gravely at Meer's frail form, bowed with sorrow.

Meer looked up. "We will not wait to be exiled. We must leave at once to join Ford and Era."

Merlin stood dumbly, astounded at the strange turn of events that had brought her to the family of Ford.

Aran began to pace. "It is unthinkable. You would never see any of our friends or family again. We would be cast out."

"And we can remain, knowing the truth?" Meer cried.

"There is another way ..." Bors began, then he made a sharp chopping movement and slipped abruptly from the tent.

He returned moments later. "There was no one, but from now on you must be careful of what you say in public. You have enemies who would be pleased to see you executed or exiled."

Aran frowned savagely. "Bors is right, we must take care. I do not excuse my guilt. Even so, no good can come of us being exiled as well. Bors, you said there was another way?"

Bors nodded slowly. "You can help us and all the scatterlings better from within – as a warden."

Aran's eyes narrowed. "Us?"

Bors drew himself up and suddenly he looked less

like a servant than a master. "Yes. Us. And now I must trust you, for what the Lady Meer said was true. I would give my life for you, and now I risk it in telling you that the scatterlings are not the only ones who fight the Offering and the Citizen gods."

"Then the rumours are true!" Meer gasped in delight. "There *are* rebels within the clans."

Bors nodded with a faint smile. "The rumours were spread by us to give hope and to encourage those who might join us and give active help. The rebels will welcome you both if you wish to offer aid. But I do not lie. There is danger in all that we do. If you, or any of us are taken, the Lord wardens will mindbond you and take all our mindprints and all our secrets."

"The Lord wardens do not mindbond any more ..." Aran protested, but Bors shook his head.

"They mindbond when they are certain their own secrets will not be told. And their precious vision-draught is at risk."

"You mean ..." Aran began.

Bors nodded. "They mindbond only those to be killed or exiled. Or those given to the Citizen gods." He nodded pointedly at Meer's bowed head.

She looked up with shining eyes. "We might be killed? I know that. My flesh is weak, not my head, dear Bors. I would embrace such an honourable death if it came to that."

Aran asked: "How is it that you know so much about the doings of the Lord wardens?"

"There is much the rebels have learned about the Lord wardens and the wardens," Bors answered enigmatically.

Aran nodded and took Meer's hand. "Then let us fight as we fight best. We will work secretly with the rebels. But what of her?" He nodded at Merlin who had stood silent throughout the long discussion.

Bors frowned. "It is possible she speaks truly and cannot mindbond. Perhaps it would be best to send her back to the scatterlings."

"We can send word to Ford with her!" Meer exclaimed.

"I . . . I can't go back," Merlin said softly.

Aran stared at her. "What do you mean? If you refuse . . ."

"You don't understand," Merlin interrupted. "It's not that I don't want to help you, but the scatterlings will kill me if I go back. They had a girl there who can see the future . . ."

"A Rememberer?" supplied Bors.

Merlin nodded. "Yes. Rememberer. I was trying to slip away, but she knew. She sent me away before we reached the scatterlings' Hide. She told me I was going to come here and she told me the way. She said she saw – Remembered – that I would bring terrible trouble for the scatterlings. She . . . said they would kill me if I went back and that something bad would happen if any clanperson killed me."

Meer turned to Aran.

"She ... Remembered that you would bring harm to Ford and Era?" he asked in a puzzled voice. "Did she say what form this harm would take?"

"She couldn't see that, but she said I would lead Ford especially into danger," Merlin said. "He ... he gave some kind of guarantee about me to the others. That was one of the reasons I was trying to leave. He had helped me and I didn't want to get him in trouble."

"He gave wordbond for you when you had only just met?" Meer asked slowly. "He stopped them from mindbonding you?"

For some reason Merlin felt embarrassed at the look in the other girl's eyes.

"There is another thing we must consider," Aran said slowly, seeming to look at Merlin as a person for the first time. "The gate-watchers did not give the alert when you entered, therefore you cannot be an exile. So who are you?"

The three stared at Merlin curiously.

"That's what I'd like to know," she said, slightly exasperated. "I don't belong here. This whole world is like something out of a story book to me. It's not the world I remember."

"Book? What is that?" Bors asked.

Merlin gaped at him. Was it possible the clans did not have books?

"What do you suppose the Rememberer saw?" Meer asked slowly.

There was the sound of footsteps but before any-one could react the tent flap was flung open. Delpha entered grandly, a curling smile of satisfaction on his lips. He was followed by two men with sharpened staves. Merlin recognized them as the men who had guarded the entrance to the Valley.

"There she is," Delpha announced, practically dancing on his toes. His long dark hair was bound in an elaborate plait and studded with jewels.

Aran and Bors exchanged a speaking glance.

"We were just about to turn her in," Aran said quickly. "Bors brought her to me because he wanted to be sure he was doing the right thing."

"*Don't give us away*," Aran's voice spoke inside Merlin's thoughts. She sensed Aran's astonishment when she did not let him inside her thoughts, but there was no time to explain.

"Of course you were," Delpha smiled. "And now the guards have come. Isn't it lucky that I heard you questioning her?"

Merlin heard Meer gasp with fright. It must have been Delpha Bors had heard outside the tent. Delpha slanted a corrupt smile at Aran. "It appears to be too much for your dear lady, Aran. Perhaps she should lie down. But of course, first we must give evidence to the Conclave of Lord wardens. On this occasion, they may resurrect the mindbond and then we will know exactly how you *questioned* her. Come, the wardens are waiting for us to join them."

Aran put his arm protectively around Meer's shoulders and inclined his head with dignity. "Of course."

Delpha smiled and made a quick elegant gesture to the guards who escorted Merlin out.

On the way through the darkness to the temple, Merlin determined to try to protect Aran, Meer and Bors. Marthe had warned her she would bring trouble to the scatterlings. Perhaps this was how it would come, since it was clear the rebels within the clans had some traffic with the scatterlings. The Citizen gods would be delighted to have information about the scatterlings' Hide. She decided to tell as much of the truth as she could, since she might, after all, find out the truth of her own identity. But if anyone was going to be exiled, it might as well be her, since she was going anyway.

Between the pool of water reflecting fire poles and the star-studded sky arched above and the temple, a long table had been set up. Seated behind it were more than fifty elderly people dressed in bright blue: the Lord wardens. All around the edges of the pool, people sat on the ground, facing the long trestle table. They parted silently to let the newcomers pass, staring up at them curiously.

Brought to stand in front of the table, Merlin and the others were clearly expected. A guard stood between each of them.

"What is this all about? What is the charge?" asked

a grey-bearded man with hair straggling over hunched shoulders. His eyes were red-rimmed as if he had been ill.

"My Lord Romino, Delpha of Fallon accuses this girl of lying about her clan origin. He further accuses his clan mates, Aran and Meer of Fallon, and their servant Bors of Gawlor, of conspiring with the liar. He claims there is a plot to undermine the sacred Offering, and demands that the Conclave mind-bond to discover the truth of the matter," reported one of the guards.

The first charge raised a small scandalized murmur from the audience, but the charge against Meer and Aran fell into a shocked silence.

"Delpha, you have cause for these charges?"

Delpha nodded eagerly and stepped forward, smoothing his immaculate plait. "My Lord, I first saw this girl just inside the Valley. She said she was of Nallar, yet she was dressed in rags. I also noted her strange appearance." Delpha spoke silkily, but his hand whipped out and pulled off the hood Merlin wore. There was a stir from the crowd at her cropped hair.

"It was burned!" Meer cried, before Aran could stop her.

"See how she defends the liar!" Delpha cried triumphantly, making a dramatic uncovering gesture.

Aran moved compulsively towards the dark man, but Delpha stepped back behind the guards.

124

"See how Aran would attack me!" he sneered. "He is not fit to rise to warden status."

"That is enough," shrilled the Lord warden. "That is not a matter for you to decide. You say you found the girl's appearance and story unlikely?" He drank quickly from a small flask of liquid at his elbow.

Delpha nodded. "Well, my Lord, when I rightly spoke my doubts these three quieted me, claiming Nallar might have fallen on harsh times. They offered to employ the girl ..." he added significantly.

Merlin realized Aran and Meer's kindness made them appear to be guilty of collusion.

"May I speak!" she interrupted determinedly.

Delpha looked startled, but before he could respond, the warden had nodded, his fingers compulsively caressing the small bottle.

"There is no plot between these people," Merlin said wearily. "I have never seen these three before today, or anyone here at the Conclave. I woke a few days ago in the Region of Great Trees with no memory."

There was a murmur of shock from those assembled. "I came here to see if I could find out who I am. I said I was of Nallar only because I did not know what clan I belonged to. These people were kind to me, but when he ..." She pointed at Bors. "When he realized I had lied, he brought me to his master and they were about to denounce me to the ... gate-guards."

"Mindbond her. You'll see then if she lies!" Delpha shrieked wildly. The assembled Lord wardens looked at him disdainfully.

"Let me understand this," the Lord warden said slowly, his voice slightly slurred. "You claim to have named yourself of Nallar only because you do not know what your clan is?"

Merlin nodded, wondering what was in the little jug the Lord warden drank so often and so convulsively. She thought she could guess.

"Then this can be solved easily. Who recognizes this girl?" the warden thundered at the audience. One of the guards made Merlin turn around, holding a torch close to her face so that all could see her.

"She must be an exile," concluded another of the seated Lord wardens, when no one spoke out.

"She is not an exile, or a runaway. We would have known," said one of the gate-guards firmly, bowing at the waist.

"Then ..." The first speaker stood again. "Who claims her?"

No one responded and the wind muttered quietly in the still valley.

"Whoever knows her clearly fears to speak out," Delpha said, stroking his plait as if it were an animal. He had removed his gloves and Merlin noticed his index fingernails were extraordinarily long and painted black.

Merlin ignored him, making a sudden decision. "I

126

told you, I woke up with no memory of who I am or where I come from. I was taken in by a group of people in the Region of Great Trees ..."

There was a sudden uproar.

"The scatterlings!" someone cried. Merlin saw Aran pale.

The noise subsided slowly. "You say you were taken in by the exiled rebels who call themselves scatterlings?" the warden asked. "You talked to them? You went to their camp?"

"Not to their camp. But of course I talked to them," Merlin said crossly. "I was trying to work out who I was and where I was, and they were the first people I bumped into. They took me for a runaway."

"She is here to spy for them," Delpha snarled. "She is here to recruit rebels!"

"I ran away from them," Merlin corrected firmly. "They spoke of the Conclave and so I decided to come here to see what I could find out about myself. I ran off before they took me to their camp."

"Only a fool would believe a confessed liar," Delpha said insinuatingly. "Mindbond her and we will know the truth."

To Merlin's surprise, the Lord warden's eyes were evasive. She was also close enough to see that the pupils of his eyes were huge, covering almost the whole coloured part of the eye.

"*One of the few pleasures the masses can afford, despite being illegal, are the multitude of hallucino-*

*genics on sale on every street corner. One of the most
obvious symptoms of drug use is the unusual dilation
of the pupil."*

Merlin was certain the Lord warden was drugged,
and she guessed the drug was the substance called
visiondraught. For the first time, she wondered if the
Lord wardens were in control of themselves.

"I am not sure we should open ourselves to one
who may be a spy, Delpha. Therefore we will not
mindbond the girl," the Lord warden said. Merlin
could tell he had no intention of mindbonding.

"What about Aran, then? I heard him plotting to
help the rebels," Delpha cried frantically.

Aran moved violently, and was restrained by the
guards. "Lords, I don't know how much of this girl's
story is true, but I did no more than question her.
What would I have to gain by shielding her? On the
other hand, Delpha has much to gain if I am executed. Perhaps it is I who should demand mindbond
to establish my innocence."

The Lord warden looked uneasily at his fellow Lord
wardens before speaking, and Merlin guessed he was
consulting them telepathically. "We do not favour
this talk of mindbonding," he said at last. "Though
we do understand why Aran would consider it.
Mindbonding is harmful and reduces the capacity of
the brain. However, I see no need for Aran to defend
himself, since there seems no substance to this charge
you make, Delpha. From a few overheard words, you

128

impugn the honour of one the Lord wardens value highly. This is not the first time you have sought to discredit Aran.''

"I heard him talk about helping the rebels!'' Delpha screamed.

The Lord warden blinked sleepily. "There are no rebels.''

"My Lord, I demand ...''

"What do you demand, Delpha?'' asked the Lord Romino in an insultingly bored tone.

Delpha bridled self-righteously. "I? I only do my duty reporting a liar and in denouncing those who traffic with her. I call it strange that the Lord wardens do not trouble themselves to examine this matter more thoroughly.''

Suddenly an old woman seated in the crowd rose. Merlin recognized her as Sheula from the Mound. She wore a green tunic with a sash of Lord-warden blue across the bodice. "I know this girl!'' she cried. "She came to the Mound tonight. She said she had a brotherblood to be Offered.''

"Is this true?'' the Lord Romino asked Merlin.

"I have told you already, I came here to try to find out who I was. How was I to do that except by asking questions? I only went to the Mound because I thought I might learn something that would help me find out who I am. If I lied it was because I do not know what the truth is.''

A man in the audience spoke out. "In my clan,

there was a man who fell from a tree. Blood came from his ears and when he woke he talked of steps into the sky and angel gods beckoning him. He looked on his friends as strangers and remembered nothing of his life up to that moment. Perhaps this girl speaks truly when she talks of an accident."

"The charge of lying is a serious one," the Lord Romino said. "Yet if she is injured and raving, that charge will be erased. Nevertheless we must find out who she is before we can pronounce judgement."

Suddenly a woman seated amongst the watchers rose. She was dressed in black, a Rememberer.

"None here will know her. She is of the clans and yet a stranger to the clans," she said in an empty voice. Her eyes seemed to look through Merlin rather than at her.

All eyes swung to the black-clad Rememberer, almost invisible in the darkness. Suddenly Merlin wondered what the Rememberers really saw. How was it they couldn't see the truth of the Offering? And if they did, why didn't they speak out against it?

"What do you Remember of her?" asked the Lord warden.

The Rememberer inclined her hooded head. "She is the stranger who remembers nothing and all things. With her coming, the visiondraught will cease to flow."

There was a stunned silence, and the Lord warden

paled visibly, his hand closing convulsively around the little flask before him.

The Rememberer raised her hand. "She must not die by the hand of the clans. That will bring death and ultimate disaster on us. She must go to the forbidden city. She must go to the Citizen gods. Her fate does not lie in clan hands."

The Lord Romino looked relieved. "So be it. It is in the hands of the gods. She will be taken with those next to be Offered."

The Rememberer turned and glided into the darkness.

"She must be questioned," Delpha burst out.

"She will be questioned – by the Citizen gods," Lord Romino said.

"But what of these three who consorted with her? If you will not mindbond the girl, then question them," Delpha cried.

The Lord warden looked at Delpha with clear dislike. "You are not unlike the carrionbird, Delpha of Fallon, always hungry for someone's misfortune. I see no evidence that Aran is guilty of more than compassion and blindness. But if you wish to plead your case you may have the honour of going before the Citizen gods."

Delpha bridled. "I do nothing more than my duty, but I see it is not enough for a man to be honest and open and that truth has no place at this Conclave."

The Lord Romino ignored the insult. "Take her to

the temple,'' he commanded the guards. Meer made a convulsive move towards her, but Aran held her back firmly, his face impassive.

8

Merlin followed the guards as they glided ahead of her through the darkness with a feeling of renewed helplessness.

From the time she had left Marthe until Bors had called her name, she had felt that she had regained some measure of control over her life. But now she realised this had been an illusion.

She walked through the broad entrance pillars into the stony darkness beyond. One of the gatekeepers carried a torch, though it threw out a meagre light, scarcely illuminating the dim, straight, stone walls carved intricately in a series of pictures. Merlin was reminded of the sort of picture writing one would find inside an Egyptian pyramid. Perhaps this was how the clanpeople recorded things, she thought with distant interest.

She shivered, though it was not very cold. She thought she should be frightened, but instead she was filled with a passive, numb acceptance.

There were a number of empty rooms leading from the hall, like museum rooms waiting for an exhibition. Where are the museums and pyramids? she wondered with a feeling of despair. Do they exist; did they ever?

The guards stopped outside one of the rooms. Unexpectedly, it had a thick door and was barred. Without speaking, one of the guards lifted the weighty bar with an audible grunt, and the other pushed the door ajar.

Merlin went in and the door was closed and barred behind her. The room was not just a single room, but another hall, from which extended other rooms. There were torches set in tall stands lighting the rooms and she walked aimlessly from one room to the other. Each contained a single trundle bed and a lumpy-looking mattress. All, except the last, were empty.

Merlin could hear the murmur of voices as she approached the doorway. Inside, seated on stools drawn up to an enormous round table, were about twenty children of varying ages.

A child seated nearest the door glanced up and

smiled. "What clan? What name?" asked a plump, big-eyed girl beside her.

"What does it matter?" asked another girl apathetically. Seated at the farthest end of the table, she had sorrowful eyes, drooping lips and limp brown hair.

The other was unperturbed. "I'm Lefka," she introduced herself. "The dying lily at the end of the table is Beta. Welcome to the temple."

Merlin nodded and looked around at the other occupants of the room. Their expressions varied from interest to boredom. A short dark-haired boy sitting near the scowling Beta smiled.

"I'm Danna," he said, catching her eye. "Former of Nallar, and soon to join my brotherblood's soul and become one of the transcended in the forbidden city."

Merlin stared, realizing that all of the children in the room were to be given to the Citizen gods to be transformed into blank-faced, drooling catatonics like the girl she had seen in the Region of Great Trees.

She felt sick.

And I might join them, she thought, suddenly afraid. It had never occurred to her that she might be sent to the forbidden city herself. She forced herself to stop thinking of what would happen to her there.

Looking back at the boy called Danna, Merlin was struck by a sadness in his eyes.

He stood abruptly and came to stand near her. "Your name?"

"Merlin."

Danna bowed and smiled. "So, another candidate for eternal bliss. How many more, I wonder?"

"*I am afraid of dying ...*" the William voice whispered.

Lefka frowned at Danna. "What's the matter with you? You're beginning to sound like her." She pointed to Beta. "Aren't you excited to be going to the forbidden city?"

Danna smiled enigmatically. "Why wouldn't I be excited? Remember when the Citizen gods first came? How they hunted the clans, and how many were killed? What joys will await us in the forbidden city?"

"But people were hurt only because we resisted," Lefka protested. "If we had only understood what they wanted, no one would have been harmed."

Merlin looked at Danna, curious how he would respond. But he only smiled again. "Where do you come from?" he asked her.

Merlin opened her mouth, intending to lie, then it struck her that there was no longer any need. "I don't know," she said dully. "I've lost my memory."

Danna frowned. "Then ... why are you in the temple?"

"A few days ago I woke up with no memory," Merlin said. "I came here in secret to try to find out who and where I was, but I gave myself away in a lie and ended up before the Lord wardens." There was no point telling them about the predictions.

"But ... didn't anyone recognize you when you were being judged?" Lefka asked. Merlin shook her head.

"If no one recognized you, that means you have never been Offered and couldn't be an exile," Danna said. "So why do they send you to the forbidden city?"

Merlin shrugged. "Beats me."

"You are bitter," Lefka said forgivingly. "There is no shame in that. The Citizen gods will come soon with the Gifts of Serenity and you will find peace."

"What are Gifts of Serenity?" Merlin asked warily.

"Collars," Beta said morosely. Merlin repressed an urge to finger the collar beneath the neck of her tunic. Surely that must mean she had been Offered. But why had the gate-guardians failed to recognize her? And if she had been Offered, why wasn't she a Blessed Walker?

"It is said the collaring is when the soul is separated from the flesh," Lefka said dreamily.

"There will be no collar for her. Didn't you hear what she said? She is not to be Offered," Beta said sullenly.

"Oh," Lefka said. "Well, never mind, perhaps they will decide to make her a Blessed Walker anyway."

"What a lucky girl! At least she is certain of being Taken."

Lefka gave Beta an exasperated look. "You will benefit from the Gift of Serenity more than any of us. Always looking on the dark side of things."

"Pah! Who says they're serene? They don't, that's for sure!" Beta snarled.

Lefka smiled loftily. "You can see it in their eyes. I don't understand you. If you feel this way, why didn't you run away and join the scatterlings?"

"Become a rebel?" Beta asked, in a curiously desolate tone. "I would if I had the courage. But I am a coward so there is no choice for me but to submit. Yet I am not a silly milk goat to gambol happily to the slaughter pen."

An astonished silence met these bitter words, but Danna at least had not been listening.

"I still don't understand why they would send someone who has lost their memory to the Citizen gods. It doesn't make sense."

Merlin was only half listening. "Don't the Citizen gods take all the people Offered?"

Danna looked at her questioningly. "Most, these days. But sometimes people are left. They are encouraged to deliver their spirits to the gods."

Merlin blinked. "I don't ... you mean kill themselves?"

Danna nodded. "And after the cycle of three moons, those Taken return – or at least, their bodies do – as Blessed Walkers. The souls stay in the city."

His voice was completely impartial, as if he were suggesting the best way to clean shoes.

"And ... the rebels, scatterlings?"

"What about them? They refuse to be Offered and they run away."

"Some kill themselves at the last minute," Beta said. "They throw themselves into the bottomless wells inside the temple."

"And these ... Blessed Walkers – what happens to them when they come back?" Merlin asked.

A terrible sorrow filled Danna's eyes, but his voice was calm. "They walk among us to remind us that their souls dwell in eternal bliss. We feed them and heal them. Some call them Voids," he added softly.

Lefka gasped. "Blasphemy! None but the rebels call them that."

Danna looked at her and after a while her eyes dropped and she moved away quickly, as if she feared he might contaminate her. There was the sound of the bolt being drawn and Merlin turned to see yet another figure enter the hall.

Her mouth fell open in astonishment when she saw who it was.

It was Ford!

"It didn't take you long to end up here," Ford said with a grin.

He had drawn an astonished Merlin slightly away from the others.

"How did you get past the gate-guards?" she asked.

"More importantly, how did you? Marthe Remembered you would get into the Valley and here you are. The guards should have declared your mindprint invalid."

Merlin had no more answers for him than she had for herself.

"As for me," he went on. "There are other ways into the Valley than through the pass. Sear had us explore the whole of this area ages ago, in the time between Conclaves, so that we could enter the Valley in secret to barter for things we needed and to attend to other matters. I came in through a tunnel in the back of the temple."

"But . . . why?"

"To see if any of those to be Offered would join us, given the choice. Of course, I don't usually come directly here unless I know someone wants to join us, then I take them out. Everyone assumes they've thrown themselves down the bottomless well," he said impishly.

"So why did you come here directly?" Merlin asked. "Did Marthe say I would be here?"

The smile broadened. "I made Marthe tell me the truth when she came back without you. I was wild at her when she told me about you losing your memory. She said I would find you in the Valley. I just had a feeling you were in the temple."

"Did . . . did she tell you what she . . . Remembered about me?" Merlin asked, wondering fleetingly at the accuracy of Ford's guesses.

Ford shrugged. "She told me. But after you left, she Remembered that you were in that flier we sabotaged. She also told me the focus wasn't clear on the Remembering. She doesn't know how or why trouble will come through you. It was she who persuaded Sear to let me come earlier to Conclave. She said she Remembered me coming after you. She said it was necessary and now I see why!"

"Then Sear knows I'm not from the Seaside Region?"

Ford nodded. "He knows you are somehow connected to the Citizen gods because of you being in the flier. He wants to talk to you."

"He'll kill me!"

"No. He wants your help in getting into the forbidden city."

"But I don't re . . ." She broke off as Danna came over, frowning.

"You told us none of the clanfolk knew you," he said.

Ford's single yellow eye turned back to Merlin. "You told him about losing your memory?"

"There was no reason not to," Merlin said in a low voice.

Ford gave the younger boy a hard look.

"Wait," Merlin said, suddenly frightened of what

Ford might do. She looked at Danna. "You wouldn't give us away to the wardens, would you?"

Danna's face cleared. "Me? Not likely. I'm just curious. You're not to be Offered, are you?"

Ford stared at him for a long moment, and Merlin sensed an unspoken exchange between them. Then he spoke just loudly enough to be heard by Danna and Merlin. "I'm a scatterling. I've come to take anyone who wants to join us. And I've come to rescue Merlin."

Merlin stirred indignantly. "I don't need rescuing!"

Ford grinned. "Oh, no? Then it was part of your plan to end up locked in the temple until you were handed over to the Citizen gods?"

Merlin lifted her chin. "At least I know now I'm not a clan person. No one recognized me."

"That knowledge will be very useful to you – when you are a Void," Ford said brusquely.

"Besides, the fact that no one spoke out to say they knew you doesn't mean a lot," Danna went on. "The clans are large and not all come to Conclave. And even if someone did know you, they might have been too frightened to acknowledge you."

"What exactly did you tell them?" Ford asked.

Merlin shrugged. "I told them I had lost my memory and that I bumped into your people in the Region of Great Trees."

Ford gave a low whistle. "You told them you came from there! No wonder they decided to hustle you off to the Citizen gods. No one but runaways and Voids go into the Region of Great Trees. The Citizen gods made it taboo."

She shook her head. "They decided to send me to the forbidden city because of what a Rememberer told them."

Ford and Danna frowned. "A Rememberer?" Danna asked.

Merlin nodded. "At the judging. She said I was a stranger to the clans and that I would put an end to the flow of visiondraught. She told the Lord wardens I was supposed to go to the forbidden city."

Ford said stiffly: "Rememberers do not always see true courses. Marthe said nothing of this."

"Rememberers do not always tell what they know," Danna reminded him. He gave Ford a look of intense enquiry. "It is said the scatterlings believe the Citizen gods are false ..."

"Are liars and murderers," Ford ended bluntly.

"You can't know that for certain," Danna said.

"The only ones who know that for sure are the Voids, and they're not talking!" the scattering said harshly.

He had spoken loudly and some of the others glanced over curiously. Ford lowered his voice. "How many here would join us?"

"None," Danna said.

"But surely you ..."

The boy shook his head. "You see, there are two

ways to end up being Offered. You can be Chosen, or you can volunteer."

Merlin gaped at him. "You volunteered?"

Danna nodded. "Last year, my youngest brother firstblood was Chosen. These days the Citizen gods prefer children, the younger the better." He paused, swallowing hard. "I . . . loved him very much. I have missed him more than I thought possible. He did not like to be apart from me, and when they took him to the temple, he wept and called out my name. They say the spirits of those Offered dwell together in the forbidden city. Sometimes I dream he is calling for me."

"You . . . believe his . . . soul lives in the domed city?" Merlin asked incredulously.

Danna hung his head. "I don't know. I pray it's true."

"And . . . if it's not?"

He sighed. "It is forbidden to try to break the sacred silence of the Blessed Walkers. When his body was brought back to us, I couldn't help myself. I tried to Send to him, but I could find nothing in his mind but a golden mist. I looked into his eyes and tried to believe the blankness was peace or happiness. But I saw nothing. That body was not my brother. My heart aches to speak to him again. I love him more than I love life . . ." He shrugged.

"But you'll end up like him! In your heart you know the Offering is a hoax!" Merlin cried.

Danna smiled sadly. "There is a rumour that the spirits of the Blessed Walkers are not dwelling of free will but are imprisoned in the forbidden city. Perhaps I will be their saviour and free them." There was a silence, then he moved away and out of the main hall. Stunned, Merlin turned to watch him go.

Ford pulled roughly at her sleeve. "Why does it matter to you what he decides? Unless he stirs the mating heat in you?"

"I don't feel anything for anyone!" Merlin snapped hotly.

"It's time we left," Ford said.

Merlin glared up at him, then she remembered something else. "I didn't find out anything about myself here, but I did find out something that might interest you. Your brother and sister, or whatever they are, want to help you and the other rebels."

"Who?" Ford asked.

"Meer and . . . Aran were their names. I was with them when the guards came. A dark-haired pig of a man called Delpha brought them."

Ford stopped abruptly, his face tight with concern.

"Apparently he has some sort of long-standing feud with Aran," Merlin went on when he did not speak. "He overheard us talking about Aran helping your people and the rebels. It was he who had me brought before the Lord wardens."

"Aran spoke of helping the rebels?" Ford asked incredulously.

Merlin nodded. "Delpha accused him and his lady friend and their servant, of conspiring against the Lord wardens and the Offering because of what he had overheard, but the Lord warden took Aran's part. He told them he had just been questioning me, and that he had meant to bring me before the Lord wardens himself. Delpha kept screaming for them to mindbond me or Aran, but the Lord warden said there was no need, since Aran was innocent. I don't think they thought much of Delpha."

"They could not accuse Aran of anything because he would have the right to demand public mindbond, as a soon-to-be-warden, and that would make their own thoughts public. Even if they believed him a traitor, they would not admit it openly. Aran must be warned to watch his back from now on. How did you get mixed up with him?"

"It's a long story. They found out I didn't belong to the clan I had told them. Aran's servant brought me to him, but when I mentioned you and the scatterlings, Meer made it obvious neither of them believed in the Offering. Then this servant turned out to be some sort of rebel. He said he knew you and Era."

"Bors," Ford said, half to himself. "But you said Aran offered to help the rebels. He told this to Bors?"

Merlin nodded. "Something he had overheard stopped him believing in the Offering."

"Meer wanted to run away and join you, but Bors told him he could help you better from the inside, as a warden."

Ford shook his head. "It is hard to believe Aran would risk warden status for us. Bors told him he was a rebel?"

Merlin nodded. "Bors said he trusted Aran but that Aran would need approval from someone else before he could meet the other rebels," she said.

"Bramble is careful," Ford said with a glimmer of laughter. Merlin remembered this name had been mentioned by Sear when she was with the scatterlings. It seemed Bramble was a secret contact within the Valley. "I wish I could be there when those two meet face to face. That will be a shock to poor Aran. You say Meer was with Aran when Delpha came?"

Merlin nodded and Ford smiled reminiscently. He did not look as if he were thinking about his sister. Merlin wondered if sister and brother meant related by blood among the clan-people. Aran and Meer behaved like lovers, but both claimed Ford as brother. And there was no mention of mother and father. She shook her head. She could ponder on the intricacies of clan society later.

"What are you going to do?"

Ford chewed his lip. "The influence of a warden would be a gift from the gods ... If I could be sure about Aran ..." He frowned. "Well, I will decide what to do about this later. We have to get out of here."

This was accomplished with unexpected ease. Apart from the barred door, there were no other security measures. Danna led her through a door concealed behind a trundle bed in one of the rooms. The temple door was unguarded since those Offered had nowhere else to go. Those who changed their mind generally did so by throwing themselves in the bottomless well. This proved to be a deep, narrow cleft in one of the temple chambers.

Grinning, Ford told her to drop a scrap of cloth into the well. A breeze blowing up from the gap suggested the chasm led to some sort of subterranean passage. The scrap of golden silk snagged neatly a short way down. Ford explained this would convince the wardens she had taken the swift way out of her dilemma. Catching sight of the finery she wore underneath the rough cloak, his eyes widened.

"Well, you certainly know how to take care of yourself, don't you? Fallon silk, if I'm not mistaken?"

Merlin couldn't help smiling at his look. His cheer was infectious and she felt less gloomy about her own fate, though she was sorry Danna had refused to come with them.

"The boy has a death-wish," Ford said callously when she voiced her regret.

"*Perhaps I have a death-wish,*" the long-silent William whispered, startling Merlin. Both the William voice and her mechanical adviser had spoken to her less since she had come to the Valley, as if the new knowledge she gained left no room for them. She felt a queer stab of fear at the thought of losing the voices for they were her sole link with her previous existence.

"Isn't this risky?" Merlin asked as Ford led her boldly out through the front door of the temple. "What if someone recognizes me?"

"Don't think about it," Ford said imperturbably.

"Why are we going back into the Valley? I thought you said there was a tunnel in the back of the temple. I suppose you want to pick up some Fallon silk too?" she enquired.

Ford leered at her humorously, then his expression changed. "As a matter of fact, I'm going to see Aran."

"What!" Merlin was aghast. "But we can't. Even if he is telling the truth about wanting to help, you'll get him into terrible trouble if I'm seen there. And Delpha . . ."

"I know Delpha," Ford said so grimly she was silenced.

In fact, it was unlikely they would be noticed. The crowds who had surrounded the temple and pool had long since departed, and the Lord wardens' table was empty. The trading area was still brightly lit and barter was apparently good for there were hundreds of people milling about.

"Most of the people will be there," Ford said as

they hurried along the dark path back to the tented area. Many of the torches that had lit the path previously were burnt out and those that remained were blown to a frail blue flicker by a cold rising breeze. Merlin pulled her cloak around her. Ford wore no more than a coarse cloak and loin cloth, yet seemed impervious to the chill in the air.

"Do you remember where the Fallon tents were?" he asked in a low voice as they approached the tent sleeping area. There was no one in sight and the wind flapped at the tents, snapping cloth and blowing a fine hail of sand into their faces. Merlin squinted against the onslaught.

"There." She pointed. "The tent they took me to is on the far side. But what if they're not there? What if they're not alone?"

"We'll worry about that when we get there."

"What if Delpha ...?" Merlin began, but Ford made an impatient chopping motion with his fingers. They made their way through the tents in silence until Merlin saw the tent Bors had brought her to, just before Aran had arrived with Meer.

"This can't be Aran's tent. It's too plain. His taste runs to the ornate."

Merlin remembered Bors' look of surprise when Aran had entered the tent. "Bors brought me here. Maybe it was his tent."

"Well, well. What have we here? An escaped criminal flown to Meer's tent like a homing bird?"

Merlin swung round in horror.

Delpha lifted a purple silk-clad arm, painted eyes widening at the sight of Ford. "And *you*! How did you get past the gate-guards, I wonder, scatterling?"

"It would be a mistake to call the guards," Ford said.

Delpha paused in the act of crying out, apparently struck by the lack of fear in Ford's voice. "A mistake for you, certainly."

Ford smiled and Delpha's smugness evaporated. "What do you mean?"

"Only that I would tell them I came to meet you, and that you had been helping us for a long time, but that your hunger to be a warden overrode everything. I would tell them you arranged to have me meet you here in a second attempt to implicate Aran."

"But this is Meer's tent," Delpha sneered. "Why would I meet you here?"

"You are very clever. I would let the warden

understand that you dared not make Aran look too much of a fool. Especially after you failed to have him charged tonight. Only a fool would meet a rebel in his own tent. You told me to meet you here, and then you called the guards to expose your plot. I would be full of outrage at your betrayal. I would tell them everything."

"You would not be believed," Delpha snarled.

Ford smiled. "I would be *very* convincing. First I would refuse to talk, and when they tortured me, just a little, I would sing like a bird."

"I would demand mindbond!"

"Would you? From what I hear, the Lord wardens are none too keen on the revealing of mindbond these days. I daresay they would find it simpler to kill us both."

There was a long silence.

"This is a bluff," Delpha said finally.

"Then call it," Ford retorted. "But remember, mud sticks. You ought to know that better than anyone."

There was another silence. Indecision showed clearly on Delpha's thin features. "What do you expect me to do?" he hissed, golden eyes blazing with malice.

"Go about your business, Delpha. Forget you've seen me here," Ford commanded imperiously.

Delpha's face suffused with angry colour. Then his expression cleared. "Very well." He turned to depart.

Merlin felt immediately uneasy at his swift capitulation.

"Oh, Delpha?" Ford called.

The dark man looked over his shoulder, his hooded eyes in shadow.

"Don't get any ideas about organizing some accidental discovery of us," Ford said smoothly. "I promise you, if the guards come, I'll drag you into the whole thing. I'm very inventive. By the time I've finished, they'll be hungry to execute you alongside me."

Delpha glared at Ford and Merlin saw this was exactly what he had intended.

"You'll barter for this," Delpha snarled. "My oath on it."

"Your oath is dung," Ford said icily.

"Do you think he'll do anything?" Merlin asked when he had gone.

The smugness faded from Ford's features. "I don't know. But I'll have to see Aran away from here. And I must warn him about Delpha."

"Then you believe he meant what he said about helping you?"

Ford nodded. "Delpha just convinced me."

The sound of footsteps outside made them freeze. The tent flap swung open. It was Bors.

"Ford!" he cried. "You are early!" His eyes widened as he noticed Merlin. "So, you spoke the truth." He looked back at Ford. "Why did you bring

her here? Delpha must not see you here of all places..."

"He has already been here."

Bors paled. "But..."

Ford slapped him on the back. "It's all right. I
threatened to implicate him if he reported me. I don't
know how long that will hold. I must talk to Aran.
Can you get him to meet me somewhere away from
here?"

"She told you, then?" Bors asked.

Ford nodded. "You believe he is truly converted?"

"It was only a matter of time," Bors said. "I'll bring
him to you. Go to Gawlor's tents. They're nearest the
temple this year. I'll bring Aran there. And Meer. She
longs to see you."

Ford smiled in a distinctly unbrotherly manner and
Merlin felt irritated. It was hardly the time for a
romantic interlude. And besides, weren't they brother
and sister?

"Are we going?" she asked crossly.

Gawlor's tents proved less glamorous than Fallon's, as workaday as the burly Bors. Without hesi-
tation, Ford led her to a small storage tent where he
said they would wait. It was almost morning before
Aran came. Bors was with him, but not Meer.

Aran and Ford stared at one another, seeming
uncertain how to begin.

"You look well, Ford, though you dress like the Hill
Region savages," Aran said.

"And you look as pretty as ever, brother," Ford grinned.

Aran responded with a sheepish smile.

"That must be why they are thinking of making you a warden."

Aran shook his head. "Once I would have been proud. Then, I honoured the wardens. I don't know how you came to be here, but I'm glad. Will you let me help you?"

"We need all the help we can get. How far are you prepared to go?"

"As far as is needed," Aran said grimly. "I was a fool not to see the truth before now. Maybe worse than a fool."

"I won't say no to that," Ford said.

Aran looked at him sharply, then laughed. "Same old Ford. You look older," he added soberly.

"I am," Ford said, equally serious. "It's a hard life. I'm glad you talked Meer out of it. You and she have made a match of it?"

Aran reddened. "I . . ."

Ford shook his head dismissively. "Times move on. This is her tent, where is she?"

"Feasting. I did not tell her you were here. She will be angry with me, but I fear for her. She is too headstrong for good sense."

Ford smiled, and it seemed to Merlin there was a flicker of sadness in his face. "It would take someone as devious as you to let her think she has her head."

Bors coughed. "Aran, you should not stay here too long. Delpha the snake will notice your absence and wonder."

Aran nodded. "He is right, Ford. What can I do to help the rebels?"

Ford turned to Bors. "How long before you can organize a meeting with Bramble and the others?"

"Tomorrow night, as luck would have it, but you will have to stay out of sight until then, for all our sakes," Bors said. "You will need to vouch for Aran before Bramble will agree to mindbond with a warden-to-be, and they will not accept him as one of us until he has mindbonded."

"Why can't you vouch for him?"

Bors smiled sheepishly. "Bramble thinks I am too partisan. I have spent too much time trying to persuade them he would join us if we showed him proof. Even now they will have none of him until you came to speak for him. I thought we would have a long wait."

Aran gave the big man a gratified look.

"Was she pleased at the thought of having a rebel warden?" Ford asked.

Bors smiled. "I think you will find Bramble has much to tell you, but I will leave that to your meeting."

Aran shook his head. "I had no idea this rebellion was so organized. And who is this Bramble?"

"Identities will be exchanged later. You will be a

real asset to us, Aran," Ford said. "I am glad you have joined us."

Aran shook his head in wonder. "I remember you as a dreamer ..."

"I'm still a dreamer, Aran. I dream now of the defeat of the Citizen gods and the freeing of our people. And when that is accomplished, I will find a new dream."

Aran looked at Merlin. "How does she come into this? Did she tell you what the Rememberer said at the judging?"

Ford nodded. "I know what the Rememberers say of her, but I do not think they read their visions clearly enough yet. Our leader, Sear, thinks her coming is a sign of luck and a signal."

Aran looked at Merlin. "Did you tell him the rest?"

Merlin nodded. "But I don't understand how it is with the Rememberers. If they can see so much, how come they can't see that the Offering is a lie?"

Ford looked pensive. "The Rememberers don't cleave to any law but their own. They see things on a broader scale. Marthe knows from her visions that the Citizen gods lie, but she says the Rememberers do not interfere with what is to come. I think they have purposes too deep for ordinary folk."

"I'm not sure I understand that," Merlin said in a troubled voice.

"Well, you can ask Marthe yourself since you'll be coming back with me," Ford said.

158

"Will you go?" Aran asked Merlin.

"I can't stay here now, or the wardens will hand me over to the Citizen gods," Merlin said tiredly. "I have no choice but to take refuge with the scatterlings. But I mean to find out the truth about myself. Whatever it takes, I must."

Merlin realized the truth of her words even as she spoke. She had tried to make herself believe it was enough to find a new life, but now she saw that until she understood her own past, she could have no future. She would go with Ford until she decided what to do next.

After Bors and Aran had gone, both Merlin and Ford slept what little remained of the night. The following day was long and tedious. To Merlin's annoyance, Ford slept most of the time, snoring occasionally and waking to wolf down the food and drink Bors brought them. He seemed preoccupied and disinclined to talk. Merlin was sorely tempted to slip out of the tent and away from Ford and the rebels and their plots, but she knew she needed Ford to get her out of the Valley. She was not sure if the gate-guardians had her mindprint yet, but they certainly knew what she looked like.

She thought over all that had happened but without coming up with any new answers or ideas. Finally she slept too, and was wakened after midnight by Ford, who behaved as if she and not he had slept the day away.

Bors whispered that they should both pull up their hoods. Merlin was to walk with him, head bowed as if she were very old or blind. Bors feared that someone would recognize her from the Lord wardens' judging. Ford was to come a little behind them, so that he could go for help if anything went wrong.

Merlin had thought Bors would lead them somewhere quiet, but instead he took them into the heart of the bustling stalls, crowded with buyers and sellers and flickering orange torch flames lighting wares and faces.

Merlin dared not do more than peep up occasionally, in case someone saw her face, but she could see they were headed for the rowdiest beer tent she had passed the previous day. Sure enough, Bors led her through the drunken, noisy throng, shoving aside a fat songster to enter the crowded beer tent, a huge dark cavern open all along one side and lit by too few lanterns.

Bors went to a flap behind the beer seller, who did not seem to notice him pass, and suddenly it was quiet and very dark. Merlin blinked, trying to accustom her eyes to the dimness. The tent cloth must be thick to cut down the outside noise so effectively. The only light in the room came from a small fire built in a pit dug into the earth. A number of hewn logs were laid about the pit as makeshift seats and two people were seated there: a man with a hood pulled forward to cover his face and a sparsely clad Amazon of a woman with dark, muscular arms and a great untidy mop of brown curls falling over one eye.

At the sound of their entrance, the woman spun on the balls of her feet into a fighting stance, her eyes dangerously purposeful, fingers reaching instinctively for a small dagger in a boot holster. But at once her expression altered.

"Bors. Where is Ford?" she demanded huskily.

"Here!" Ford announced, coming through the flap with a flourish.

"As usual you are late!" she responded. "Who is that? Bors said only that you would bring Aran to us. I presume you do vouch for your pretty-faced brotherblood?"

"There is more to him than golden curls and fine clothes, Bramble," Ford said. "And, yes, I do vouch for him."

Merlin stared at the woman, realizing she was the rebel leader. She had quick darting eyes and a determined looking chin that hinted she was the leader for good reason.

"And her?" Bramble asked, seeming to sense Merlin's scruting.

"I vouch for her too," Ford answered. "There is no need for mindbonding since she will be coming with me when I leave."

"Fair enough," Bramble said dismissively. At a nod from Ford, Bors slipped from the tent and Merlin guessed he had gone to get Aran.

Bramble brought forward some mugs and a huge skin of beer and poured a drink for herself and Ford. Merlin had shaken her head in response to the beer, not speaking since it appeared Ford had no intention of revealing who she was. The rebel leader had offered nothing to the only other occupant of the tent and Merlin looked at him curiously, wondering at his silence and downcast air.

"So," Bramble said, sitting and inviting Merlin and Ford to do the same. "What brings you to Conclave so early? Or did you Remember your brotherblood was about to develop a conscience?"

Ford gave the rebel a sharp look, and Bramble burst out laughing, pushing the curls impatiently out of her eyes. "I am not a fool, Ford. Just because women are generally Rememberers, does not mean men are not sometimes able too. But since it embarrasses you, I will speak no more of it."

Ford said shortly: "Bors said you had news for me?"

Bramble grinned and Merlin noticed a deep dimple crease her cheek. "As to that, I have much to tell. Let me introduce you to my companion. Helf?"

Roused, the hooded man leaned forward and firelight lit his melancholy features. Merlin was startled to recognize the old man who had sat with Sheula on the Mound of Wisdom.

"I know your face," Ford said slowly.

The old man nodded. "You should. I am a warden

of Sadik. Have been for thirty years. I was a warden when the Citizen gods first came."

"I am Ford and a scatterling," Ford said. "What makes a warden turn?"

The old man told Ford about his servant boy. "It took his return as a mindless Walker to open my eyes. To begin with, I said nothing of my loss of faith. But each day I saw greed and lies and treachery in the wardens about me. Until I could stand it no more."

"Fortunately, one of our people got to him before he could do himself too much harm, though he is known as a warden who thinks too much," Bramble said, smiling fondly at the old man.

"If I think too much, then most of the wardens think too little," Helf said.

Bramble leaned forward. "Helf was at the Lord wardens' judging table tonight when your old friend Delpha denounced Aran and a girl."

"The girl came to the Mound," Helf said.

"While she was being judged a Rememberer announced she was to bring about the end of the visiondraught. She claimed to have been with the scatterlings. At present she is in the temple ..." Bramble began.

"The girl is no longer in the temple," Ford interrupted.

"You have got her out? Then she spoke truly when she said she had been with you? But how is it that the gate-guardians let her through?"

Before Ford could respond, Helf stared at Merlin, obviously recognizing her. "You!"

Bramble reached out and pulled the hood from Merlin's head, staring critically at her hair. "It does not become you, girl. Is it true that you came past the gate-guardians?"

Merlin nodded.

"Helf told me you claim not to know who you are."

Merlin nodded again.

"Curious," was all the laconic Bramble said. She turned to Ford. "So, she was with you, and then she came here alone, and now you have her. What will you do with her? And how is it she left you?"

"There was a misunderstanding," Ford answered simply. "Our Rememberer believed she would bring terrible strife down on us. But the reading was blurred. What Helf will not have told you is that when she woke with no memory, she was in a crashed Citizen gods' flier."

"Wha-at!" Bramble showed her first real surprise. "Then she must have been Offered ... but ..."

"Exactly," Ford said. "If she was Taken, how is it that she is not a Blessed Walker? And why didn't the gate-guardians have her mindprint?"

Bramble eyed Merlin with curiosity. "A puzzle ... And the Rememberer said she would go to the Citizen gods, not that she had come from them. Perhaps she got it around the wrong way."

"No doubt," Ford said. He drank deeply from his mug and Bramble filled it again. The air smelled sour with spilled beer and Merlin wondered how they could drink the foul-smelling stuff.

"What other news?" Ford demanded.

Bramble's eyes became grave. "Helf is not the only warden to have joined us. We also have a Lord warden."

Ford jumped to his feet in astonishment. "A Lord warden?"

They all stared down at the man lying on the pallet bed. Bramble had taken them through the back of the tent to the tiny alcove where he slept. Merlin thought she had never seen anyone so ancient. His cheeks were sunken and thick blue veins wound like cords beneath papery skin. His arms and legs were little more than frail bone and the scant flesh that covered them was mottled with scabs weeping a yellowish ichor. The heat radiating from his wasted body was intense. That and his shallow breathing were all that told he lived. The stench in the room was foul.

"The truly amazing thing is that he is this way by choice," Bramble whispered, her eyes shining with pity.

"Who is he?" Ford asked softly.

"Don't you recognize him, Ford? He is the Lord warden who condemned you to exile."

"Ranulf!" Ford guessed faintly.

Bramble nodded, the orange light from the torch she held glinting on her dark curls and smooth cheeks. She reached out and gently shook the old man's arm.

With an agonized moan, his eyelids slid open to reveal the faded sallow glint of his eyes. For a moment he seemed not to know who Bramble was, and where he was. His eyes flickered fearfully from her face to the billowing darkness of the tent walls and Merlin held her breath, certain he would cry out. But then he smiled, a macabre twist of wasted lips.

"Bramble ..." he whispered, seeming to see no one but her. "Sweet Bramble ..."

Bramble stroked that hideous face as tenderly as if it were the face of a lover. "Ranulf, how goes it?"

The old man swallowed, his lips folding over pink gums innocent of teeth. "It is well with me. And you?"

"I, too, Ranulf," Bramble said softly, dropping to her knees at his bedside. Merlin wondered how she could bear to be so close to that living corpse.

Then the old man's eyes slid shut slowly and Merlin wondered if he had died. But Bramble rose and pulled the blanket up over his emaciated form to his neck and kissed his withered cheek. Then she gestured for them all to go back to the other section of the tent. They did so without speaking, but it was some minutes before Bramble joined them. Merlin was astounded to see the rebel leader's eyes bright with unshed tears.

"What is wrong with him? He looks so old," Ford said, as Bramble joined them around the pit fire. Merlin felt icy cold and stretched her hands out to the flames. She noticed Bramble did the same.

She filled a mug with beer and drained it in one long drink before answering. "I stumbled on him one night when I was returning from a hunt," she said. "You remember how he was? Tall and strong. Arrogant mouth and sneering eyes. He rode like a god and that was his only redeeming feature. I had hated him for as long as I could remember, since he killed my sisterblood for loving someone else. But that night, when I came on him, he was grovelling on the ground, half mad with delusions. I could see from the way he held his leg that it was broken and guessed he had been thrown from the black beast he rode. He was filthy and looked as if he had dragged himself far, yet I looked on his broken body without compassion." Her eyes were bleak with the memory.

"Naturally my first thought was to slide a knife into his belly while there were no witnesses. I would never have such a chance again. Do you know what he did when I came to him with my hand on my knife?"

Mesmerized, both Ford and Merlin shook their heads.

Bramble stared into the dying flames as if the story were written in the embers. "He begged me to kill him." She shook her head. "He looked up at me, his haughty face twisted, his eyes wet with tears, and he begged me to put my knife in him. He said he would bless me for it."

"Why?" Ford asked. "Surely a broken leg would not cause so much pain."

Bramble gave him a strange smile. "Of course, I thought as you do that he was over-reacting to the break. I thought him a coward. I did not kill him. Don't ask me why. Perhaps because he asked it and I wanted to do nothing for him. I took him back to my hovel. He wept and begged all night to die. Then, he slept. When morning came he was lucid but fevered. He demanded in his old proud way that I return him to his home. Again, I don't know why but I refused. Maybe because it pleased me to have a Lord warden at my mercy. And I still toyed with the thought of killing him. He threatened me with death if I did not return him to the other Lord wardens, but I closed my ears to him. And he began to convulse. He was racked for hours. It was the most terrible thing I have ever seen. He *screamed* with the pain for hours, and I could do nothing. I tell you, after that night, all my hunger for revenge was burned away by what I saw him suffer. I had decided I would get a Lord warden to come to him in the hope that they would know what ailed him, but as I prepared to go, he asked me to stay with him. He said ... he said he was afraid to be alone. He said it was worse at night ... so ... I stayed and we talked.''

There was a long silence and Merlin pictured the young Amazon and the stricken Lord warden talking together in the darkest hours of night.

''We talked of many things and of nothing. Not of the Offering or of my sisterblood or clans, but of places where we had ridden and streams where we swam as children and ...'' She shook her head. ''That night, Ranulf changed in my eyes. For the first time, I did not see him as my sister's slayer, but as a man who had once been a boy.''

But the pain and the convulsions had come again, and strange fits filled with nightmare visions that had reduced the Lord warden to gibbering terror. In between were lucid hours, and in these hours, he had told Bramble about the visiondraught.

The rebel leader looked at Ford. ''Understand that like you I thought the visiondraught was a thing one could lust for like fine clothes or gold: a luxury paid for in the blood of the innocent. But it was not long before Ranulf taught me the truth. Visiondraught is a terrible potion which, once taken, is craved for ever. It is this dreadful crazed hunger that blinds the Lord wardens to the Citizen gods, for though the drug gives visions and wondrous ecstasy to those who drink it, it becomes a necessity to the body and the mind and without it ..." She waved her hand significantly towards the alcove.

"A drug ..." Merlin murmured, but no one heard her.

"Don't you see?" Bramble asked Ford. "He ... they, had no choice. Later, in between the bad times, he told me the Citizen gods had held them down and pushed the visiondraught into their bodies with hollow needles that first time when they had been taken into the forbidden city to speak with the Citizen gods under truce. After that the hunger for the potion ruled their souls. They would do anything for it. Anything."

There was a devastated silence, then Ford nodded towards the alcove. "Why did you bring him here? It is obvious he is dying."

"He wanted to come. You see, he ... he wanted to get free of the potion, and so he would not take it. The other Lord wardens think he suffers from some mysterious illness. They believe he has the mating heat for me, or I for him." She shrugged. "They bring him the visiondraught, and I pour it away. Where it touches the earth, no plant grows. In the beginning, he fought the hunger for the potion because he believed if he could overcome this, he could convince the others to do it. Now, I think he lives only because he says he refuses to die until his soul is his own again." She blinked rapidly and stared into the fire.

"How long has he been like this?" Ford asked gently.

Bramble looked up in anguish and Merlin saw that she loved the dying Ranulf. For the first time since she had wakened in the Citizen gods' flier, Merlin felt real sorrow for another human being, and a searing anger for the terrible things done by the Citizen gods. She was startled and shattered to realize she had not really thought of the clanpeople as human before then. She could no longer tell herself the Citizen gods were the scatterlings' problem.

"I found him not long after we returned from last Conclave," Bramble said. "He has been fighting the potion for almost a year now. Still, he suffers as he did in the beginning, but each day his body grows weaker, less able to fight. I think he has begun to accept that this is a battle he cannot win. He wanted to come to Conclave because he wanted you and the rebels of the other clans to see what the Citizen gods have made him. He wants everyone to understand that the Lord wardens were not weak or greedy men and women, but that they were trapped and poisoned against their will or choice. He wants you to understand that the enemies of the clans are not the Lord wardens, but the Citizen gods."

The tent flapped open and Bors entered with a heavily cloaked Aran barely recognizable in plain garments.

Bramble seemed to draw herself together with an

effort, but she managed to greet a clearly astounded Aran. "Welcome to the underworld, pretty boy. I'm Bramble," the rebel woman announced.

Aran did not react to her scorn. "So, Bramble is a woman?"

Bramble stared at him belligerently. "Does that not please you, sire?" she asked in a wheedling voice.

Aran bridled, but his voice was calm. "I do not blame you, my lady. But I offer my aid sincerely, and I will mindbond to prove myself true."

A flicker of surprise showed in Bramble's gamine face. "Very well. So be it. Perhaps there is more to you than meets the eye, *Aran*."

Aran smiled faintly. "Perhaps there is . . . Bramble."

After a moment, Bramble smiled reluctantly. "Very well." She drew herself up to her considerable height, hands on her hips. "I offer the honour of mindbond," she intoned formally.

"I accept the honour of mindbond," Aran responded with equal dignity. Merlin watched with interest as the two faced one another, less than a hand span between them. Slowly, like dancers timed, each clasped their hands behind the other's head, thumbs bent forward to rest under the chin, and they stared intently into one another's eyes.

"This is the formal stance," Bors whispered to Merlin. As he spoke, both Aran and Bramble began to hum in low breathy tones. "That is the trance song,"

Bors explained. "You have to be in the right state of mind and the trance song ensures it."

Aran's eyes unfocused and he began at once to sweat.

"What exactly are they doing?" Merlin asked quietly.

Bors drew her back to the edge of the tent. "Mindbonding. Bramble will tie all of her sensations and thoughts into Aran's, and then she will examine his thoughts."

Aran groaned.

"Is it painful?" Merlin wondered.

Bors nodded fractionally. "Sometimes it is worse than others. It is difficult to simply allow someone complete access to your mind. It's easier the more often it is done, but the Lord wardens have banned it."

Merlin realized the Lord wardens could not afford to have their own consuming lust for the vision-draught exposed.

Aran groaned again.

"There is an even more intimate mindbond but that is part of the mating heat and involves body as well as mind," Bors said.

At last the pair fell apart. Aran sagged to a log chair and Bramble swayed on her feet.

"A good journey?" Ford asked her.

She nodded. "You were right, Ford, there is more to your brotherblood than met the eye."

Aran looked up at Bramble and Merlin was surprised to see admiration and wonder in his expression. Then his eyes darkened and he looked unerringly towards the hidden alcove where the old Lord warden lay. "We must fight them for what they have done."

Merlin was startled to realize Aran must have got the knowledge of Ranulf from Bramble's thoughts. Bors poured two mugs of beer and Aran and the rebel woman drank thirstily, Aran with a grimace.

Bramble turned to Merlin. "I do not know who you are, but I salute what you will bring about. The end of the flow of visiondraught," she toasted. The rest raised their mugs and Merlin shrank from their expectations. They acted as if she were supposed to defeat the Citizen gods single-handedly.

Merlin asked: "Did . . . Ranulf say why the Citizen gods turned your people into Voids?"

Bramble shook her head.

Ford set his mug down purposefully. "I must return to the Hide. Sear must know of this."

Bramble caught him by the arm. "Tell him Ranulf said the only way is to fight the Citizen gods. He said there was no possibility of dealing with them."

Ford nodded abruptly and drew his cloak about him. "We will meet before next Conclave. No more clanfolk must be sacrificed. In the meantime, you must make sure all of the rebels know of Ranulf and the visiondraught."

Ford embraced his companions, then Bors and Aran left the tent. A little time later, Helf departed.

"Good luck," Bramble said when Ford decided enough time had passed for it to be safe for them to leave.

Ford grinned. "I make my own luck – or find it," he added with an oblique glance at Merlin.

There were still a few people around the stalls when they slipped out of the tent. Most seemed to be stall holders packing up for the night. Looking at the pale horizon, Merlin guessed it was close to dawn. Suddenly she felt exhausted. Ford made them go carefully, but they reached the deserted temple without trouble. Just as the sun began to rise, they passed through the temple doors and into the honeycomb of caves behind the main rooms.

It was pitch dark, but they carried no light. Ford explained that Sear had designed a series of guiding marks in the caverns which marked the route which would take them out of the Valley. Great blustering draughts of wind along the tunnel made it impossible to keep a torch lit so those who did not know the secret of the guiding marks would be unable to find their way through the dark labyrinth, and would be forced to turn back once their torch blew out, or risk becoming lost inside the hill.

Coming out at last into the daylight, Merlin and Ford rested, each silent with their own thoughts.

Merlin felt strangely isolated. Ford's parting words

to Bramble frightened her. What did they expect her to do? She had not even been able to find out who she was. This wasn't her world, though it might once have been. The Rememberers called her a stranger and predicted that she would bring disaster. Ford and Sear and now the others, decided this meant she was an omen that would work in their favour against the Citizen gods, but was that really what the Rememberings meant? What if it were the other way round? If she knew who she was and why she had been in the flier, she might know.

She pitied the clanfolk and wished them luck in their struggle against the Citizen gods, but she was not one of them. Until she knew who she was, what she was, she could commit herself to no one, and the predictions surrounding her only made it worse.

She had to find out the truth, and she would not find that in the Hide of the scatterlings.

And then it came to her!

There was only one way to discover the truth about herself. She had tried every other way. The only place she hadn't tried was the forbidden city. The Citizen gods had to know why and how she had come to be in the flier. They had to know who she was and where she came from. If she wanted to know who she was, there was only one avenue left open to her.

She would have to go to the forbidden city.

Ironically, she found herself resolving to go where she would have gone if Ford had not rescued her, and there was a rightness in the thought of returning to the beginning.

She did not think of going back to the temple. It was one thing to approach the forbidden city as one of a number of prisoners. Another entirely to travel there under her own volition.

ord was too full of excitement at the prospect of working with his brother to notice how quiet she was.

"This will make a great difference to us," he said. "As Bramble said, we have always regarded the Lord wardens as the first rank of the enemy. We thought of them as deceivers and traitors, when the truth is that they are victims. I wonder how much Marthe knew of this?"

They were walking along the border of the Region of Great Trees and the Treeless Plain.

Ford looked sideways at Merlin, sensing her pre-occupation. "You need not be afraid of Marthe's threats. I told you Sear does not think you will bring trouble on us, but that you are a sign that we must become more aggressive in our harrassment of the Citizen gods. And with the news of Ranulf, he is certain to want to attack them in full force."

"Yet Marthe meant it," Merlin said quietly. "I think you would have killed me, if Sear ordered it."

Ford shrugged. "If it were true that you would bring disaster on us, what else should she have done, or I?" He seemed baffled by her attitude, while Merlin found his simple savagery repellent. Even to save her own life, she did not think she would be able to kill anybody. She felt suddenly removed from Ford and the events of the night. She had been carried away by her emotions.

"*Humankind kills,*" said the William voice. "*It is an instinct we have and no matter how we try to tame or divert it, how civilized we become, there are moments when anyone will kill.*"

Merlin wondered if her decision to go to the domed city had somehow resurrected the William voice.

"What if Sear is wrong?" she asked Ford. "What if I do bring disaster down on you?"

Again, Ford gave her a perplexed look. "Then we made a mistake. A person can only act as he sees best. You have a strange way of thinking about things. Your mind is like trying to put together the pieces of a cracked birdshell."

"That's exactly what it's like," Merlin said feelingly. "You can't imagine, can you, what it's like to be in my place – to wake up in a savage world that makes no sense, without any memory."

Ford stopped. "It is true that I can't imagine that, but I do not believe that you are evil or bring evil with you like a sack of flourseeds. Marthe said only that you were a stranger among us. If it is so important to you, we will find out who you are."

"How?" Merlin demanded. "Do you think I will find the answer in the Hide of the scatterlings?"

Ford shrugged. "We will ask Marthe."

Merlin shook her head. She felt as if a great gulf separated her from Ford.

He took her silence for resignation and whistled softly as he walked behind her. But Merlin was silent because she could not think of a way to make him understand what she had decided to do. It would be easier to slip away unnoticed but Ford's hunting skills made that impossible. Besides, he would need to give her directions to the domed city.

But how to make Ford with his simple, direct motives understand what she meant to do?

She decided to draw him into talking about the dome, but very gradually so that he would not wonder what made her ask. Perhaps she could trick him into giving directions.

"Why do you call Aran 'brother' and Meer 'sister'?" she asked.

"Because that is what they are," Ford said.

Merlin shook her head. "But if Meer and Aran have

... have made a match of it, then they can't be related."

Ford laughed aloud. "What mad ideas you have. Why shouldn't they be together? Only firstbloods may not marry. Aran and I are firstbloods. Meer is secondblood to us both. For a time, I was with Meer. We shared a greenstick mating heat."

"I don't understand," Merlin said, still puzzled by the relationship of the two youths. "Do you and Aran have the same parents?"

"Parents?" Ford echoed blankly.

Merlin stared. "Mother and father ... the woman who gives birth and the man who ..." She floundered to a halt, much to Ford's amusement.

"Women bear children in the clan birthing house, and the children are then assigned to a brother or sister firstblood, or secondblood, if there is no firstblood available."

"You mean ... you don't know who your mo ... who the woman who gave birth to you is?"

Ford shook his head. "Why should I care? There are so many things in the world to wonder about greater than that. Besides I daresay I could find out if I wanted."

"But what about ... well, this mating heat? What if a baby comes?"

"Truly your Region must have strange customs. When Meer is fat with child, she will go to the temple and be cared for and pampered until the baby comes out, then she will return to Aran, or to some other if she has tired of that relationship. Once suckled, the babe joins brother and sister firstbloods."

Merlin was shocked. "No wonder there is no great protest when the children are Chosen, if no one knows who they belong to."

Ford bridled at the criticism in her tone. "Do you think I need to know who spawned a child to care for it? It may seem to you that no one cares since they do not protest the Offering, but you are wrong. Brother and sisterbloods grieve deeply, yet are shamed by their grief because they believe those Offered will have a better existence, immortal and cherished in the forbidden city." He gave her an odd look, squinting his single eye as if to see her better.

"You have forgotten much. It must be a queer matter to wake thus," he said, as if for the first time trying to understand how she felt.

Merlin nodded slowly. "I can't remember anything about myself. When I woke in the flier, I didn't even know what I looked like. I don't know what I'm like as a person, what I've done, where I lived or who I lived with. But I can remember lots of things that have nothing to do with this world of clans and Citizen gods. Yet some things in your world are familiar. That city where you first saw me – except I remember it when thousands of people lived there and the roads were new."

"No one has ever lived there," Ford said, a curious

note in his voice. "In the stories from before the beginning of time, it is said the firstborn of the world left the old places in great flying boats to seek a place called Eden. But these are no more than stories. Perhaps you have muddled up Remembering what will come with what has past," Ford said kindly.

Merlin opened her mouth, then closed it.

"I think the Citizen gods were taking you to the city when the flier was caught in our trap. I think they caught you and took you, though you had not been Offered. That would explain why the gate-guardians had no mindprint of you. I think they had no collar to put on you and that is why you are sane. As to the forgetting, perhaps your brains were scrambled in the crash," Ford suggested seriously.

Merlin suppressed a frustrated urge to hit him on the head.

"What does it matter anyway? Past is past," he said dismissively.

Merlin swung to face him in a sudden rage. "You stupid savage! Of course it matters! It matters more than your clans and scatterlings and schemes. Are you so simple that you can't understand why I need to know who I am?"

Ford blinked as if she had struck him.

"Look!" Merlin shouted, rolling down the neck of her tunic and showing him the collar. "I'm sure you recognize this! I don't know how it got there. But I have learnt enough to know who put it there. Your

Citizens did! How do you explain that I wear this, and can think still?"

"But ... how can you ...?" Ford looked dumb-founded. "It must be broken," he said in wonder.

"Somewhere along the line your Citizens put this collar thing on me but it didn't sedate me, or it did and was broken in the accident."

Ford's single bright eye filled with excitement. "They must have been taking you to the forbidden city. They put these collars on all those Offered. Perhaps there are other clans far away where the Citizen gods also find Offerings. Maybe that's why no one at Conclave knew you." He frowned. "If the collar worked you would have stayed near the wreck. I have never heard of collars being broken. That's why the Citizen gods were so quick to search for you. The Citizen gods say that the collaring separates the spirit from the body, and that they can never be rejoined. The Citizen gods themselves conduct the ceremony. You are proof that this is a lie. That collar might bring them unstuck."

"Just before I ran into you in the ruined city, I overheard one of the Citizen searchers talking to another. They were trying to work out if the collar was broken. They seemed scared that I might stumble onto someone," Merlin said, now understanding why they had been so frantic.

"Sear must know of this. It means we can attack the fliers which bring the children who have already been collared. We did not bother before because we thought them beyond saving. All it would take is one child back and the wardens would have to demand an answer from the Lord wardens. The clans would force it ... We must hurry. You'll be safe when we reach the camp."

Merlin shook her head, making a sudden decision. "I'm not going to the Hide, Ford. That's what I've been trying to tell you."

Ford turned to her, his face tight and unforgiving. Merlin sensed she had offended him by calling him a savage, but there was no point in apologizing for something she believed.

"I have to know who I am, and there is only one place left for me to try," she said. "The Citizens are the only ones who can know where I come from, and why I have no memory."

"The forbidden city!"

Merlin nodded. "It all started with the Citizens. They must know who I am."

"If you go there, they will kill you or worse, they will make you a Void," Fort retorted. "You call me a savage, but it is better to be a savage than a fool who will die for nothing. You don't understand how they are!"

Merlin shook her head. "It's you who doesn't understand. I'm not going to the dome full of blind hopes. I have to know who I am. It's worth the risk because right now, I don't have a life anyway."

They glared at one another.

"Then why did you come with me at all? Why didn't you just stay and go with the others to be Offered?"

Merlin smiled wryly. "I'm not a complete idiot. If I went that way, I'd be re-collared and witless before I got a chance to speak. This way, they should be curious enough to give me a hearing. I have no intention of turning up like a trussed chicken."

"Cheeken?" Ford echoed.

Merlin shook her head impatiently. "I need to know how to find the domed city."

"And you think now I will tell you?" Ford asked expressionlessly.

Merlin said nothing.

"I wonder why you think that. Sear would be angry if I fail to bring you to him. He might even kill me. That is the sort of thing savages do to people who betray them. Or do you think savages have no sense of loyalty?" His voice was full of contempt.

"I think Marthe was right about me bringing trouble on the scatterlings. It would be better for all of us if you told me where the domed city is and let me go. You could tell Sear you didn't find me."

Ford smiled nastily. "We savages do not lie as easily as you." He glanced at the sky thoughtfully, his eyes remote.

Merlin bit her lip. "Listen: if your Rememberers can see the future, and they say I'm going to stop the flow of visiondraught, doesn't it follow that this will happen whatever I do? Maybe I'm meant to go to the forbidden city."

Ford gave her an enigmatic look.

"Will you tell me the way?" she asked softly.

"I will take you there," said Ford.

Merlin shook her head firmly. "No."

"Yes," Ford said. "I do this because I have given my bond for you. It is a savage custom, but I am a savage and must live with my own honour."

"I didn't ask you to make any sort of agreement over me so it doesn't count."

"If you refuse, I will not tell you how to find the dome," Ford said. "I will gag your mouth and tie your hands and that is how you will arrive at the Hide."

"What about the others? You have to tell Sear about Aran and Ranulf."

"I will tell him later. As you said, the Rememberers saw that you would stop the flow of visiondraught. Perhaps I am part of it too."

Merlin glared at the scatterling for twisting her logic.

"Sear will contact Bors to find out what happened to me, then Bors will tell him about Aran," Ford said.

"I don't *want* you to come!" she shouted.

"You have no choice," Ford said coolly.

The following morning Ford wakened her before dawn. After his refusal to leave her he had said little.

Somehow the events of the previous day had changed things between them, and Merlin found herself regretting the loss of the old Ford with his banter and smiles.

"You told me before there was a story that said the people who once lived in the old places had all gone away. Tell it to me," she asked impulsively, hoping to restore their comfortable intimacy.

"They are stories. No one has ever lived there," Ford said tonelessly. Merlin felt like shaking him. Since he had forced her to let him come, he might make an effort to behave normally.

"Did the stories ever say where they went?" she asked.

"To Eden," Ford answered. "To Eden in the clouds."

"What about the Citizens? The domed city was there for a long time before they came out."

Ford nodded. "One day the flying vessels came out like seeds exploded from a pod. At first no one knew there were people inside. They hunted and killed many of us before the pact of the Offering. Many died, but at least then we fought with honour and died in honour. Yet I am happy to know the Lord wardens did not betray us that day when they met with the Citizen gods."

Merlin shivered, trying to forget where they were going. "What do you suppose they really want your people for?"

Ford looked at her. "No one knows. But there must be a reason. Maybe we'll find out," he added ominously.

Having given up trying to convince Ford to leave her, Merlin admitted her relief at his presence, despite his sullenness. From what she had seen and heard of the Citizen gods they were a long way from being kind or benevolent. If they were at all like the searchers she had overheard, they were unlikely to regard her questions with sympathy, especially if they realized the scatterlings knew about the failed collar. Maybe Ford was right about that being the reason for their hurried search for her, although she had the feeling the searchers were worried about what she would hear, rather than what she could say to the clanfolk.

She knew the danger but was resolved. Somehow though, she had to make sure Ford was not taken as well. "Is there a way to enter this domed city other than by flier?" she asked.

"There is a place that opens in the side of the dome. We have seen them go in that way." His voice was even and untroubled, as if the danger no longer bothered him.

Merlin felt less composed. She was frightened first that the Citizen gods would simply turn her into a Void without telling her anything. And she was frightened of what they would tell her if they did decide to speak. Maybe Ford was right and the truth was that easy. Maybe she was simply from a remote area where life went on as she remembered. But what of the ruinous city she remembered as whole?

So many questions. Would she find the answers in the forbidden city? And what of the Citizen gods? Had they been inside the dome all that time before they came out? And why had they come out?

More importantly, why had they hunted the clan-people, then made up the whole Offering charade? What did they do to the children that turned them into mindless Voids? Experiment on them?

Merlin shivered and rubbed her eyes wearily, tired of the blazing glare of the sun. Surely it had not always been so bright and white and painful? Even though they walked in the shade as much as they could, the sun set up a fierce glare that made her eyes and head ache.

Walking beside her, Ford was lost in his own thoughts.

Merlin thought of Danna, the boy they had left behind in the Valley temple, and wondered if the Citizen gods had taken him yet. She tried to imagine Danna reunited with his beloved brother, but could not. She saw his face slack and witless, his eyes empty of all expression and sanity, and shuddered. At the same time she knew Ford was right in saying Danna had a death-wish.

Sensing her movement, Ford looked down, his tanned forehead sheened with sweat. "What is it?"

"I was thinking of the children in the temple," Merlin said. "This is a terrible world."

Ford looked at her without warmth. "Don't pity us too much. When I was very young, before the Citizen gods came, I remember a warden getting honey from a stinger Hide. It was early in the morning and there was a mist just above the ground. He lit a fire under the nest and the stingers flew away. He dipped a stick in the honey and gave it to me. I remember how sweet that honey tasted. I can smell the smoke in the cold air." He looked at Merlin whose mind was reeling. She had told that story to Meer to prove she knew Ford, yet she knew she had never heard Ford speak of the stingers before that second. Was it possible this was Remembering?

"*Déjà vu is the illusion of remembering events and scenes which are taking place for the first time.*" Only this had not been an illusion. She had remembered Ford's story before he told it to her. Remembered, she thought. *Remembered!*

"I was happy then, but I was not always happy," Ford went on. "Now that I am grown, I am sometimes happy, but not always. Do you think it savage to accept that I cannot be happy always?"

Merlin stared at him, struck by his words and the feeling that he was telling her something important. Everything that had happened since waking seemed bad, but when she thought about it, there had been good times. Sitting in the warm tent bath, eating with

192

Bors at the food stalls, the moment of triumph when she had succeeded in joining the Valley road unseen. Moments of happiness, and maybe that was all anyone ever had.

"You must grasp the chance of happiness when it flutters by like a bird," Ford said, looking at her.

Merlin shrank back from the longing in his face, frightened by his intensity. A shutter fell over the brightness of his eyes and he looked back the way they had come.

"How far now?" Merlin asked, to fill the uncomfortable silence.

"Not far ..." Ford began, then his eye flickered sideways and he stopped.

"What is it?" Merlin asked, automatically lowering her voice to a whisper.

Ford held his finger to his lips and crouched down, pulling her beside him.

"What ..." Merlin began.

"Run!" Ford hissed, lurching into a hunched, soft-footed run.

Merlin's heart thundered and her breath rasped in her throat as they ran bent low through the flicking, stinging bushes. She was so intent on running she ran headlong into Ford who had stopped unexpectedly.

"What is it?" she began.

Directly in front of them was Sear with more than fifteen other scatterlings ranged on either side, all carrying weapons.

Ford raised his staff threateningly. "Get out of our way," he commanded, but Merlin could hear a pleading note in his voice.

"Ford!" It was Era's voice, shocked, as she stepped out beside Sear.

"Would you spill scatterling firstblood for her?" Sear asked gently, his face stern.

"I don't want to spill anyone's blood, but I am oathbound to her. Let us pass and no one will be hurt," Ford said.

"Marthe has seen more, Ford," Era shouted. "She has seen that you will walk a path of terrible danger if you walk with her!"

"We must talk, Ford," Sear said urgently. "There are things that have happened since you went. Mora has been killed by the Citizen gods, and Keha. They hunt us on foot now, in groups. They have grown steadily closer to the Hide. It is only a matter of time before they find us."

"Because of the flier?" Ford asked.

"In part," Sear answered. "They seek us not because we harmed their flier and killed a Citizen god, but because they think we have the treasure that was carried in the flier." He looked deliberately at Merlin. "Her."

Ford's face hardened. "And now you would hand her over to them?"

Marthe's voice rang out: "Does it matter, when she is bound to go to them anyway?"

194

Ford looked startled, then angry. "She is going because she chooses it. I'm not making her and neither will I stand back while you do it." Ford's eyes darkened. "And tell me, Marthe, what do you know of Ranulf?"

Sear looked at Ford incredulously. "You would *question* a Rememberer in such a way?" He shook his head. "It is just as Marthe warned. You have changed, Ford. We did not come to take Merlin to the Citizen gods. Marthe Remembered that she would go to the forbidden city of her own accord."

"Then why did you come, if you knew there was no need to force her?" Ford demanded.

Sear stepped closer, ignoring the raised point of Ford's staff. "Because I saw that we could make better use of this matter. They want her badly, and she means to go to them. What is wrong with our gaining an advantage from it? If she did not intend to go to the forbidden city, I would fight to keep them from her."

"I don't understand what you mean by advantage," Ford said warily.

"They want her badly enough that they will bargain with us. They don't know she means to go to them. We can gain much in this exchange and we can make her safe return part of the bargain," Sear argued.

Ford was clearly troubled, though he lowered his staff. Merlin realized he was torn between his bond to her and his alliance with the scatterlings. He said:

"But can they be trusted in a bargain? There is much I have to tell you about the Citizen gods and their *bargain* with the Lord wardens."

"And I will hear it all," Sear answered soothingly. "But for now, we must travel."

Before Ford could respond, Era came up to him, her face full of scorn. "I do not know you, Ford. You threaten your sister and brotherbloods with weapons; you demand answers from a Rememberer; you accuse us of cowardice and treachery. Your time with this girl has changed you."

"It ... wasn't her," Ford murmured. He sounded confused and Merlin guessed his old clearcut notions of right and wrong had blurred so that he did not know what to trust.

"It was," Marthe said without anger. "I tell you, Ford. It is not too late to turn from the path where she will walk. It is fraught with danger and you will be changed forever by what you see."

"Whatever you believe," Sear broke in. "You meant to take her to the forbidden city. Nothing has changed and wherever your loyalties lie now, you owe us this chance to change the balance in this war. Once I am inside the city who knows what I might..."

Enlightenment filled Ford's face. "So. The bargain – now I understand. It has nothing to do with the scatterlings. It's for you."

"It's a chance that will never come again. We will

offer her to them on condition that I may go with her into the city."

Ford nodded at last, his expression unreadable. "I will agree, but only as long as they will agree to let me go with you both."

"No!" Era shouted.

"I think they will agree," Sear said slowly, and Ford nodded.

Merlin was troubled by the rift between Ford and the leader of the scatterlings, yet she felt incapable of doing anything about it. Marthe's awareness of her decision to go to the forbidden city had plunged her into despair, for how could the Rememberer know what she had decided unless the decision had never been hers to make? Again she was swamped by a feeling of helplessness, propelled by forces beyond herself.

It no longer seemed to her that going to the forbidden city was the right course, only that she had no choice in the matter.

"They want a puppet, but I will give them a mind which is capable of thinking and choosing," the William voice vowed softly. For the thousandth time, Merlin tried to guess who William had been and who the "they" were he often referred to.

When Ford turned to her, she felt as if she were looking at him from a long way off. "What do you want to do?" he asked in a low voice. "If you don't want to go, I'll fight him."

Merlin shrugged apathetically. "It doesn't matter."

Ford gave her a baffled look.

"There, you see?" Sear said, sounding relieved. "There is no conflict. She wants to go to the Citizen gods, they want her, and we can profit from the barter."

"But what will they do to her?" Ford asked still looking at Merlin.

"Can we go?" she said wearily. "Maybe they'll just take their precious collar and let me go." She did not believe this, but Sear, puzzled by the reference, distracted Ford by questioning him. Before long, the scatterling leader was convinced the faulty collar was the sole reason for the Citizens' search for Merlin.

"They know that once the collar is removed, we'll have no proof and they're safe," Sear said reasonably. Ford told him of Aran and Ranulf.

Sear paled. "So, that is the answer. It has always troubled me that the best of us should be turned into traitors so easily. All the more important for me to enter the forbidden city. You say the Rememberer said she would put an end to the flow of vision-draught. I wonder exactly what that means ..."

He and Ford walked either side of Merlin, talking, but there was no friendship in their voices. They spoke like wary allies.

At midday, Sear called a halt and they roasted strips of meat over a fire.

"What about the eyeballs?" Ford worried.

Sear grinned, teeth white between grease-smeared lips. "That was part of the bargain. The eyeballs are not to fly, nor Citizen gods to kill any scatterling in the time of truce when we bring Merlin to them."

Ford's eyes narrowed. "You have spoken to the Citizen gods before we had agreed? Then you must have intended to give her to them all along."

Marthe reached out a bony hand and squeezed Ford's shoulder. "Do not look for deceit to cover your doubts. *I* told Sear that you would be taking Merlin to the forbidden city. It was his idea to convince the Citizen gods we had her and to make them call a truce to prevent more killing. The final bargain will be struck at the dome."

Sear bit into another strip of meat. "Once I saw how badly they wanted her alive, and Marthe told me she would go to them by choice, I saw what must be done. I went to the dome and convinced them we had her and would kill her rather than give her up. I said we would persuade her to come to them if they would allow entry to the city. Then we came to find you."

"I do not trust these Citizen gods in any bargain," Ford said.

"You have lost your ability to trust," Era broke in suddenly, looking at Ford from the other side of the fire. "Where is honour without trust?" She threw the strip of meat she was eating into the fire as if it had become bitter in her mouth. Ford watched her go with regret and Merlin thought: where is trust without honour?

They walked well into the night before making a rough camp. This time Ford did not sit at the fire, but strayed about as if he were more restless than weary. Sear and the scatterlings sat around the fire talking and making plans while Merlin sat apart, leaning against a tree.

Marthe came and sat beside her. "You set yourself apart. That is not good."

Merlin looked at the Rememberer squarely. "You think sitting with them would make me one of them?"

"You choose to set yourself apart, so do not blame them when you find it a lonely choice. Whatever happened to you before the accident cannot be undone, and you must live with what you are. You choose to walk alone. You draw Ford away from his brother and sisterbloods. You must accept responsibility for your actions."

Stung, the fog of despair in Merlin's mind dissipated slightly. "I didn't ask Ford to do what he did. He did that on his own. It's nothing to do with me."

Marthe laughed. "Of course it has something to do with you. It has everything to do with you. And you know it."

"I tried to make him leave me!" she said angrily.

"Did you?"

Merlin flushed at the Rememberer's tone, recalling her secret relief when Ford had insisted on taking her to the dome.

"You try to pretend to yourself that you have no choice, only so that you need not take responsibility for the things you cause to happen. But that does not make them any less your fault."

"If you know what I'm going to do and think, then I don't have any choice in the first place," Merlin cried.

The cold anger faded in the Rememberer's eyes. She reached out a grubby hand and touched Merlin's arm. "The choice is always yours. Just because I can see what you will choose, does not mean the choice was made by someone else. And Rememberings change constantly as one action affects another. I told you once before it is not a certain business."

"You said you know I'm going into the dome."

Marthe nodded. "But I don't know what will happen there. Remembering is a matter of seeing outcomes, not ordaining things to happen."

Merlin bit her lip. "I ... I felt it didn't matter what I decided."

The Rememberer sighed. "You must not give up choosing, else you might as well be a Void."

Merlin hung her head.

"And, girl, be gentle with Ford. He is a dreamer

with a soft heart and a head that is sometimes softer. You hold him in your hand now, and that cannot be undone either."

Before Merlin could respond to this, Marthe rose in a rustle of cloth, and walked into the shadows of the night.

Though enormous beyond imagining, they were almost on the dome which covered the forbidden city before they could see it, because it was built in a deep depression. For this reason, and in spite of its enormous dimensions, the dome rose only slightly above the tallest of the giant trees. It was exactly as Ford had described. Made from milky glass, it had a pearl sheen which rendered it almost opaque. Indistinct shapes within the dome gave it a mystical air and Merlin saw how easily such a city would give rise to superstitions.

The dome alone was enough to excite wonder. The coming of the Citizen gods would have seemed miraculous to the unsophisticated clans.

The domed city reminded Merlin of something she

had once seen: a miniature town set in a half dome of glass and filled with water. When shaken, the air was filled with glittering fragments making it seem as if silver rained from the skies. She could not recall when she had seen the tiny dome, but understood instinctively that it belonged to the hidden other part of her mind.

As if evoked by the memory of the tiny dome, the William voice spoke: *"This is all that remains of the knowledge of the lost world."*

Merlin trembled at the thought that she might very soon have the answer to that voice and her lost memory and found herself wishing Sear would lead them more quickly.

Marthe had not come back the previous night, but Sear merely said it was the way of Rememberers to come and go unexpectedly. He was too full of anticipation about what he might find inside the forbidden city to think of anything else. Merlin realized Ford was right about Sear's motivation. At least half of his hunger to get inside the city stemmed from his fascination with the Citizens' technology.

Since her talk with Marthe, Merlin was no longer weighed down with hopelessness. There would be danger in the city for her and for any scatterlings who came with her. Sear thought he had it all worked out, but though he hated the Citizen gods, he still thought of them as he did himself. He did not see how different they were. Merlin thought she did.

She had to try to stop the scatterlings coming in with her.

Ford was still uncommunicative. The meeting with Sear and the scatterlings had not altered his new coldness towards her. She now regretted that she had been so blunt in her disparagement of him, but Ford would not allow her to apologize.

"There is no need. You think I am a savage. This has not changed. Once this deed is done, I will recant my oathbond and there will be an end to it." He looked away as he spoke and a chill fell over Merlin, as if some great harm had been done in losing his friendship. Yet she could not lie to him. She did think he was a savage. She could not give him what she sensed he wanted from her, so there was nothing more to say.

The ground all around the dome was cleared, and Sear called a halt where the trees ended.

"Wait here. I will go and speak to them." His eyes glittered and Merlin felt a sense of terrible foreboding.

"Sear, be careful. These people are not like you and the other clanpeople. They don't think the same way as you do," Merlin pleaded. But her words fell on deaf ears.

"No one breaks a blood oath."

Merlin tried again. "To make an oath with anyone is easy. It's just words. You have to respect and maybe even fear the person you make the oath with before it will bind you. Do you think the Citizen gods are afraid of you or care about how you judge their honour?"

Sear's face was stony. "Your words fly on a breath of corruption. Even a warden would not break an oath bound in blooding. I don't know what clan spawned you, but keep your foul words behind your teeth."

Merlin felt the blood drain from her face. She noticed that all of the scatterlings were watching her with hostility, except Ford, who seemed to be concentrating on the dome, taking no part in the conversation. She saw they blamed her for Ford's defection. Merlin wished the dark Rememberer were present.

Sear disappeared into the trees and re-appeared some time later on the other side of the trees. He was clearly trying to conceal their hiding place, but Merlin was sure the Citizens knew exactly where they were. They wanted to take her alive, and that was the only reason they did not simply attack. They were afraid the scatterlings would kill her. They understood the clanpeople as little as Sear understood them.

Sear walked fearlessly up to the edge of the dome.

"That is where the dome will open," Ford said tonelessly.

"I, Sear, leader of the scatterlings, am come to bargain with the leader of the Citizen gods," they heard him shout. He had lifted his hands in a ceremonial manner and Merlin thought how absurd he looked in his dirty rags. How was it that he and the others did not see how unlikely it was that the Citizens who named themselves gods, would honour a contract with such a figure?

But immediately there was a loud humming sound that made Merlin's teeth ache and a small regular section of the dome close to the ground shimmered and dissolved.

Around her the scatterlings tensed, aware that this was the moment of truth. If the Citizen gods meant to attack, they would kill Sear.

One of the Citizens, clad in a white suit and glass helmet, walked out through the gap and crossed to where the scatterling leader waited. The suit flared in the sunlight to dazzling white. Sear's words were inaudible now, but after some moments the Citizen handed him something. Sear crossed his fist over his chest. The Citizen responded with the same gesture.

"That means the bargaining is done," Era whispered, relief in her tone. Merlin's own heart began to beat faster, knowing her own moment of truth had arrived. Any minute now she would be inside the dome.

Sear crossed the grassy expanse and blended with the trees. The dome gap remained open and the suited Citizen stood waiting. Sear appeared suddenly from the trees behind them, panting with excitement.

"What has been decided?" Ford demanded. "What have you told them?"

Sear frowned impatiently. "I told them we know about the broken collar and why they want her back. They told me her mind is damaged because of the broken collar and that's why she can't remember anything. They want the collar back, but they have promised to heal her mind and you and I are to go with her as guardians. Once they have finished with her, we will all be set free."

"How do you know they'll let us go?" Ford asked. Merlin thought of Ranulf and the other Lord wardens being drugged, but held her tongue.

"We are oathbound," Sear said.

"And if they simply kill us and keep her?"

Sear snorted angrily. "Do you think I am leader of the scatterlings for nothing? See this." He held up a small wafer-thin metal disc. He squeezed the disc, pointing it into the trees and a great patch was instantly burned and obliterated. The smell of the burning leaves was acrid and dreadful, but the path of destruction was worse.

"They gave you a deathweapon," Era said, seeming more horrified than elated.

Sear nodded proudly. "You see now? They have given this weapon to me as a signal of their honour. I will keep it trained on them all the time we are in the forbidden city."

"Perhaps we should just take this. We can hurt

them badly with such a weapon, perhaps even destroy the dome,'' Era said.

"Any other suggestions?'' Sear sneered. His yellow eyes scanned their faces. "Good, now that we've had this little Conclave and you're all satisfied, let's go.''

Merlin took a deep breath. She did not believe the broken collar was why the Citizens had been so desperate to have her back, but there was no way of convincing Sear. His rigid belief in the clan honour system made him incapable of understanding how the Citizens would look on that custom. She looked at Ford whose brows twitched up questioningly.

"Ford, I don't want you to come,'' she said.

His single good eye blazed for a moment with something very near to hatred, then it was hard, like a piece of stone. "I don't think you have anything to say about it. Let's go.'' He turned his back on her and walked purposefully into the glaring sunlight. Sear took her arm possessively and followed, pointing the lethal disc at her head.

"Of course I won't shoot you,'' he confided. "But they have to think I might until I get close enough to aim it at them.''

As they approached the opening, Merlin saw there was a kind of airlock just inside and level with the ground outside the dome, though the rest of the city lay below. It seemed very dark in the dome, yet what could be seen was wondrous. The city was less like the ruined city in the Region of Great Trees than something from a science-fiction movie. Though she did not remember going to such movies, she could recall them.

The buildings in the forbidden city soared to much greater heights than the buildings she remembered and were frequently surrounded by a spiralling outer lattice of stairs. Outside, she had thought the world regressed, but inside the dome, she felt herself primitive in comparison.

If she was amazed, the two scatterlings stared around with their eyes starting out of their sockets. Sear was dazzled out of his senses.

The waiting Citizen stepped inside the dome and beckoned for them to follow. Suddenly Merlin wondered whether the air inside the dome were breathable, but it was too late to ask as the dome wall recoalesced and the world outside became a dim, blurred shadow. The dome glass cut off almost all outside light. There was a hissing noise as the outside air was replaced with dome air. She breathed tentatively and found the air cold and metallic.

Once the hissing ceased, the airlock began to descend and Merlin realized it was an elevator. The two scatterlings flung themselves against the transparent walls, wild-eyed with fright.

"You are quite safe." The Citizen god spoke slowly, as if to very young children or fools, the voice distorted by the helmet.

The elevator descended into the city and Sear lost

his fear, eyes devouring the forbidden city with its soaring buildings, convoluted towers and walkways. Unlike the cities of her memory, there were many layers of paths at various levels passing from building to building. There were numerous trees growing at all levels but they were not real, and gave the dimlit city a forlorn air.

Ford's face was grimly unimpressed. Absurdly Merlin wished she could think of something to say that would make him smile. There was something very real and reassuring in his lopsided grin.

The movement ceased and there was another hissing sound. The suited Citizen touched the wall and it opened straight onto a broad, spotless street. They had come right to ground level, which was far below ground level outside. Buildings soared above on all sides, shadowed and silent. The street was lit by dull artificial lights and was dreadfully cold. More of the artificial trees were planted along the centre of the streets.

The Citizen pointed to a door on the other side of the road.

Shivering, Merlin wondered how the Citizen gods could bear the cold. Sear went eagerly through the door, pulling her along behind, so the blast of gas hit him in the face first and he dropped like a stone. Merlin was dragged from his grasp and the suited Citizen who held her pointed the weapon at Ford's startled face.

"No!" Merlin shrieked as he fell hard at her feet. She whirled to face the Citizen who held her. "You made a bargain with them!"

The Citizen released her arm, and removed the helmet with a faint clicking noise. Inside was a very beautiful woman with bone-white skin, cropped dark straight hair and dazzling sky-blue eyes. "We do not honour contracts with apes," she said in a familiar voice.

"Sacha!" Merlin whispered.

The blue eyes widened. "Well, well, how do you know my name, I wonder? I thought you could only read what I was thinking."

"I didn't read it from your mind," Merlin said defiantly. "I heard you speak when you were all looking for me after the crash."

"So, you were restored then. Remarkable," she said.

The other Citizen had also removed his helmet. He had dark hair and white skin too. "She'll have to be decontaminated."

Sacha nodded. "You take care of them. I'll take her."

Merlin looked down at Sear and Ford. "Are they dead?"

"No," Sacha said. "There was no need. *We* are not the barbarians, Merlin." Seeing Merlin start, she smiled. "Nor do I read minds, more's the pity. Your name was known to me. Now come with me."

Merlin did not move.

"You might as well come. You will sooner or later, walking or ..." She looked significantly at the crumpled forms on the floor.

Defeated, Merlin followed her to the door.

They walked along the empty barren street, their footsteps sounding loud and intrusive. There was no real greenery, no trees or bushes or flowers, and no natural light to brighten the dreary city. The deadness was accentuated by the lack of people. Not a single Citizen was visible. Where were all the people who lived in the forbidden city? Even the windows in the buildings were dark, as if the city were a magnificent, lifeless tomb.

Sacha climbed into a small vehicle like the cars Merlin could remember, and motioned Merlin to climb in too. In response to the touch of a lever, the vehicle rose with a faint hum, and they soared over the tops of the dark buildings towards a single lighted tower.

Merlin wanted to ask questions, but stubborn pride kept her silent. When the vehicle came to rest on the roof of the tower, Sacha gave her an amused look and climbed out. Again, they descended in an elevator which opened onto a white passage. The carpet was soft and thick beneath her thin sandals.

They passed one door and stopped outside the next. Sacha passed her hand over a small red light set at eye-level in the door and it slid into a recess, opening the way to a pristine laboratory filled with gleaming bottles and tubes. It was very white and clean, and in the midst of the room stood a red-faced man with ginger-coloured hair and faded brown eyes.

"At last, Merlin. You've given us a lot of trouble, but now you're home," said Andrew.

Decontamination meant a series of unpleasant smelling showers in water that burned her skin and left it sore and red. Dressed in a white tunic which was an exact copy of the garment she had worn in the wrecked flier, Merlin padded barefoot from the shower room into the small adjoining laboratory.

Sacha inspected her as before by running a small square box which ticked slowly up and down her body. This time, the clicks were very faint.

"Not bad," she decided. "Andrew wants to talk to you, then you will be fed."

Merlin did not respond, but her mouth watered. Sacha shrugged and led the way back down the corridors to the laboratory.

Andrew beamed at the sight of her. "Much better."

Merlin gaped, staring at the cages behind him. She had not noticed them previously because they had been empty, but they were no longer empty.

Ford and Sear were in two adjoining cages.

They were awake, squatting on their haunches since the height of the cages made it impossible for them to stand. The sight filled Merlin with a terrible impotent rage and she wondered why they were so passive about their captivity, until she noticed the dull gleam of collars around their necks.

Unwittingly she fingered her own collar.

Andrew smiled at the movement. "Their collars work," he assured her.

Merlin whirled to face him. "You lied! They trusted you to keep your word."

Sacha stared at her with mild interest. "They bargained to enter the city – they entered it."

"That was not what they meant and you know it. I tried to tell them you wouldn't honour any bargain you made with them but they wouldn't listen."

"Fascinating development, wouldn't you say, Sacha?" Andrew asked. "She was able to stand outside the beliefs of the savages and see the truth, yet they would not be warned. It's amazing what a civilizing effect knowledge can achieve. If she had been with them longer, she would have begun to change them."

216

"An unfortunate development is what I'd call it. A disastrous development!" Sacha said.

"How so?" Andrew asked.

"Surely it's obvious. If things had gone as planned, she would have been completely malleable. Now, she sides with the scatterlings. She is useless to us because she looks on us as an enemy."

"I'm not so sure that matters," Andrew said evenly. "There are advantages in this outcome. After all, if things had gone according to plan, there was always the possibility that her natural telekinesis and telepathy would have been suppressed. I believe we will find both those abilities functioning in her."

"But what good is it if she will not do as we ask?" Sacha protested mildly.

Andrew smiled. "Perhaps it is not necessary to ask. In choosing to align with the scatterlings, she makes herself vulnerable to other persuasions. Her mental processes appear undamaged, and that is reassuring."

"Persuasions?" Sacha echoed curiously.

"As I see it," Andrew interposed smoothly, "there are two courses open to us. One, we can regard this as a failure, and simply use her as if she were any other outsider, which will almost certainly render her useless. Or we can use her as she is."

"*What*!" Sacha began.

Andrew smiled and something in his eyes reduced the woman to silence. "The point is, though she has aligned herself with the primitives, she would not be able to help feeling superior. For instance, she foresaw the possibility that a Citizen would lie – the others are incapable of that. This means she would be an outsider with them, until they came to think the way she does: the way we taught her to think. That tells me she is developed enough to interface with the computer and intelligent enough to be convinced."

"But even if she is capable, you can't mean to use her when she regards us as the enemy," Sacha protested.

"That is exactly what I propose," Andrew said pleasantly. "She will do as we ask, precisely because if she doesn't, her little playmates in the cages will suffer."

Sacha's eyes widened appreciatively. "We will still need to make sure the psychic abilities are developed enough for our purposes."

Andrew nodded without taking his eyes off Merlin. "What do you say, girl? How much do these savages mean to you? Enough for you to want to save their lives?"

Merlin felt a stab of shame at the realization that she *had* thought of the scatterlings and the clanpeople as Andrew did – as savages. Now, Merlin saw the error in her thinking. Andrew was not a good man, though he might call himself a civilized man. She felt confused about her own reactions, and found herself wondering whether it was so terrible to be a savage if that meant one was honest and naive and believed in the word of another. Maybe it was better to be a savage than civilized, if it meant being like Andrew or Sacha.

Merlin wished with all her heart she could have spoken to Ford one last time just to tell him she had been wrong.

But it was too late. Merlin blinked away tears of helplessness, because she was not completely helpless. Whatever it was the Citizens wanted her to do required her co-operation. She would refuse until the scatterlings were freed. She might not save herself, but she had the power to save Ford and Sear, and because of that, she had the responsibility to try, even if she failed.

She felt Marthe would have approved and, strangely, that gave her courage.

"I won't do anything until I know who I am and until you free them," Merlin said, looking at the caged scatterlings.

The two Citizens stared at her with as much astonishment as if she had been a chair that had begun to speak.

Andrew recovered first. "Extraordinary. See how strongly she wishes to know the truth about herself? I believe she would have come to us eventually of her own accord, since she is intelligent enough to work out that we would be the only ones who could fill in the blanks." His eyes widened in sudden comprehension. "Of course. She *was* coming to us. She cares enough about these youths to allow them to bargain for her. She was not their prisoner. The savages asked for her safe return. I daresay they worked it out between them." He shook his head in admiration and Merlin felt a savage urge to scratch the cool clinical interest out of his eyes.

"I think you will find it best to do as we wish, for the sake of these two creatures. There are worse things than being collared. I'm sure you understand what I refer to."

Merlin thought sickly of the Voids.

"As for knowing who you are, you will be told the truth, but only because it suits my purposes for you to understand your situation exactly. Therefore, I will arrange for your questions to be answered." Andrew looked at Sacha who turned to a small intercom built into the wall. There was a barely audible crackle as someone responded.

"If she makes a mistake . . ." Sacha said, replacing the receiver.

"The simulator will ensure that doesn't happen," Andrew said. "If she can succeed there, she will have no trouble with the real thing."

"And if she fails?"

"I don't think she'll fail given the possible consequences," Andrew said, peering into the cage holding Sear.

He reached through the bar and scratched the leader of the scatterlings under the chin.

Merlin shuddered with revulsion.

Andrew looked up suddenly at Sacha. "Have you looked at the collar yet? With luck, we won't need it any more, but it should not have failed. I have warned Sedgewick about his carelessness."

"It was probably damaged in the accident, but I'll have to dismantle it before we can find out exactly what went wrong," Sacha answered. Casually she lifted her hand and pointed a tube at Merlin, who flinched.

The collar fell apart from her throat and onto the floor with a clatter. Sacha gathered the two halves, taking them to a bench.

Andrew waved his hand grandly, and before Merlin could see what was coming, Sacha had fastened another collar on her from behind. "Unlike the collars your friends are wearing, this one has to be activated. It won't be used as long as you behave yourself," she warned.

Merlin lurched forward as a shock of pain filled her head. Then it was gone.

"Just a little demonstration to ensure we understand one another," the Citizen woman said.

"Take her now," Andrew said, suddenly brisk. "There is much to be done before tomorrow." He smiled and Merlin's stomach seemed to curdle at his false warmth. She wondered why he bothered.

They rode another elevator several floors down in the same building before stopping in a pale green hallway. Seeing her reaction to the colour, Sacha smiled. "The savages responded best to that colour."

Merlin's anger faded into bewilderment. From the sound of things, she had been in the city in the first place for some task which only she could perform, and which was somehow vital to the Citizens. She had been prepared in some way for this task, and had never been intended to come into contact with the clanpeople because this had damaged the preparations. For some reason, they had not wanted her to know about the people living outside the dome.

She couldn't imagine what they wanted her to do, that they with all their technology, could not. But thinking it through, she knew it lay behind the taking of clanpeople.

With a chill, she guessed whatever she had to do was dangerous, and might reduce her to a mindless, drooling Void, too. That answered her question about why the Citizens did not use themselves.

"Here," Sacha said, passing her hand over the blinking red light on the door and it slid smoothly aside. Merlin felt her mouth drop open at the green painted room filled with plants and hauntingly familiar classical music. There were paintings and prints on all available wall space, some of which she recognized, and books piled in shelves and on benches.

Rather slow, dragging footsteps came slowly closer, then another door opened and a very thin boy with white blond hair came out. The dragging noise was the sound made by two metallic rods he was using to hold himself up. His legs were visibly withered, incapable of supporting even his slight weight.

He stopped dead at the sight of Merlin.

"Andrew wants you to tell her everything," Sacha said, her voice faintly conciliatory. This told Merlin the sickly looking boy was important.

"Sedgewick will come over later, but if you have any trouble with her, use this." Sacha handed the boy the activating switch for the new collar, turned on her heel and departed, the door closing after her with a faint electronic hiss.

The boy dragged himself nearer, eyes questioning. "We've met before but I don't suppose you'll remember."

"I don't remember anything," Merlin said coldly. She didn't care how important he was.

"Do you mind me calling you Merlin?" the boy asked, again with a quick apologetic smile. "My name is ..."

"I don't care who you are or what you call me," Merlin retaliated.

"Let's sit down," the boy said gently. "This will take a while and we may as well be comfortable." He walked very slowly to a chair and lowered himself awkwardly, carefully laying the metal supports across his knees.

Merlin flung herself into a seat facing him. "Andrew said you would tell me who I am."

The boy seemed not to mind her unfriendly tone.

"I don't actually know who you were originally," he said. "In fact, I don't even remember you coming here. You first came into the dome about the same time I was learning to talk. Andrew found you wandering half starved and witless. I suppose your parents had been killed somehow. You were very young, and the trauma of seeing your family die had taken away your senses. But that is only a guess."

"Then I *am* a clanperson?" Merlin interrupted.

"Your body is the body of a clanperson," he corrected. "Your mind ..." He shook his head. "This is no good, I'm telling it in the wrong order. You come into the story later. We have to go back a long way before then. How much have the clanpeople told you about us?"

Merlin frowned. "Only that the dome was here for as long as anyone could remember, then one day your people came out and started murdering everyone in sight. Then you turned yourselves into gods, drugged the clan leaders and made them sacrifice their people. You told them the spirits of those you took would live forever in perfect happiness. In truth, you made them mindless idiots and sent them back, calling them Blessed Walkers." Merlin's tone was accusing.

"You did not learn those things from the clan-people," the Citizen boy said, his eyes alight with a curious pride. "You worked all that out for yourself." He sighed. "It's true of course. I don't say that what happened was right in a moral sense, but I can see how Andrew and the others believed it was their only choice." He looked into Merlin's eyes and she had the fleeting impression that he was much older than he looked.

"They believe using the clanpeople was not just the only thing to do, but also the right thing. But I'm not a scientist." He smiled unexpectedly. "My father was a historian. I think I should have been a historian, too, if things had been different. Do you know what a historian is?"

Merlin nodded coldly. "I don't know how I know, but that's one of the things you're going to tell me, if you ever get round to it."

He pretended not to hear the hostility in her voice. "It must have been odd to wake with memories that have nothing at all to do with the world you find yourself in."

He broke off, coughing violently. Then he sat back and his face was so pale his eyes were like burnt ashes. He gasped air in a shallow jerky rhythm until his breathing became closer to normal. Merlin felt an unexpected stab of pity for him.

"This whole mess has more to do with history than anything else," he went on as if the coughing fit had not occurred. "We, the Citizens, are all that remain of the old earth. That's the world you remember. Think about that world. Can you remember the pollution, the damage to the air and water, the thinning of the ozone layer?"

His words evoked a vivid set of pictures in Merlin's mind, as if he knew exactly which words would trigger memories of industrial chimneys belching black smoke and spewing invisible poisons into the atmosphere and pipes leaking oily sludge into the sea.

"What you remember is only the beginning," the Citizen boy said. "It became much worse, and happened faster than anyone expected. The scientists had warned people, but the industries and technological people refused to listen. They persecuted the scientists and conservationists, calling them greenies, and saying they cared more about trees than people, never seeing that humans are just part of a complex infrastructure of lifeforms where the death of one has repercussions for all." He shrugged, seeming exhausted by his eloquence.

"When the scientists' predictions started coming true, the technologists came up with the idea of building domes because the atmosphere had become poisonous. For a while that was all right, except there were a lot of people who were too poor to live in the dome cities, so they stayed outside, dying slowly and horribly of disease, squalor and hunger.

"But that wasn't the end of it. The earth's weather pattern changed dramatically causing tremendous upheavals: hurricanes, tornadoes, and earthquakes which damaged the domes and killed thousands of people."

Merlin sat forward, sickened by the tale of destruction. "What has all that to do with me, or with your barbaric treatment of the clanpeople?" she demanded.

"Everything," the Citizen boy said simply. "Your clanpeople are the descendants many times removed of those people who were refused admission to the domes, and who somehow adapted to the poisons, the increased strength of the sun, and the heat. We are not descendants – we are members of the survivors who lived in the domes." He closed his eyes for a moment.

"When it was clear the domes would not protect us for as long as it would take the earth to heal, scientists and technologists came up with the idea of going somewhere else; finding a new clean planet and starting again, except there weren't any close enough. Then an astrophysicist invented the Dimension jump. I don't really understand how it works, but it meant a spaceship could travel billions of light-years across the universe in only a couple of centuries of real time. With frozen sleep, travellers only aged about ten years in a journey that otherwise would have taken generations to complete. Of course, the co-ordinates fed into the ship computers were based on minimal data since it was impossible to know what existed so far away. Even the best telescopes only showed information that was already a long way out of date by the time it reached earth.

"It was a gamble because a ship might just as easily come out of a D-jump in the middle of a star or a black hole as find a planet that could sustain life. Another likelihood was for ships to end up in a dead solar system, in which case they could just turn around and come back, guided by a signal transmitted continuously by a homing device. The real time for the round trip meant that although they would only have aged about twenty years, centuries would have passed on earth, and there was a good chance the planet would be clean again.

"Given the alternative of staying on earth, trapped in degenerating domes, it seemed the best hope. So they built ships and started D-jumping people who could afford the passage all over the heavens. The pollution and the tremors got worse, and civilization started to decay completely, especially since the people who hadn't been inside the domes began to revert to savagery, and ancient terrible diseases like the black plague started again.

"Then a couple of the last scientists started to worry about what would happen to humanity if none of the ships that D-jumped survived the journey to carry on the human race either on a new planet, or back here on earth. So they spent a tremendous amount of money building this special dome around the homing device which would guide the D-jumpers back, sinking it in the ground to protect it from tremors. Then they froze hundreds of volunteers too poor to afford to fly away, or wealthy people too scared to D-jump, to repopulate the earth in case none of the D-jumpers survived to come back. They designed a super computer to nurture the sleepers through their endless night, and to wake them when it was safe."

Merlin was transfixed by the queer story.

The boy smiled a melancholy smile. "It seems I am ever destined to be telling you stories. Well, you might guess what happened next. The super computer tried to wake the sleepers but five centuries too soon. Something went wrong and it ended up killing all but twenty people. I'm one of the lucky ones," he said with bitter irony.

"We woke to find ourselves on the verge of extinction, with no hope of reprieve in a world filled with lethal poisons."

There was a long pause, and Merlin seemed to come from a long way off, back to the present, and her own dilemma. "Then the whole city . . ."

The boy nodded with a bleak smile. "Is empty, except for this single building."

Merlin shook her head. "But what has any of that got to do with me?"

The Citizen boy stirred, as if from a deep sleep. "Well, once we realized how things stood, most of us accepted that we were a kind of postscript to humanity on earth, and set about like good scientists to make a record of the last days, just in case some of the D-jumpers ever did return. Then we discovered we weren't the last." He smiled. "It's a bit of an irony when you think about it that the people left for dead were the real survivors. No one had suspected that. It was Andrew's idea that we take a closer look, for research purposes, and note the changes that made them able to cope with the environmental upheavals. It was then we found that the clanpeople, your people," he added with gentle emphasis, "had developed more than an immunity to atmospheric poisons. They had a primitive form of telepathy and telekinesis.

"That changed everything," he said grimly.

Merlin stared past the Citizen boy in amazement. On a small table sat a tiny village trapped in a dome-shaped glass ornament.

The boy looked around to see what had caught her attention, reached over and picked up the ornament. The movement disturbed the water inside, showering silver rain onto miniature roofs. He watched Merlin's expression with a strange smile.

"So, you *do* remember? I always wondered if you saw anything I showed you." He shook the ornament and then set it down on the chair between them.

Merlin opened her mouth to speak, but found her lips were dry as paper. She felt suddenly frightened, as if she had reached into a familiar corner and touched something completely unknown.

"My name is William," the boy said.

"*You* are William? But . . ." Suddenly many of the whispered memories made sense. "What did you do to me?" she said at last. The words seemed curiously limp in contrast to the surge of questions in her throat.

William took his time answering. He shook the ornament and watched the silver rain fall, mesmerized by the slow movement. "This is us," he said softly. He looked up into Merlin's eyes, his expression grave.

"I don't understand," she said flatly, sick of his hints. It was hard to accept that the William of her innermost thoughts was a Citizen god.

William sighed heavily. "Sometimes I envy the outsiders not needing to bother with words. Words are so slow. If I could just tell your mind . . ."

"It's not like that," Merlin said, without meaning to. She knew little of how the telepathy worked, but she seemed to have the ability anyway, and that meant she knew a great deal more about it than William. The pallid boy seemed to imagine it meant a whole lot of grand things, as if it were the magic Sear lusted after. Because of her memory of a world in which telepathy was nothing more than a story, Merlin could understand exactly how the Citizen boy felt. That seemed an important and significant realization, but there was no time to think it through. William was staring at her expectantly.

232

"It's like someone whispering inside your head. You still have to have the words," she said.

The boy smiled. "So, the teacher is taught. That's the way it should be." He looked sad again. "So. The dome people, my people, were curious about these new powers. Andrew more than the others wanted to know everything about them. You see, he understood what it meant long before the rest. He had always been strong, but when he told us his plan, he became the leader of the dome. Not much of a kingdom, but Sedgewick envies it and styles himself as Andrew's successor. Andrew thinks him a fool," William added with faint disparagement.

"His plan?" Merlin echoed, feeling certain they were about to get to the heart of the story. She had a sudden desire to stop William from speaking, an irrational fear of what she might learn.

"I said before that all the ships D-jumped, but that's not exactly right. One last ship was built and set to D-jump before the last scientists went. That ship was a final safeguard just in case the calculations were wrong and the earth never did heal well enough to support humanity again. It gave the sleepers a chance for life, since the dome life-support systems would not last forever."

"Why don't your people fly away, then? Or aren't there enough of you to fly this ship?" said Merlin with the sudden suspicion that Andrew was trying to train the clanpeople to help pilot the spaceship.

"The ship is set to D-jump," William said. "That means one person could fly it, if they had to, with the right code. The problem is that the computer won't let us near the ship."

"What?"

"There was a flaw written into the computer program as far as it concerns us humans, but there was nothing wrong with the ship protection part of the program. You see, the ship was set to be released from the force-field protecting it in twenty centuries, at the same time as we were to be wakened. But we woke five centuries too soon.

"The computer won't let us near the ship for another five centuries."

"Can't you switch the computer off?"

William sat back and looked up at the roof. "There's the rub. You see, the master computer and an auxiliary powerpack are inside the force-field with the ship. You can't switch it off because you can't get to it. And we daren't try to upset the computer linkups because the whole city is booby trapped to explode. If the computer is tampered with there's a good chance the city will be destroyed."

"Why explosives?" Merlin demanded. "In fact, why a forcefield to protect the ship if you were all supposed to be asleep?"

William shrugged. "History again. Apparently the people who put us to sleep were afraid of other people. Not the outsiders, but people from another country. In those days the world was all divided up into . . ." He stopped. "But you know that, don't you? You remember that world."

He seemed tired. "Waking was dreadful. Most of us had friends or family who had died. The outside world was still poisonous to us, and once we started sorting it all out, we understood why. And then someone shouted that we were saved because there was a last ship which existed solely in case all else failed, so that we could follow the last D-jumper and join their colony. Only we couldn't get to the ship because of the computer, and we couldn't alter its program because of the danger. We couldn't repopulate the earth because it was poisonous, and because there was too small a gene pool.

"Most of the survivors resigned themselves. Only Andrew refused to accept that there was no hope for us. He would stand for days without taking his eyes off the ship inside the force-field, staring like a madman. He said there must be a way. No one believed him until he called us altogether and suggested that the clanpeople with their telepathy might be able to do what we couldn't."

William looked around as if he were frightened of being overheard. Merlin wondered why, since Andrew had instructed him to answer her questions. "He believed that an outsider with telepathy might be able to reach the computer's mind without having to touch it and alter the program so that the computer would switch off the machine.''

Merlin was confused. ''But why take so many? Why not ask the clanpeople to help. They would have.''

William shook his head. ''You don't understand. To begin with, to Andrew and the others, the people outside weren't – aren't – human. They are a corruption of true humanity. Garbage left over from the old world.

''The religion thing was a second thought. In the beginning, Andrew had outsiders rounded up, stunned and brought in. Naturally they went mad when they woke up and found themselves in here. They had to be killed or stunned again. He tried all sorts of ways to get the people here calmly so that he could tell them what he wanted them to do. But he treated them like animals and they reacted like trapped wild things.'' A flicker of revulsion crossed the pale bony face.

''There was always a lot of violence until Sacha dreamed up the collar whose circuitry introduced a current which interfered with brain waves. It was a much more efficient way to control the outsiders, since, collared, a captive would do literally anything they were told. The trouble was that the business with the computer couldn't be forced. It had to be voluntary.

''The other big problem was that some of our

236

people were killed in the raids, not many compared to the outsider death figures, but with so few of us, it couldn't go on.

"It was Sacha who came up with the idea of making the clanpeople want to come into the city. She designed a mythology which focused around the city and the Citizens, and she brought in and brainwashed a number of tribal wardens using a highly addictive drug to ensure they stayed obedient. But you have discovered that, though Sacha said it was impossible. She had been examining their society to identify key figures. She did this by watching their tribal meetings in secret, and photographing those to whom the rest deferred, those who made judgements or gave commands. These were later captured. Those successfully addicted were freed, and allowed to go back to their tribes to tell stories of the generous, misunderstood Citizen gods, who wanted only to offer immortality and paradise to a lucky few who would be taken into the mysterious domed city. In return, Sacha supplied them with the drug."

"But why turn the clanpeople into mindless idiots at all?"

"Can't you guess, Merlin?" William asked. "Those who come to us are tricked into attempting to access the computer telepathically. But for some reason, their minds are unable to cope. Andrew refuses to accept that his great plan might not work, and so the trying goes on."

Merlin was appalled. She could accept, almost, the desperation of the doomed Citizens to find a way out of their dilemma. But not their callous abuse of the clanpeople. She wanted to scream her disgust at William, but something in his expression was ambivalent, as if he liked all that had happened as little as she. Merlin found herself wondering about the loyalties of the sickly Citizen boy. Belatedly she remembered that he had said "they" far more often than "we" when he spoke of his fellow Citizens, almost as if he had mentally divorced himself from them. She thought of his furtive glance around, and wondered if he would help her.

But there was one question he had not answered. "What about me?"

William looked up. "Yes. You were the next stage. You came to us without a mind, so there was nothing to burn away, but also nothing to think with. Andrew had the idea that if we could raise you as one of ourselves and give you a mind that would help you align with us, you would be able to access the computer where the others couldn't.

"He appointed a number of us to organize a sleep-learning program that would plant in your mind all the technical information you would need to access the computer program. We also had to give you enough of a social background to act as a foundation for the personality we meant to create." He smiled. "I proved to have an unexpected talent in this. And since all the people who knew about computer learning had died, I became valuable in spite of everything.

"I did not have enough knowledge to reprogram the learning computers with anything new. But I could use what was available, and that turned out to be old history tapes of a time long before ours, but it was better than nothing. We planned to tell you that you had been in cryogenic sleep and we had woken you, to explain the gaps. I even planted information that would make it seem feasible.

"After a long time, I put together a patchy program, the best we could do considering what I had to work with. Then we linked your mind up to the computer and waited."

Merlin had a vivid memory of the dry inner voice offering her information, and realized it had been the voice of the sleep-teaching computer. It struck her that she had scarcely heard the voice after meeting the scatterlings. And now, she supposed, the William voice would fall silent.

Merlin looked up at the Citizen boy. "You ... your voice was in my head too," she whispered.

"You remember?" he asked simply, his eyes shining inexplicably. "You see, it was I who watched over you all the long years of sleep learning. Once the program was set there was no need for a team. Just one was needed to watch to make sure nothing went wrong, and I was useless for most other things.

"The others thought it a tedious job and pitied me, sitting and watching you for hours and weeks and years. They never understood that I had shaped the learning that went into you. It was a painstaking job, like piecing together a jigsaw puzzle. And I had done much more than they guessed.

"Andrew only wanted you to have enough of a mind to be able to understand what they wanted. They didn't care what went into you, as long as you could function and reach the computer when you were wakened. But I wanted more than that. I wanted you to have a real memory, and so I pieced together a world for you to remember. Not just a world of places and things, but a world of songs and voices that disagreed and argued, and books and stories, and plans that worked and plans that didn't work. Some of it I fed through the computer, but more often, I spoke to you myself. There were times when I spoke to you of my own thoughts and problems. I never knew if this would go in. Sometimes I really felt like a god, creating life out of nothingness and chaos."

"And then?" Merlin asked.

"And then came the day of waking," William said.

"You were unhooked from the computer and taken by flier to a smaller dome where you were to be 'found' by Andrew and Sacha. It was reasoned that you could be brought in over the dead city, to make the story of your being 'found' more plausible. Andrew also wanted you to see the dome from the outside, so that you would understand the dome was all that remained. You were never meant to see that there was life going on outside the dome. You would live among us, and bond with us."

"But you never got to the small dome."

"The accident!" Merlin hissed. Then it dawned on her what she had been told. "Then ... I never lost my memory because I never had a memory." She felt a terrible anguish at the realization that there was no memory to be found, no self to rediscover. She was nothing more than a programmed human being who had returned to her masters.

"If Andrew had not brought you here, you would have died," William reminded her.

"I *am* dead," Merlin shouted. "I thought coming here would make it right. I thought knowing the truth about myself would fix everything. Instead I find I'm programmed like a robot. I would be better off if I had never asked any questions."

"Impossible," William said with such insistence Merlin looked up at him.

"What?" she asked dully.

"It would have been impossible for you just to accept your memory was gone," the Citizen boy said indignantly. "I told you. I didn't just throw a lot of facts into your mind and hope you'd come out all right. Your mind is a delicate, complicated jigsaw puzzle that took me years to weave out of broken bits of computerized memory, and I had to do it mostly in secret in case they stopped me. I wanted you to be able to think, and to have something, somewhere, to think from."

"I don't know what you're saying," Merlin said hopelessly.

William sat forward eagerly. "The fact that you were capable of saving yourself in the accident, and of finding and communicating with the outsiders could only happen because of the way your mind was put together. You were able to think and reason. That was why you had to search for the truth. I made you a mind hungry for knowledge, a mind that would wonder and ask questions. A mind that would demand answers, that would search for them."

"What about the collar?" Merlin asked, trying to take in his words.

William smiled. "You never guessed? I tampered with the collar circuitry after Sedgewick installed it. Andrew wanted it done in case you woke before they were ready, but I could not bear to think of you collared."

Merlin stared at the youth, wondering why he looked so happy. She felt empty. "Why?" she asked.

To her astonishment, a faint blush stained the boy's cheeks. "You were so strange and beautiful when they gave you to me. So still. Like a sleeping princess. I didn't see you as the others did. I did not want them to cut your hair, but it had to be done because of the computer electrodes. I didn't start out to disobey

Andrew, but bit by bit, that's what I did." A shadow crossed his features. "I think he has guessed some of it, but there is nothing he can do to punish me." He looked into Merlin's face with a dreamy tenderness that reminded her vividly and painfully of the way Ford had stared at her.

"I used to watch you and talk to you and play you music. I tried to imagine what you would be like. I didn't let the others know how I felt, in case they took you away and gave you to someone else. I used to call you "princess", and in the end I think I actually believed that was what you were. And one day, you would wake up, and ..." His eyes flickered away, hiding whatever he might have said.

Merlin had a brief vision of the sickly Citizen boy, sitting in the endless twilight of the dying city, watching over her sleeping body, telling stories to a corpse. It was a sad and rather pathetic picture, reminding her of Bramble's vigil with the dying Ranulf.

"But I remembered the ruined city!" Merlin said suddenly. "How could that be?" She clutched at the flaw in his tale, wanting desperately to believe that he was lying, and that she was normal.

But William shook his head. "You remembered a hologram. Sometimes the learning required you to see. Your eyes were sewn open and bathed. You saw pictures and heard sounds. That's when I showed you the little dome ornament. You were never really in that city."

Merlin slumped back in her seat. "I wish I was dead," she whispered.

At last something of her reaction filtered through to William.

"What's the matter?"

Merlin laughed at the smallness of his question, as if he had offered a bandaid for an amputated limb. She felt the laughter bubble shrilly into hysteria and stopped abruptly. William looked at her uneasily.

"I'm not going insane," Merlin said, sinking her head in her hands. "I probably can't, or did you program me with that too?"

Comprehension filled his eyes. "No! No, what you are thinking is wrong. You are not programmed like a machine. Your mental processes are your own, and perfectly normal. If you were really a machine you couldn't think for yourself. You wouldn't be capable. I didn't program you. If you like, I fertilized the ground and you planted the seeds. Not the seeds you were meant to plant. The scatterlings put paid to that. You made yourself what you are and your thoughts are your own."

Merlin shook her head.

"Merlin . . ." William's voice was shockingly intimate, and Merlin was shaken from her mindless despair by a tone so knowing that she felt naked before those burning eyes and his utter knowledge of her. "My sleeping princess," he murmured, and reached out a frail hand to her cheek. "Do you know, I even gave you your name. There is a story behind it. Do you know what it means? Do you remember?"

Merlin shook her head dumbly and the boy looked disappointed.

He said: "In the olden days, there was a legend about a city. The most beautiful, peaceful, perfect city in all the world, ruled over by a wise and good king. But the secret of the wondrous kingdom really lay in the king's advisor, a sorceress who had been born outside time and contained the wisdom of all ages, because she was confined by no era. Her name was Merlin.

"I called you after her because you don't really belong to any time either. Your body is like an outsider's, immune to the poisons of the old world. But you are also the inheritor of the wisdoms and dreams of the old world and the new. You are of both times and no time. You are outside time," he said, a note of triumph in his voice.

A stranger who remembers nothing and everything ... the Conclave Rememberer had said. And it was true. But she had also predicted Merlin would bring an end to the flow of the deadly visiondraught.

"If I survive," Merlin whispered.

William looked taken aback and Merlin realized the boy lived in his dreams and stories. He had not given a thought to why she had been programmed.

"The computer. That's what it was all for, wasn't it? I may be your special creation, but that's what it was for. And maybe I'll end up Void as well. Then you can lay me down and tell me stories forever." Merlin had an inexplicable desire to disturb the dreamy calmness in the boy's eyes.

William's face told her she had succeeded. "You hate me that much?" he whispered.

Merlin stared at him for a long moment, wondering if the terrible emptiness was a kind of hate. "I don't feel anything for you," she said in a thin voice.

"It doesn't matter what you feel," said a voice Merlin remembered as vividly as waking in the flier. Sedgewick. She turned to find a thick-set youth with flat, sleepy, green eyes, coarse black hair and a soft small mouth. She had thought herself incapable of feeling, but she reacted to the boy's arrogance with instant antagonism. No wonder Andrew saw him as a poor heir.

"Sedgewick." William greeted him in a neutral tone nothing like the gentle, eager way he had told her the story of her past.

"So, it doesn't matter," she hissed, and from the corner of her eye, she saw William gape at her tone. Her rage focused on Sedgewick. "Then it won't matter either that I have no intention of trying to mind-read your rotten computer and you can tell your precious Andrew that."

Sedgewick grinned with infuriating complacency.

"We'll see. Perhaps you have forgotten that the lives of the two savages you brought with you depend on your behaviour."

Merlin was taken aback. For a moment she *had* forgotten Sear and Ford. Then her expression hardened. "I won't do anything unless they go free and I see them go free. I don't want any of your worthless lying promises. I'm not as gullible as they were."

"I don't think you understand," Sedgewick said pleasantly. "You don't have any say in what will happen. You will do exactly as you are told and no more, or else your two friends will die, and then we will hunt up the scatterlings one at a time, and put them to death in front of you until you get the point. Andrew believes in reason, but I favour more direct persuasion. Either way, you will do as you are told."

Filled with impotent fury, Merlin opened her mouth and closed it again. She looked down at William, willing him to defend his sleeping princess, but he only looked at his hands, folded loosely in his lap.

A ndrew was leaning over Sear's cage when they entered the laboratory the following morning. Merlin had spent the night in a cramped cubicle locked from the outside.

Though a new day had begun, there was little change inside the dome. It was still dimly lit and cold, and inside the tower there were no windows. Almost all the tower rooms were lit by the bright artificial lights of the city. Merlin wondered if Sear would admire the forbidden city so much if he could understand how barren it really was. She began to long to feel the sun on her face.

"This one is taming nicely, but I'm afraid the other is just too wild," Andrew observed, hearing them enter.

Merlin felt a queer thrust of triumph to see that Ford refused to allow himself to be petted like an animal. It seemed the collars had degrees of effectiveness. Neither Ford nor Sear were like the Void zombies, but then, the two scatterlings were not mindless. Yet.

"I've brought her," Sedgewick announced.

Andrew turned to face them with a smile which did not reach his eyes. "I think we can call Merlin by her name, Sedgewick." The Citizen boy's hand tightened painfully on her forearm at the rebuke, but his expression showed nothing.

He's learning to control his face, Merlin thought. He's learning to be a liar and a cheat, like Andrew. He's becoming civilized.

The word "civilized" had taken on a whole new set of meanings since she had entered the dark city. She was not the same ignorant girl who had entered the dome the day before. She saw the true worth of the scatterlings and the clanpeople now, but that awareness made her feel even more of an alien than ever. William believed her to be a sorceress who stood outside time, outside the rules of those bound by time, but it was more than that. Being on the outside meant she could never truly be one of either the Citizens or the clanpeople. She had lain awake for hours the previous night, thinking about all she had seen and been told, and had woken with a clear knowledge of what must be done.

Strangely, although she felt very alone, she had a

purpose which her life had previously lacked. She wanted to do as Andrew demanded. If she were able to get the Citizens their ship, they would go, and the clanpeople would be free of their tyranny. So if she could, she was going to do as they asked. If.

She also wanted to make sure Sear and Ford were freed, and she would have to convince Andrew that she would do nothing unless they were let go. She was certain he would not free any of them if she succeeded.

She wasn't the person who had lain down to sleep in the Citizen sleeping cubicle. She understood that even if Andrew refused to free the scatterlings, she would do as he wanted so that the Citizens would fly away in their spaceship and leave the clanpeople in peace.

She clenched her teeth, trying to decide how to frame her words to the scientist. But Sedgewick spoke before she could announce her ultimatum, repeating her words to him.

"She wants them freed before she'll do anything," he said.

"She doesn't believe you'll free them after. I say they should be kept. She will obey as long as we have them," he announced.

"I do not remember asking for your opinion," Andrew said.

Merlin thought that the Citizens were a cold people. Had the long sleep made them that way, or had they been like that before? Had all those thousands of D-jumpers been so unfeeling, so remote, so cruel? Was that what humanity had become?

"I do not bargain with savages," Andrew said.

"They are descended from you, and you from apes," Merlin snapped, the information unexpectedly offered by her computer-designed memory.

"Not quite," Andrew said calmly, wiping his hands on a cloth. "They are descended from the refuse that was left to rot outside the dome societies. Criminals, lunatics, drug addicts. Walking rubbish. Against all odds they survived, as did the hardiest of other life-forms which also adapted to cope with the changed world. In a sense, we should have foreseen it. After all, cockroaches survived the nuclear holocausts."

The impregnable coldness in the scientist's face rendered Merlin speechless. Unlike Sedgewick, he seemed incapable of anger. She guessed this stemmed from his essential attitude to her. He might order Sedgewick to use her name, but his eyes told her she, like the clanpeople, was a worthless, expendable savage.

She forced herself to answer calmly, feeling a display of emotion would weaken her in Andrew's eyes. "I don't care what you think of the clanpeople, or of me for that matter. Either they go free, or I won't do a damn thing to save you."

Her blunt demand had succeeded as nothing else

had in making Andrew look at her as a person, but even so, his expression was curious rather than angry.

"So. The worm turns," he said softly. "I wonder what exactly William used in the sleep-teaching program. I doubt the brief time spent among the savages could have made you so independent without a little help in other quarters. Perhaps I should have kept a closer watch over the process."

Merlin felt sorry for William, for she felt that Andrew guessed the truth already about his illicit programming. But she had to think of Sear and Ford before the dreamy Citizen youth who seemed incapable of applying himself to the real world. She had to make sure Ford and Sear got out of the dome safely, otherwise the Rememberers would be right about her bringing destruction and death on them.

"They will be freed. It is a small matter," Andrew said indifferently, after a slight pause.

Merlin looked into the smooth, calm features of the scientist. "I want to *see* them freed."

He nodded. "But first, you will demonstrate that you are capable of doing what has to be done. I assume William told you all you needed to know?" He seemed to be staring closely at her and Merlin felt herself flush. Andrew nodded as if her reaction had confirmed something.

"I must have a few words with young William," he said. "Nevertheless, I think we understand one another."

Doggedly, Merlin pointed at the caged scatterlings. "I want proof that they're still all right," she said, her throat dry with fear. There was nothing she could do if Andrew refused, but she had to try.

He smiled. "Of course. Sedgewick will deactivate one of the collars. Which one?"

"Both," Merlin said.

Andrew laughed. "One. You choose."

Torn, Merlin stared at the two scatterlings. More than anything, she wanted to speak to Ford, to tell him she had been a stupid, prejudiced idiot, and to say she was sorry. She would have given much to see him smile his lopsided smile and to hear him laugh out loud.

But she pointed at Sear.

Andrew smiled. "So be it. As soon as the simulation has been successfully completed, we will return, and you will see that he still has his mind, such as it is."

Merlin shivered with hatred, seeing Andrew had no intention of letting her talk to the scatterlings. She nodded, as if believing the illusion that she had a choice.

The simulation room was a square divided in two by a thick wall of glass which represented the force-field barrier. On one side were a number of instruments and a chair facing the glass; on the other was a computer on a desk.

Andrew pointed to the computer. "It has been

programmed not to allow entry to the room by blocking any command to raise the glass. It has control of the mechanism which moves the glass wall. Your task is to access the computer and to alter the programming. If you succeed, the glass will slide away and allow entry to the other side of the room."

On the way to the laboratory that morning, Sedgewick had taken pleasure in telling Merlin that none of the few who had managed to access the simulation computer had survived the experience with their mind intact. Those who had failed to access at all had been killed. Disposed of, Sedgewick said. Merlin had the feeling he would like to see her fail, even if it meant the Citizens were doomed to extinction.

Sacha, clad in a white coat and carrying a clipboard, directed her to sit in the chair facing the glass wall. A number of tracers and measuring wires were taped to her forehead and temples.

"What we need to know is can your mind survive the computer linkup, and if so, is it possible for you to actually alter a program telepathically," Sacha said. "You were sleep-taught a great deal of computer knowledge which should help you deal with the programming, and that should surface under the stimulus of this test."

Merlin remembered fleetingly the rush of computer knowledge that had assailed her immediately after the accident, and her naive assumption that this meant she was "something to do with computers".

"Can we start?" she asked, her mouth dry with fear. It had not escaped her that all Andrew's hopes might lead to nothing if the computer burned her mind out. She thought it would be like dying, and if that was the case, then she had already died once and been reborn. Would they bring her back again?

A thought struck her. "How come you didn't do to the Voids what you did to me? Build them a new mind?"

Sacha looked preoccupied, checking the monitoring devices. "A waste of time," she said briskly. "There was no mind left to build on, whereas your mind was simply empty."

Merlin swallowed, and looked at the computer through the faceted glass. The scene reminded her disturbingly of her dream of being trapped on one side of a wall of choking smoke. Perhaps the dream had been a kind of premonition. Or a Remembering, since it was obvious she now had a touch of that strange ability too.

"Theoretically, it should be possible for you to interface with the computer. We have not been able to discover why the attempt destroyed the telepaths' minds yet, since there is no physical evidence in any autopsy," Sacha went on.

"The subjects in the past have always been completely receptive, because we made sure they experienced a very pleasant time in the city. They woke in beautiful surrounds, exposed to music and art. They ate magnificently and certain drugs were introduced to their food to heighten their sensory capacity so that ordinary pleasure became a kind of ecstasy. When they attempted interface, they were always relaxed and receptive because they trusted us and believed we were about to help them understand the magic of the Citizens." Sacha seemed to be talking more to herself than to Merlin.

"In every case, access ended up destroying their minds.

"I suspect the reason for the failures is something to do with the way the telepathy works. Unfortunately we haven't done enough research to understand it fully yet." She looked at Merlin with chilling speculation, as if deciding how to dissect her skull.

"Andrew is of the opinion that the failure is connected to culture shock – that the computer is simply too complex an artifact for the primitive minds. If that's so, you have a better chance than any of the others."

Merlin laughed harshly, and the Citizen woman looked at her in mild astonishment.

"Can we get on with it?" Merlin said.

"Of course. One last point though. If you do succeed in accessing the machine, avoid the red circuitry areas, since these coincide with the areas of the program dealing with retaliation. It's no good if you get in, then accidentally blow us up. You might remember that you and the two in the laboratory, not to mention the group hiding outside the dome, will also die if that happens. In the simulation, the tripping of the retaliatory system will be represented by an alarm bell.''

Merlin nodded without looking at the other woman.

''Very well, we'll proceed. I'm activating the monitors which will tell me if you have any success in altering the computer. Begin. Remember, use the knowledge in your own mind if you are able to access the program.''

Merlin nodded. She looked at the computer, thinking how small and unimportant it looked. Just the same, she was frightened, not only for herself, but because if she failed, Sear and Ford would face mindlessness or death.

She was also frightened because she knew as Sacha and Andrew couldn't, that she had scarcely used her telepathic powers, and had generally refused access to others trying to Send to her. The ability was as alien to her as her yellow eyes. It was possible she did not know enough about how to use her own ability to do what Andrew asked.

The other Offerees might have lacked knowledge of computers, but they knew how to use their telepathy. They used it easily and continually.

On the other hand, that hadn't helped them when it came to the crunch.

She took a deep breath and tried to think positively.

"What are you waiting for?" Sacha demanded with a trace of impatience.

Ignoring the scientist, Merlin tried to imagine her mind with a hand. She envisaged reaching the mental hand out through the glass to the computer. She made herself concentrate as she had when forced to respond telepathically to the guards at the gate of the Valley of Conclave.

Then, all at once, she felt a surge and suddenly she seemed to be two people, one seated on the chair, and the other floating just above the computer panel.

She questioned her memory about how computers were constructed. It told her the computer was operating. Again she thought of her mind as a hand, and tried reaching inside the machine.

It was no good! She was inside the machine all right, but not inside the program.

She withdrew, wondering how she was to do that. She searched her knowledge until she discovered that computers spoke in a language of numbers and codes and electrical impulses. She felt a rush of despair. How was she to reach a mind that wasn't a mind?

Then she thought of the mechanical voice that characterized her implanted memory. It spoke to her, had spoken to her. How had it managed to communicate with her unconscious mind? If the computer could access her mind, there must be a way to access it. She wished she had asked William for more detail as to how the sleep-teaching worked.

She hovered above the panel uncertainly. Curiously, she found she could "see" herself on the other side of the glass, sitting still with her eyes closed, when she turned her mind that way.

She focused her attention on the computer.

In order to issue a command, it was necessary to touch the keyboard in the same way you had to make noises out loud to be able to speak to someone. Telepathic communication was a thinking to, rather like throwing a ball to someone with your eyes closed.

She tried thinking to the computer in the form of a command, imagining the command running from the keyboard along the wire and translating into the computer's language.

Nothing happened.

She felt sweat running down the side of her face, and wondered what would happen if she couldn't even get inside the computer, let alone change its program.

She stared into the winking green eye of the computer screen, and her memory told her the screen was the input point. A tiny cursor winked in the top left corner of the screen. Merlin stared at it curiously. Her memory told her the cursor was manipulatable by her or any human user. That was where human and computer language was translated. With a tingle of excitement, she directed the hand of her mind towards the cursor, imagining going inside and merging.

To her astonishment, she felt her mind rushing forward into the screen, into the cursor. She had the distinct physical sensation of being somehow connected, or linked up, then suddenly a great surge of energy rushed at her like a tidal wave. Already tense, she withdrew instantly out of reach, closing her mind deliberately to the computer as she had closed it to Ford.

At the same instant, she understood with dazzling clarity why the others had failed. In fact, they had not failed to access the computer at all. It was what happened after access that destroyed their minds.

The problem was that the clanpeople were natural telepaths, never questioning their ability or looking at it as something that might be dangerous. It was as much a part of them as their tongues. Their lives, she realized for the first time, were shaped by their ability to know completely what another person meant. They had no capacity for mental deception. That was why the Lord wardens had discouraged mindbonding, because it was a complete revealing.

There had been no reason to set boundaries on their abilities, or to try to curtail them since telepathic communication at both a simple and mindbond level was a matter of mutual decision.

But Merlin had woken with a mind bereft of

memory. Her telepathy existed outside the framework and moral direction that ruled the clanfolk, for what she remembered was an older, more corrupt world. Her first reaction to telepathic contact had been to prevent Ford from accessing her mind. Instinctively, she had refused him entry, and from that moment she had gone on blocking out all other minds, regarding the telepathic ability she possessed with fear and distrust.

Her attitude to telepathy had created an ability to block and this saved her from the computer which, once accessed, simply dumped its vast reservoir of knowledge into the accessing mind, as it would into another computer.

Andrew had been right in believing she could do what the others had been unable to do, but he had no idea why.

Merlin was sickened as she imagined the duped clanpeople trustfully reaching their minds out, unaware of what would happen to them. They had no power to protect themselves, and so they had been destroyed as completely as the death-weapon had cleared the thick trees outside the dome.

Merlin turned her mind back to the screen and again cautiously imagined sinking into the cursor, but she pictured her mind screened on all sides by thick walls, except for a tiny hole.

The computer accepted the limitation, and began to feed information through the tiny hole at an incredible pace. She requested the computer to slow down, and the information became a harmless trickle.

Then she began to push out again, following informational bypaths and streams by moving the cursor, using the reservoir of knowledge available within her mind to guide her around the program.

She realized very quickly that the computer's simulated program was laughably simplistic. Unlike a human mind, the computer hid nothing, and was extremely logical. All it required was correct access. It would refuse her nothing within its power. But she hesitated to make the alterations, sensing this was a safe moment to stop and think about what would happen after she had done as they asked.

She let the electrical impulses which made up the voice of the computer jostle her gently.

Unexpectedly, she left the computer via an input line. She found herself inside a program designed to recirculate air. She moved quickly to the input line, and into a program which supervised the elimination of dust.

She realized what the Citizens had not: all the computers were linked by input lines which were in turn linked to the main computer program which oversaw the city. Like a fish swimming against water she followed the input lines back to their source.

In no time, she found herself inside the main program. It was enormous, but essentially designed along the same principles as the small simulator program. Merlin was startled to realize she could free the ship or switch off the air and light in the city, or open the electrical doors to the cages which held Ford and Sear if she chose.

She felt a sense of incredible power at the knowledge that she held the lives of all the Citizens in her hand.

But it was not as simple as switching off the forbidden city. The computer would not accept that instruction because it had a series of red-linked circuits designed to emulate human decision-making processes. It would think of the changes as sabotage and set off the explosives which riddled the city. She could alter the programming slightly, if she were very careful. If she made a wrong move, the computer would retaliate. It was the same if she simply switched off the air. In the first place she and the two scatterlings would be suffocated along with the Citizens, and as soon as she passed out the computer would resume the air flow.

She noted absently that the computer had a line which moved outside the dome. Curious, she followed the output to discover that the main computer was also linked up with the other, smaller dome William had mentioned. The program told her the dome was designed to serve as an emergency dome, but beneath one layer of programming lay another, which revealed that the dome was a secret weapons cache left by the scientists who had designed the two domes. This suggested the D-jumpers who would return in five centuries were preparing themselves for a less than complete welcome.

That gave Merlin a frightening idea.

She withdrew her mind carefully back along the circuits and input lines, thinking furiously. By the time she reached the tiny computer in the room with Sacha, she had decided what to do. With insulting ease, she altered the simulator's programming as she withdrew into her own mind.

There was a loud click and Merlin opened her eyes to see the dark glass slide up and into the roof.

"You did it!" Sacha cried.

Merlin felt tired, but not from her immersion into the maze-like computer linkages that controlled the forbidden city.

"I want to see Sear uncollared," she said wearily.

Sacha seemed not to hear. "Andrew will want to know the result of the simulation," she said in a preoccupied voice, unsticking the monitoring wires. They went straight back to the laboratory.

While Sacha described the test to Andrew, Merlin pretended to be far more exhausted than she was. She was surprised to find William in the laboratory. He looked pale and grim and she guessed Andrew had been questioning him about her sleep-learning. Little did he realize that without William's programming and her exposure to the clanpeople, she would not have been able to think enough to protect herself from the computer.

She no longer blamed the Citizen boy for what Andrew had done. She understood that William had behaved as morally as he was able, given his circumstances.

Andrew asked her a lot of questions about the simulation, but she pretended to have hardly understood what she had done. A number of times she stared at him blankly, trying to imagine herself as a Void. Andrew appeared to accept her story, but she noticed William staring at her curiously. He knew better than Andrew what her mind was capable of understanding. She prayed he would not give her away.

At one point she found Andrew watching her suspiciously and she warned herself not to underestimate the scientist. If he had the slightest idea of what she intended, he would kill her without a second thought.

"Well," Andrew said at last, but the coldness underlying his voice was unchanged. "Tomorrow you will access the main computer."

Merlin looked up mutinously. "I already told you, I'm not doing anything else until you free my friends. And you promised to let me talk to Sear." Even to herself, she sounded childish. She prayed Andrew's superiority would make him accept her outburst.

There was a curious tense silence, and Sacha and

Andrew exchanged a brief glance that made Merlin uneasy.

"Wait here. Sacha, find Sedgewick and have him bring the deactivator to me." Sacha nodded, a faint smile playing around her lips. She departed, and Andrew went out too saying he wanted to look at the simulator monitor.

Merlin looked questioningly at William, thinking she was paranoid for wondering if Andrew could somehow listen to what they said to one another.

"I was afraid for you," William confessed in his soft wheezing voice. At the same time, he pointed to the door and shook his head vigorously and made elaborate hand signals.

Merlin got the hint. "What for? I'm nothing to you," she said sulkily. "I just want to get out of here with my friends."

"I created you," William said in a pompous voice. He smiled and patted Merlin's hand, and she found herself smiling too.

"I don't care what you did to me. When are they coming back?"

"Andrew was right, you're an ungrateful savage!" William was very white and Merlin moved towards him, concerned he was about to faint.

He shook his head urgently and looked towards the door. Merlin stepped away from him just in time. Andrew returned, beaming, followed by Sacha and Sedgewick.

"Can I go?" William asked.

Andrew smiled. "I think you had better wait and take Merlin back with you. We won't need her again until tomorrow."

"I don't want to," William said with a scowl.

Andrew smiled even more broadly. "You will do as I command. Now, you wanted to speak to that one?" He pointed at Sear and Merlin nodded.

The scientist made a sign to Sedgewick, who pressed a small square device in his palm. Immediately, Sear's expression changed. He shook his head, looked around and threw himself at the bars of his cage with a howl of anguish.

"Betrayed!"

From the corner of her eye, Merlin saw William flinch. She moved forward and Sear begged her: "Let me out!"

"I can't," Merlin said. "They won't let me. They will let you go once I do something for them."

"What?" Sear demanded. "What do you have to do?"

"Nothing that will hurt you or anyone outside," Merlin promised. She was talking more for Andrew's benefit than for Sear's, wanting him to believe she was malleable.

Sear looked around at Ford. "What is the matter with him? He's not . . ." he began, dawning horror in his eyes.

Merlin shook her head. "He's not Void. He's collared."

At once Sear felt his own throat. "No!" he cried in rage. Then his face changed. "You say they have agreed to free us when you do what they want?"

Merlin nodded. She was stunned to realize the scatterling leader was prepared to accept the word of the Citizens yet again, so powerful was his belief in the honour of a person's word.

"Time's up," Sedgewick announced, and Sear's eyes glazed over, his expression slackening into blankness.

"No!" Merlin cried. She turned to find them all watching her: Sacha and Andrew expressionless, Sedgewick smiling in triumph, and William pale and shocked.

"I won't get your ship free unless you free them. I swear it," she said. "And I am a clanperson so my promises are more than just words," she added with pride.

"Very well," Andrew said. "They'll be freed tomorrow morning. In the meantime, there is much to be organized. We will be leaving as soon as the ship is freed."

Merlin bit her lip. That they would want to leave immediately was something that had not occurred to her.

A ndrew would not permit Merlin to speak to Ford and Sear before their release. She was surprised at the pettiness of spite, but she insisted on seeing them leave the dome and watched their departure on a narrow monitor in the laboratory.

Sacha led the scatterlings into the elevator which would take them to the outside. They were both still collared and walked slowly. Sacha put her helmet on as the elevator air-lock rose to ground level. Seconds later, the dome opened. Merlin felt a fierce gladness at the sight of the two scatterlings walking into the harsh sunlight. Clad in a white suit, Sacha lifted her hand and Merlin held her breath in fear that Andrew might have them killed at the last.

The Citizen woman retreated immediately and the

dome closed over just as Sear and Ford shook their heads and looked around them.

Merlin saw Sear's lips move quickly, perhaps telling what he had seen in his brief caged wakening inside the domed city.

Ford whirled and stared at the dome with anguished eyes. He flung himself against the place where the dome opened, but it was immovable. Sear pulled the youth away, his lips moving rapidly. Merlin wondered what he said that made Ford allow himself to be drawn away.

The two began to walk away, but Ford looked over his shoulder and for a moment it was as if he stared directly into Merlin's eyes. Her heart felt as if someone had squeezed it. Ford's lips moved and though she could not hear, Merlin read the shape of her name on his lips.

Her nails bit deep into her palms with the effort of controlling her expression. She could not bear for Andrew to witness her grief.

Now let them go, she prayed. Sear, take them far away. Marthe, see what is to come and take them away from the danger.

The scene of green trees and dazzling sunlight faded into black on the monitor screen. Merlin's reflection looked out at her.

"Very well," Andrew said with the merest trace of impatience. "Let's get on with it." He looked at Merlin speculatively, then told Sacha to organize food for her. Merlin had no illusion that he cared whether she might be hungry. All he wanted was to make sure she was as ready as possible to tackle the real computer program.

Sacha, clearly irritated at being assigned such a domestic task, called William and instructed him to see she was fed.

In a very short time, Merlin was sitting in a kind of eating hall filled with a huge number of empty tables, eating more of the bland paste-like matter the Citizens used for food.

"It's all right," William said in answer to her suspicious look. "I don't think Andrew knows Sacha sent you off with me. And besides, I think he accepts that I'm sorry for disobeying him about the programming." He smiled. "He thinks I'm bitterly disappointed that you don't appreciate me more. You don't, of course, and he's right that I didn't foresee that. But I'm not disappointed."

He smiled sadly. "Even so I doubt he would have been so lenient on any of the others. He's a vengeful man. But what can he punish me with that would mean anything?"

"He could kill you," Merlin said bluntly, irritated by the boy's inability to see reality.

He smiled. "What for? I'm dying anyway."

Merlin's mouth fell open stupidly.

"I thought you realized," William said apologetically. "Like the computer, I was frozen with a fatal flaw. If the scientists knew, they would have put me outside. Sickness was not allowed. It seems I've lived my whole long life on borrowed time. Maybe that's why I never saw things the way the others did."

"You . . . you seem very calm about dying," Merlin stammered.

"I've had some time to get used to it. And I'm different because of it. I see things more clearly than the outsiders or the Citizens because none of it matters to me personally. Whether you get the ship for us, or don't, whether the D-jump succeeds in taking us to the others or not won't make any difference to me. As it is, I'm dizzy with the drugs Sacha feeds me to keep away the pain. The D-jumpers who went before might have developed enough of a technology to help me, but I won't live long enough to take advantage of it. The D-jump takes ten years in frozen time, centuries in real time. I barely have one year."

"Is that why you did what you did with me?" Merlin asked.

William shook his head, then shrugged. "I don't know. Maybe it started out that way. But there's more to it than that. The others see themselves as the prime species. That's the old world's way of thinking, the kind of thinking that poisoned everything. That's why they can use the outsiders without feeling it's wrong. But I'm not so certain our species is the most important thing, or that any species is more important than the rest. It seems to me Nature weeds out the ones that don't live in harmony with the others. I think we, the old kind of human, were slated for extinction, except we won't lie down and die. The scientists who created the domes and the ships to D-jump, believed it was the most important thing in the world to make sure humankind survived, and they even went so far as trying to make sure the best survived. But maybe Mother Nature was ensuring it in her own way because the people rejected by scientists as unfit to live survived and altered so they could live on the new poisoned earth."

He sighed. "Andrew and the others think it's a bizarre mistake. But I'm not so sure. I don't think Mother Nature makes those kinds of mistakes. I think she knew exactly what she was doing when she created the new people. The outsiders are not like us in many respects, but the one thing that makes them utterly different from us is their telepathy. It means they can tell if someone is lying."

"I have known clanpeople who would lie," Merlin protested, thinking of Delpha.

William shook his head. "It's not that they can't lie, but that if they swear to be telling the truth, they can be checked, and that sort of makes lying obsolete. The old kind of human was good at telling lies, because there was no way of really knowing if a person lied or spoke the truth. Ever. The whole justice system of the old world, the whole corrupt political structure, was based on that, and look where it brought us. Your outsiders are not very good at telling lies. Why bother since they can always be checked? Those who lie will never be permitted to prosper, except where we have interfered with drugs and coercion. But once we have gone, things will go back to being the way they were.

"There was a great man born years ago who said survival of the fittest was what it was all about. I think the outsiders are fitter than the old kind of human." He coughed, a dry racking spasm that sounded worse than before.

"For all their technology, the Citizen gods are nothing more than a few rag-tag leftovers of a people who first ravaged then abandoned this earth. This world doesn't belong to them any more. It belongs to your people. You and the outsiders are the inheritors."

"Why are you saying this to me?" Merlin asked.

William looked around as if the answer to her question were knitted in the air. "I don't know. Because you might be able to do this thing Andrew wants. And if you do find the way for us to follow the D-jumpers, you might also be able to find a way to stop them from coming back."

"Back?" Merlin echoed.

"When the D-jumpers come back, and they *will* come, they will have had centuries to develop if they don't destroy themselves first, and they will come back because human beings are like that. They will come back to reclaim old earth. Maybe they will have changed and become better, but I don't think so. I think Mother Nature knew what she was about when she tried to make them extinct. Like me and the computer system, old humanity has a fatal flaw. They don't want to live in harmony, they want to dominate and control. You've seen how they look at the outsiders. What do you think they will do if they come back and find people like your clanfolk living on an earth they regard as theirs?"

"What are you trying to tell me?" Merlin whispered.

"Warn the outsiders. Help them prepare for when the D-jumpers return. They'll have to pass the warning on, generation to generation. They must be ready to fight when the D-jumpers come. They must be ready for war," he said urgently. "But first we have to make sure you get out of the dome safely. Andrew has planned . . ."

Sedgewick burst through the doors leading to the eating hall, his eyes excited. "Bring her. It's time."

"All right," William said, immediately rising. He beckoned indifferently to Merlin who followed, mind reeling. It was as if William had read some of her own thoughts, and clarified them. But what had he been about to tell her about Andrew?

The entire Citizen community was assembled in the gigantic launch room at the centre of the dome. For the first time, Merlin saw them all together. There were less of the Citizens than the scattering rebels. She thought of the hundreds who had congregated in the Valley of Conclave, and wondered that so few had managed to dominate so many. In a way it was all a bluff. If the people outside knew how few there were in the city and concentrated all their efforts on killing them, the Citizens would have been forced to retreat.

She thought of what William had said of the Citizens' ability to lie. That was what had fooled the clanpeople. They could not conceive of anyone creating such immense lies, and so they had never questioned them.

The ship was visible through the dancing laser-field which cast a bluish light over the faces of those assembled. Shaped like a fat cigar, it was gleaming gold. Not all that different, she mused, from the science-fiction spaceships in her memory of the movies. The memory planted in me, she corrected. For a moment, the memory had seemed so much her own that she had forgotten it was false. For the first time it occurred to her that the memory base carefully planted in her mind by William lay under her thoughts, helping to shape them. Though false, they were part of her now and forever, and in time, the dividing line between what was her own memory, and the memory grafted into her empty mind would blur. When I am old, she thought, I will probably forget everything and think these things my own memories. Children will call me mad and a witch.

She smiled. Then she remembered what she meant to do, and the smile died on her lips.

Andrew came to meet them. His sharp eyes moved over her face, then William's.

"I've brought her," William said wearily. Dismissed by Andrew's curt nod, he crossed the floor to where the other Citizens waited.

Andrew looked at Merlin and smiled his cold smile. "Why so grim? If all goes well, soon we will be gone. And you will be free."

Merlin thought uneasily of William's interrupted words. *"We have to get you safely out of the dome. Andrew plans . . ."* Andrew plans what?

"You don't think I would kill you?" Andrew said with mock horror, reading uncertainty in her face. "I am no savage. Besides, I made a promise to your scatterling leader to return you to them." He smiled and Merlin remembered Sear talking to Ford, perhaps telling him what the Citizen god leader had promised. She felt a deep and abiding sense of unease at that promise. Why would Andrew bother to promise anything? He was more the sort to want revenge for having his hand forced.

"From the tragic little scene of their departure, I am sure the scatterlings will wait for you outside the dome," Andrew continued.

Merlin repressed her shock viciously, and tried to smile, but her lips felt stiff.

"She doesn't look too happy about that," Sedgewick observed.

Andrew frowned. "She doesn't, Sedgewick. I wonder why that is?"

Merlin forced herself to meet the flat stare of the scientist, thinking fast. She mustn't let Andrew guess what she planned. "I don't trust you to let me go," she said. That was true enough, but not the whole truth.

Unwittingly, Andrew had exacted a cruel revenge. She thought of Ford and Sear waiting outside for her and wanted to scream with despair.

Andrew's face cleared. "I will keep my promise. You will be freed from the dome before we leave this place. But now, you will keep your part of the bargain. The ship."

Merlin wondered what he would do if she simply refused. It might be worth it to see the tables turned on him. In spite of his own behaviour, he had not taken into account that she might not keep her end of the bargain. She shook her head. She had more important things to think about than revenge. Besides, Andrew's promise to free her had a ring of truth. Maybe that was what William had been trying to say. Her heart rose with hope. Maybe she would be able to get out in time.

"Where is the computer?" she asked.

From the corner of her eye, she noticed Sedgewick

turn away quickly, but not so quickly that she failed to see the smirk twisting his lips.

The slight hope was extinguished. The smirk told her something was wrong. For a moment, she considered refusing, and making Andrew tell the scatterlings to leave the area. But then he would wonder why, and what she had to do was more important than her life or the lives of the scatterlings.

She stood like a statue as Andrew spoke to the Citizens, trying to think if there was another way. If the launch were delayed somehow and Andrew kept his promise to free her, she might have time to get to the scatterlings and warn them. Or they might think Andrew had lied, and go back to the Hide. But that was a huge "if", and she knew in her heart they would not leave while there was a chance for her. That compassion and honour would see them killed. And Sedgewick's smirk told her that Andrew had something unpleasant planned for her.

Coldly, she fixed her mind on the ultimate aim.

"To conclude," Andrew said. "I see no reason for us to delay our departure if the experiment succeeds. We will be on our way home tonight." He turned to Merlin and nodded regally.

As if he's a king, she sneered inwardly. But she turned obediently to face the computer and a silence fell around her as the hand of her mind reached out, and she poured herself into the cursor.

It did not take long to do what she had to.

There was an excited hum as the blue glowing corona surrounding the ship winked out. For a moment no one moved. Then Andrew stepped forward eagerly, the first to walk within the circle of protection in hundreds of years. His face was flushed with triumph as he turned to face the others.

"At last!" he shouted.

Then the other Citizens came forward, hesitantly crossing over the line, as if they feared the blue mantle would suddenly reappear and incinerate them. But nothing happened. The spell was broken, the sleeper awakened.

"How does the ship open?" an old man asked Andrew tremulously. His face filled with awe, as if Andrew were truly a god.

"I will show you," he said.

"What about her?" Sedgewick reminded him.

Andrew looked down as if from a great height. "As promised, I will set her outside the dome."

"But . . ." the boy began.

"But first, her reward," Andrew said. He smiled and made a gesture. Merlin turned to see Sedgewick lift his hand, grinning maliciously.

There was a click as the collar around her throat activated, and then there was nothing.

Merlin woke with a sour taste in her mouth, her limbs sore and heavy. She felt disorientated. The last thing she remembered was Andrew signalling Sedgewick to activate the collar. And now she was chained, hands to collar, but where was she?

It was pitch dark and she was on the ground. It was hard and cold and so was the wall her shoulders rested against. The metal walls and floor told her she was still inside the dome. Andrew had lied when he promised to free her. Perhaps his revenge would be to leave her to rot in a room inside the dome when he and the Citizens flew away. But she would not rot, nor die of starvation. It would be quicker than that and for this she was bleakly grateful.

She moved experimentally, trying to ease her

numb hands, and found her legs were also chained. A faint hiss told her the room was air-conditioned. Even so, above the metallic scented air of the dome, there was another smell. She sniffed, trying to decide what it was.

Abruptly, she wondered why the collar had stopped working.

There was a sliding noise and she froze, terror like a cold knife between her shoulder blades.

"Is anyone else there?" a voice asked.

Merlin almost fainted. She recognized the voice. It was Danna, the boy she had met briefly in the temple. That was something she had not expected.

"Danna?" quavered another voice. A chorus of voices followed and Merlin's heart sank.

"Is this hell?" a girl asked in a quavering voice.

"Stupid, there's no such thing," said another. Beta, Merlin thought. "We are inside the forbidden city."

There was a hiss of indrawn breaths.

"Why have they chained us?" someone asked.

No one had an answer to that question. Finally Danna answered and Merlin thought how odd that leaders arose, regardless of age or personality, in times of stress.

"We are not dead, and we are not Void. There is hope in that," he said.

"Blasphemy," someone hissed, sounding on the verge of hysteria. "They're probably testing our faith and you have doomed us all with that foul word."

There was an aghast pause while this was absorbed.

"I don't believe we are being tested." Again Danna.

"The Citizen gods do not lie! Beg forgiveness or you will be the cause of killing us. Quickly."

Someone began to sob.

"Danna, beg for forgiveness," pleaded a girl. Someone else moaned in fear.

Merlin bit her lip. She had not spoken only because she could think of nothing to say that would help the children. They were doomed and so was she. But now it looked as if Danna would be murdered if she stayed silent.

"There is no one listening and there is no forgiveness," Merlin said, her voice sounding flat and loud in the room. A shocked silence greeted her words.

"It is the voice of Citizen gods," breathed a girl. "We must pray."

"No," Danna whispered. "Didn't you hear what she said?" There was a pause. "Besides it came from in here. Who are you?"

"I was in the temple with you for a short while. I am Merlin."

"Merlin. Yes. They said you had thrown yourself down the well. But you escaped with that scatterling boy," Danna said.

"Are you a ghost?" someone asked.

"Of course not," Merlin said. "Danna told you, I escaped."

"Then why are you here?" someone else enquired.

"I came here for the same reason I went to the Valley of Conclave: because I have lost my memory. To find answers to who I am."

"Did you find answers?" Danna asked.

Merlin hesitated, knowing they would not understand all that had happened because they did not understand what the Citizens were.

"I found that the Citizens are evil demons, not gods, and their magic is black."

"They lied?" someone asked. "But what will happen to us?"

"They will eat us," someone squealed. "That is what demons do."

Several people began to weep hysterically at this.

"Stop it," Danna said firmly. "There's no point in screaming and wailing. Besides, they gave us back the bodies of the ones who were Offered so they couldn't have eaten them."

"They ate their souls," a girl whispered. Merlin shivered because it was close to the truth.

"Stop that hissing and moaning," Danna snapped. "You're frightening everyone and it does no good."

"What do you suggest we do?" a boy snarled. "Sing praise?"

"Do any of you know how long we've been here?"

Merlin interrupted. It was possible the ship had gone already. If so, there was little time left to sing or wail.

"They collared us," Danna said. "Then we were here. That's all. I just woke up."

"I'm hungry so we must have been here a while," said one of the older boys.

Merlin felt a slow anger at the realization that the Citizens had left them all to die a slow horrible death of starvation or suffocation, trapped like rats. She wondered if there was any way of getting into the computer so that she could free them, but was forced to recognize that she had to be able to see a screen to access it.

A mechanical sound filled the air and everyone was silent, listening. Merlin's heart began to thump. Has it begun? she wondered.

Then a light went on: a pinkish glow, dimly illuminating the group of dirty, huddled clan children. The room they were locked in was little more than a cupboard. Holding the wavering light was William.

"Merlin?" he whispered, peering around.

"It's a ghost ..." whimpered a small boy.

William ignored the whispers, scanning the group until he spotted Merlin. He stepped over the others and came to kneel beside her. Amidst all the gold-skinned clanpeople, he did look ghostly pale.

"Must be quick," William said, his breathing shallow.

"Who are you?" Danna asked.

William looked around and smiled. "I don't think there's much time for introductions, but I'm William."

"How long have I been here?" Merlin asked.

"Only a night," William said, rummaging in a pouch bag over his shoulder. He pulled out a key with a grunt of satisfaction. "Ah." He bent to unchain Merlin's hands and feet, then he threw the key to Danna.

"Unlock the others."

"Thank you, William. I am Danna," the clan boy offered. William solemnly shook his proffered hand.

"Are you a demon?" a little girl asked.

William turned to smile ironically at Merlin. "That's as good a name as any for us." He lowered his voice. "The ship had to be stocked. In all the excitement, no one had thought of that so the launch was delayed a day. We're going any time now."

"Can you get us out of the dome?" Merlin asked eagerly.

In answer, William stood and aimed a familiar plastic square at Danna.

"No!" the clan boy cried, hands rising to the collar at his throat.

There was a loud click and Danna slumped back, silent. Merlin gaped incredulously as William aimed the device in turn at each of the clan children, until all were vacant-eyed and silent.

Then he turned to Merlin.

"What have you done?" she asked, horrified.

"I had to free them all to free you. Andrew sent me," William said, taking the key from nerveless fingers. "You're all to be released, but with activated collars."

Merlin touched her own collar. "But that means we'll be Voids."

"As good as, since the collar can't be removed or altered. That's Andrew's revenge. It pleases him to think of you walking amongst them, mindless."

Merlin stared at the Citizen boy in horror. "I would rather be dead!"

"That won't be necessary. You'll have this," William said with wry humour, his bones seeming to press out against his scant flesh. He reached out and pressed the deactivating slide into her hands, then he bent and unlocked the chains on the remaining children.

Merlin blinked, closing her fingers around the device.

"That will deactivate the collars," William said over his shoulder. "Of course, it would be no good to you if your collar were activated, since you wouldn't have the wit to use it. That's why you're going to have to pretend."

"If Andrew finds out . . ." Merlin began.

William's face was grim. "You would be killed, and probably so would I. But we have to take the chance. There is no other way."

Merlin opened her mouth, but was prevented from speaking by the wail of an ear-splitting siren. "What is it?"

"Launch mode," William said. He turned to the clan children and ordered them to stand.

He looked at Merlin. "Don't fail me, Merlin. You're their only hope. Remember, you have no mind. You can't think, and barely feel. Do you understand?"

Merlin nodded, swallowing dryly. Her heart galloped in her chest as she schooled her face to blankness, clearing her mind of all thoughts.

William reached in his pocket and brought out a collar. "Put this on instead of that one. This is the old broken collar. Even if someone tries, it can't be activated. Just in case."

He helped her remove the collar she wore and replaced it with the old one.

"Thank you," Merlin said.

William smiled sadly. "You know, I wish I could have stayed here, even for the time I've got left, but if I asked, it would make Andrew suspicious."

Merlin felt tears come into her eyes. She blinked hard, willing them away as William reached out and touched her cheek. His fingers were longer than hers, but thin and cold like sticks of ice.

"My sleeping princess," he murmured. "I always imagined I was the prince who would waken you with a kiss. Perhaps death is not the real end, and only a different kind of sleeping. If so, I will dream of

288

waking to the kiss of a princess." He leaned close, his shallow breath fanning her hair, and pressed his cold lips to hers.

William's eyes were closed. Merlin stared at his long dark lashes curled against the pale curve of his cheek and thought that was how he would look when he died. She shivered and instantly he moved away. "A salute from the old world to the new," he said, his ironic tone giving lie to the unspoken words in the kiss.

Merlin could think of nothing to say.

"Don't forget me," he said gravely. "That's a kind of immortality too."

Merlin nodded, slipping the precious plastic square into her pocket.

"Come on, we'd better hurry or Andrew will start wondering what is taking me so long," William said briskly, ushering the collared Offering children before him.

"Line up," he commanded. Merlin stood third in line. "Walk," William instructed. They walked out of the cell and into another adjoining cell, and then into another. Merlin gasped aloud as she saw that the final cell was also occupied – by Aran and Bramble! Her mind reeled as she tried to understand what possible course of events could have brought them to the forbidden city.

"What is it?" William asked anxiously.

"We have to take these two. We can't leave them."

William shook his head firmly. "Impossible. Andrew said only you and the children."

"I'm not leaving them," Merlin said.

William stared at her in exasperation, then laughed in defeat. "Well, I gave you the will, and now you use it to defy me. So it goes." He knelt to unlock the chains that held them to the floor. Merlin wondered fleetingly why they bothered with chains when they had the collars.

"I want to release the woman," Merlin said determinedly.

"There's no time!" William protested.

"Please," Merlin insisted.

After a pause, William sighed. "This is probably our undoing, you know that. I'll have to make Andrew think I got his instructions muddled and hope he won't bother making me bring them back."

Merlin took out the deactivating switch and pointed it at Bramble.

The Amazon rebel shook her head groggily, and reached instantly for a non-existent knife. Then she recognized Merlin.

"What . . ."

"There is no time to explain anything, Bramble. Are you two the only ones here?"

Bramble pushed back her waist-length mop of curls and glanced at the still-collared Aran. "The guardians surprised us. Delpha brought them. Meer and Helf were killed. And a lot of others. I killed

Delpha but they managed to stun me. Aran and I were the only ones who survived. They chained us up and handed us over to the Citizen gods with the Offered ..." her eyes flickered to the collared children. "Them!" she said.

"Yes?" Merlin prompted.

Bramble tore her eyes from the children, her fingers pulling at her own collar. "Apparently the Lord wardens were frightened out of their wits at the thought of the visiondraught being stopped. They had Delpha watching Aran ever since the night of the judging. They were frantic over your disappearance. They sent us here because they thought that's what the Citizen gods would want. How ...?"

Merlin shook her head. "Ranulf?"

Bramble's eyes darkened with pain. "I cut his throat," she said in a harsh voice. "He did not want them to drug him again. When he knew we were caught, he asked it. This time I could not deny him. It was for this that I killed Delpha the snake."

Merlin reached out and touched the rebel woman's muscular arm. "I am sorry. But, Bramble, for now you have to forget that and everything. I need your help to get us out of here. We can talk later, if we get out of all this alive." She looked at William. "I want her to be awake too, in case something goes wrong. She can fight if we are exposed and if something happens to me, she can deactivate the collars on the others."

"All right," William said with obvious reluctance. "But it increases the danger." He looked at the rebel leader seriously. "Bramble, if that is your name, I hope you are a good actor because our lives depend on you being able to convince anyone we run across that you're a Void."

"I will not fail you," said Bramble with a soldier's quick grasp of the essential. Merlin knew she must have a thousand questions about how she had got into the city and how it was that a Citizen god was helping them, but she kept them to herself.

William nodded. "Let's go, then."

He led them single file along a number of passages and down steps, gradually working his way round the edge of the dome to the airlock. She prayed they would not run across Andrew, but almost as if he had been summoned up by her fears, he stepped out from a doorway in front of them.

"What do you think you're doing?" he demanded.

William instructed the sluggish walkers to stop. "What do you mean? I'm doing what you told me." His voice had the faintest suggestion of a whine.

"You have brought all of the outsiders from the cells."

"You told me to bring all of them!" William protested indignantly.

"All of the outsiders in the *last* cell, you dolt!" Andrew snarled.

"I'll take the others back, then," William said sulkily. Merlin hoped he wasn't overdoing it and her heart beat hard. She felt as if Andrew would hear it or see it thundering in her breast.

"No, don't bother about that now. I suppose it's just as well to put them out," he said irritably, running his eyes along the line. Merlin forced herself to stare ahead, her eyes unfocused as his eyes stopped on her. Andrew came along the line and ordered her to face him. The rest of the line turned with her in unison. Fortunately, Andrew was too busy to note that Bramble's reaction was a split second slower than the rest.

"So, your little creation," Andrew sneered.

He was close enough for Merlin to see the tiny broken blood vessels which gave his cheeks their ruddy, unnatural colour. The satisfied smile faded abruptly and he frowned.

Merlin had a sudden dizzyingly vivid memory of Andrew slapping her violently across the face. She wondered when that had happened, then realized it had never happened. It was *going* to happen. She had Remembered it. She steeled herself.

Without warning, Andrew raised his hand and slapped her viciously in the face. She neither flinched nor blinked, thanks to the Remembered warning. She felt blood trickle from her nose. Her mouth hung open and a dribble of saliva ran down her chin.

Andrew grimaced in disgust. "Get them out of here. Launch in thirty minutes."

He marched off without a backward glance.

"Turn. Walk," William ordered indifferently, but Merlin thought his voice trembled slightly. Her own legs shook uncontrollably, and she hoped they would meet no one else.

But there were no further mishaps. Soon they were crowded into the elevator airlock leading to the outside, pressed close together. Merlin took her lead from William who was staring blankly out over the dark forbidden city.

He had changed into a white suit and he clipped the helmet on before opening the dome. Sunlight streamed in and Merlin forced herself not to shade her eyes with her hands. Her neck prickled and she sensed they were being watched.

"Walk," William commanded.

They walked out into the hot brightness of the outside world and Merlin realized with a fierce regret that she had not said goodbye to the frail Citizen youth, without whom she and the others would have died.

She wished she had told him what she planned to do. He deserved that much. But it was too late.

"Don't look around, either of you," William said softly. "There are directional microphones, but they aren't very good. They won't hear me unless I face them. When I order the others to walk, walk with them. Don't drop your pose until you are deep in the trees. Goodbye and remember what I have told you about the D-jumpers, Merlin. They will come back."

Merlin squinted against the sun, resisting the urge to turn and face him.

"Walk," William commanded in a loud voice. The others began to shuffle towards the treeline. Merlin thought of William reaching to kiss her, and she felt tears spill out of her eyes and run down her cheeks as she shuffled with them.

Near the treeline she sensed a movement in the trees. She dared not speak, and though she knew it was possible to think to someone unseen, she did not know how.

At last they reached the trees. The walkers straggled dully to a halt.

"Walk," Merlin commanded softly, and they walked.

They were deep in the trees before she dared call a halt. The bushes rustled and Ford burst from them, followed by Sear and the Rememberer, Marthe.

"It's Aran! And Bramble," Sear cried incredulously. "But they're all ..."

"Void! No!" cried Ford.

"*She* is not Void," Marthe said. "She hears you."

Ford stopped dead and looked closely into Merlin's face, his own chalk pale. Merlin was touched by his concern for her.

"I'm all right," she said gently. Something in her voice made Ford stare at her oddly.

"What about the others?" Sear demanded. "Aran ..."

"Will be fine!" Bramble said triumphantly. They all stared at the rebel woman in wonder and she burst out laughing. "Can I act!"

"But, how ...?" Ford asked.

"Someone in the city helped us. A Citizen," Merlin said. "We had to pretend."

"There is more . . ." Marthe prompted urgently.

Merlin stiffened, remembering what was about to take place. "Of course! We have to get away from here now. Fast! As far as we can. Something is going to happen!"

"The Citizens will return to the heavens," Sear said. "The blue-eyed Citizen god told me."

Merlin nodded, thinking fast. "That's true. But when the ship flies, the air will be filled with poisons. There will be a terrible explosion."

Sear looked uncertainly at Marthe.

"We must go now or we will all die," the Rememberer advised.

Her hard-edged voice galvanized the scatterling leader. He looked at the blank-faced Offering children. "What about them?"

"They're all right," Merlin cried. "We can bring them back to normal later. There's not enough time to explain. We have to find high ground. We must put the earth between the dome and our bodies."

"That way," Ford said, pointing towards the sun. "There is a ridge."

Merlin nodded. "Run," she ordered Danna and the others. "Run towards the sun."

Aran and the collared children broke into a trot.

"Faster!" Merlin shouted after them, and she began to run too. The rest followed.

Merlin was not fit. Very soon her breath jagged painfully in her chest, and a sharp cramp bit into her stomach.

"Keep going," Ford shouted into her ear. He took her arm and began to drag her so fast she could barely keep her feet.

"Run fast for the ridge!" Sear cried as they encountered the other waiting scatterlings. They did not ask for explanations. The wild faces of the runners warned them, and they ran too. The air was filled with panting and gasping.

"I can't," Merlin murmured.

"Unless you want to die, you must," Ford hissed, and dragged her on. Two of the collared children had begun to fall behind. Without breaking her stride, Bramble swept them up in her arms.

"Further, this is too close!" Marthe called, and they stumbled on.

Now they were running up a hill which grew steeper. "Over the other side of this hill we will be as safe as we can be," Ford gasped. "It is only a little further."

He lied, but it was as well. And still they ran. Merlin began to trip, too tired to lift her feet any more.

Some of the others had begun to walk, and no amount of cursing and driving would make them run again. Then a rumbling noise filled the air.

"What is it?" Era whispered, slowing to a walk.

Marthe looked up. "It has begun."

"Run!" Merlin cried. And though she was breathless, the terror in her voice gave even the weakest strength and they ran the last few painful metres to the top of the ridge.

Merlin flung herself over the crest of the hill slamming into a very solid tree trunk where she lay gasping air into her aching lungs. After a moment, she crawled to a position where she could see the dome.

A great roaring filled the air around them.

Bramble had deposited the two collared children lower down the hill and now flung herself down next to Merlin. "I hope this is far enough," she said, peering critically at the distance they had come.

The dome arc gleamed above the trees in the dusk sunlight, as smooth and enigmatic as a pearl. It looked no different than it had when they had approached it days before, and for a moment, it seemed to Merlin she had dreamed or Remembered all that had happened.

Then the ground began to tremble.

Sear bellied up next to Merlin. "Are we safe here?" he asked urgently.

"I don't know," Merlin admitted. "As safe as we can be." She noticed that all of the scatterlings had crawled to the lip of the hill and were staring down at the dome, the sun gilding their faces and reflected in their golden eyes.

The low rumbling noise increased steadily in

volume until the air vibrated eerily. A little quiver of fear went through the watchers.

"It is the ship of the Citizens," Sear said, eyes alight.

There was an earshattering burst of sound, and a terrific whoosh of air, and the ship burst from the top of the dome, seeming to pass straight through the arc without touching it. Unlike the much smaller white fliers, it flew straight up, a trail of fire streaking out behind.

The noise was deafening for a long minute, and then it began very slowly to fade as the ship rose ever higher.

"It's over," Bramble said, exalted. "We are free of them!"

"No," Marthe murmured.

No one but Merlin heard the soft word and she looked around to find the Rememberer staring at her with a knowing intensity. Ford had told her no one could read a person's mind without them knowing it, but Merlin guessed the Rememberer's strange foresight allowed her liberties the other clanpeople could not take.

The others were getting to their feet, laughing in relief and staring up to see the golden ship flying higher. Merlin did not rise, but she looked up too, bidding a silent farewell to William, and praying he would understand what she had done.

"They have gone, all of them?" Era asked.

"All," Ford echoed.

"Then we are free," Era said gladly.

Merlin noticed that the leader of the scatterlings alone had not watched the ship for more than a moment before returning his gaze to the dome. With a sinking heart she noticed the greedy hunger fill his eyes and saw that even after all that had happened, he lusted still after the Citizens' powers and arcane knowledge. Catching Merlin's eyes on him, Sear grinned. "They have left their dome and we are well rid of them, but think of what they have left behind in the forbidden city. Think what magic devices might be there ..."

The ground began to shudder again.

Sear's eyes were puzzled and he looked up to where the ship was little more than a golden dart high in the sky. "What is it?"

Merlin shrugged, sliding her eyes away from Sear's searching gaze.

"Perhaps it is the end of the world," Era said, staring back at the dome.

"It is the end of a world," Marthe whispered, and Merlin understood that the Rememberer knew what she had done, and why. Merlin heard the satisfaction in Marthe's soft words, and yet the Rememberer gave her a dark, enigmatic look.

The ground heaved violently, and those standing were thrown to their knees, crying out in fear and clutching at the twitching earth as if they feared it meant to throw them off into the sky.

"It must be the Citizens," Bramble said.

Sear looked at her sharply, then he stared down at the dome.

"Get down," Merlin said. "Don't look at the dome!"

The collared children obeyed instantly, but the scatterlings looked from Merlin to their leader uncertainly.

"The dome? What are you saying?" Sear shouted the question at Merlin.

"Get down and close your eyes or you will die, all of you," she said fiercely.

Sear cursed, then dropped to his hands and knees, closing his eyes and ordering his followers to do the same.

There was a waiting silence, then the ground heaved again. Merlin prayed silently that the ancient instructions and warnings she had read inside the computer's programming were accurate.

"What is happening?" Sear demanded.

But before anyone could venture an answer, there was a terrible clap of sound and then a smaller boom from a different direction. Only Merlin understood that this was the smaller dome. Her ears were pierced with agony. Dimly, she heard screams from the others, and a wetness trickled from her nose. Blood.

Then there was a brightness that burned her eyes,

even through tightly closed eyelids. The heaving earth slowly settled to stillness, and the rumbling in the heavens faded into nothing.

Gingerly, Merlin opened her eyes. She saw that everyone's noses were bleeding, and Aran was also bleeding from the ears. Two of the Offered children and a number of the scatterlings were lying on their backs, unconscious, and Era was rocking back and forwards, holding her ears. There was a deep, abiding silence, but gradually the deafness caused by the explosion subsided, and Merlin realized the scatterlings were moaning and weeping.

She stood shakily, and looked over the ridge. Where the dome had risen above the tree tops, there was nothing but black seared earth. No dome, no trees. Anything exposed to the flare of the explosion had been obliterated. Even the tops of trees and bushes which had risen above the crest were singed black. Merlin thought with a shudder how they had all lain looking at the dome. If it had exploded at that moment they would all be dead, except the Offered children, who would be doomed to be imprisoned forever in their own minds. The same devastation would have taken place where the smaller dome stood.

Those capable of standing stared open-mouthed at the black earth.

"It's all right now," Merlin said, as much to reassure herself as the others.

She walked on rubbery legs to where Aran and the Offered children sat, blankfaced, their eyes still shut tight. She took the deactivating device from her pocket and neutralized the collars.

One by one, they came to themselves.

Predictably, Danna was first to speak. "What happened? We were in the dome and that Citizen boy ..." He wiped the blood from his nose and looked at it in bewilderment. The children who had passed out stirred and groaned.

Aran looked around and Bramble clapped him heartily on the shoulders. "Welcome back from the dead, my friend."

They stared at one another, and Merlin guessed they both thought of those who had died, of Meer and Ranulf and the rest.

"They have gone," Bramble said. "The Citizen gods have gone forever."

"The Citizen boy collared you only so that he could get us out of the dome safely," Merlin told Danna. She felt oddly weary and even talking required a great effort of will, but she did not want Danna and the others thinking badly of William when he had done so much for them. She forced herself to go on. "Now the Citizens have flown away and the dome is destroyed." There was much more than that, but she felt too tired to explain more fully.

"Nooo!" Sear shouted, looking over the blackened ground where once the dome had stood. He stared down at Merlin, white-faced with fury. "You knew this was going to happen. You warned us. How did you know?"

Merlin lied without shame. "I Remembered."

Sear looked taken aback. "The Citizens did this. They have made sure we cannot ever know their secrets." Era moved to stand beside him, and slid her hand into his.

"Does it really matter?" she asked softly. "Look at that ugliness. That is what their great powers could do. We don't need such things. They have gone and the dark times are ended. The clans are free, and we must return to tell them what has happened."

The rigid anger melted from Sear's face and he smiled ruefully. "Yes. You are right. I let my hunger for the magics overcome me." He looked around, and for the first time everyone noticed that the shadows were long and gold-edged.

"Soon it will be dark. It is too late to return to the Hide. We will make camp here tonight and tomorrow we will go home."

"Why not go straight to Conclave?" Bramble suggested. "It is not over yet."

Sear shook his head firmly. "If we appear now before Conclave and tell our story, no one will believe us. The chances are they will think we sabotaged a flier and stole you and Aran and the others. We would be executed. It is too big and too strange a thing to tell. We must wait until the clans have begun to notice the absence of the Citizens and wonder at it. By then, the Lord wardens will have run out of their precious visiondraught and their agony will give weight to our accusations."

The others nodded. Danna rose and faced Sear.

"I am not one of your followers."

Sear looked at the boy thoughtfully. "This is true. I do not wish to force you to join me, yet we need time to prepare ourselves. The Citizens have gone from the Region of Great Trees and I claim this Region for my own clan."

"What?" Bramble asked, looking startled.

"Why not?" Sear said. "It would not be easy now to go back to the old clans and live under the wardens' rules, even without the Offerings. I am a man now, not a boy." He looked at Aran. "It is one year until next Conclave. For that year I ask you to stay, and when that year is over, you may choose to remain with us, or return to your old clan with gifts of goodwill from the scatterlings."

"Perhaps you will not mind too much the loss of your fine tents and jewels," Bramble grinned.

Reluctantly, the sad-eyed Aran smiled.

"Perhaps the wilderness will offer other compensations."

"What will you call your clan?" Danna asked. "Scatterling clan?"

Ford hesitated thoughtfully, then he shook his head. "Scatterling was a name for rebels. We need a new respectable name if the other clans are to take us seriously. I think we will call ourselves ..." He grinned mischievously. "Dome clan."

There was a shocked murmur, and then laughter.

Bramble said: "We cannot have a clan without barter. What shall we barter?"

"We must explore this Region to see what it offers for trade. We must see what skills are among us. That is not a thing we should decide lightly."

"Who will be wardens?" asked Beta.

Ford looked at her. "We will choose. Wardens will be chosen for wisdom, not age, and by all the clan."

There was a murmur of agreement. Again Sear looked at Danna. "What do you say?"

Danna frowned. "Wordbond that we may leave without strife at the end of a year?"

"Mindbond," Sear said solemnly.

Danna turned to face the others. "I think we should accept this offer. If we return, the clans will think we have escaped and kill us. Even if we submit to mind testing, they will not believe. They will think us demon-filled and we will die anyway." Gradually the others nodded, and Danna turned to Sear.

"We will accept your offer and your laws if they are fair," Danna said.

Merlin sighed and turned away, wondering why she felt so flat and dispirited. She looked at the sun as it sank like a molten gold disk in the west, seeming at the last to melt into the indistinct horizon.

It was dawn and those in the makeshift ridge camp slept, exhausted from the singing and exaltations of the night before.

Only Merlin was awake, and she stared at the black earth lit by the clear crisp dawn light. She thought she had never seen anything so ugly in all her life, and wondered if it were the ugliness that depressed her.

Somehow she had the feeling it was not all over. There was a feeling in her of things undone.

She looked up and wondered if the Citizens had D-jumped before seeing the dome explode. She hoped not. She hoped William had seen and understood what she had done. She smiled wanly, thinking how easy it had been to link up the retaliation programming of the master computer with the ship launch, so that when the ship was launched the dome and its smaller brother would be destroyed.

And the domes, which would have acted as beacons to the D-jumpers when they returned, were no more.

I did what I wanted, and no one was killed, so why do I feel that something is still left to be done? she wondered.

"Because there is something else to be done," Marthe said.

Merlin started, for the Rememberer had come to stand beside her so softly she had not been aware of her presence.

"I don't understand," Merlin said. "What else is there? The dome is destroyed. The Citizens can never come back and the earth belongs to the clans. The clans are safe from them."

"Are they?" Marthe demanded.

Merlin was puzzled. "What more can they do? Even the small dome and all that was in it is gone. There is nothing left."

"Isn't there?" Marthe asked.

Merlin felt suddenly irritated. "What are you trying to say?"

Marthe looked around at those sprawled out beside the fire, then she walked over the ridge crest, signalling for Merlin to accompany her.

"My Remembering tells me that there is danger still," she said in a conversational tone.

"Perhaps the Remembering is wrong. It was wrong before," Merlin retorted, recalling how the Rememberer had sent her away.

"*Was* the Remembering wrong?" Marthe questioned.

Merlin stopped and faced her. "Look here. Stop doing that."

"What?" Marthe looked startled.

"Making the things I say into questions," Merlin said angrily.

Marthe shrugged. "It is the Rememberer's way. We learn not to give answers but to help others find their own answers. This matter is not ended and the means to end it lie in your hands. My Remembering still warns that you are a danger and might destroy not only the scatterlings, but the clans."

Merlin stopped and stared blankly at the Rememberer. "In case you don't know it, I *saved* them all from the Citizens. I got rid of the ones who were here, and I got rid of the ones who would have come," she said indignantly.

"Tyranny is not the only danger," Marthe said firmly. "If that was all it was, the clans would eventually have dealt with it themselves. Know that there are more subtle dangers offered by the decadent old world to this fledgeling one."

"Even if that were true, the Citizens are gone," Merlin said, exasperated.

"Are they?" Marthe murmured, then she smiled ruefully. "I'm sorry. The answer to your question is that no, they are not completely gone. A piece of them remains, and that piece is enough to destroy the clans. Think about that, Merlin. Only you can remove the danger."

The Rememberer turned back to the camp, leaving Merlin staring after her.

She means me, Merlin thought incredulously. She opened her mouth to challenge the Rememberer, then she stopped.

Suddenly, William's words came to her. He believed the greatest difference between the old corrupt people and the new was the telepathy which prevented their world from being based on deception. He believed telepathic communication could not lie. So did the clanfolk.

But Merlin could lie and hide her mind from probing. She had telepathy, but it did not stop her lying. That very ability had enabled her to access the computer and free the Citizen ship.

And it set her apart from both Citizen and clan.

She thought of the way Sear had immediately believed her the night before when she had sworn she knew nothing of the destruction of the dome. And she had done so without a qualm. For good reason, but, still lies.

William's wonderfully created mind graft had given her a weapon which had enabled her to free the clans from the domination of the Citizens. But now that weapon remained. The clanpeople were defenceless against her lies, and how long before they would begin to see that lying was useful and easy. How long before she would teach them how to lie and cheat?

She shuddered, understanding.

She was the last danger. The Rememberer's seeing was true. All along it had been true.

"But what can I do?" she whispered.

"Only you can remove the danger," Marthe had said.

Merlin's eyes filled with tears. "I have to go," she said, and spoken, the words seemed to hover prophetically in the air.

She returned slowly to the makeshift camp, her heart heavy and bitter.

Marthe sat by the fire, feeding it twigs, restoring it to life. Her eyes searched Merlin's face for a long moment, then she nodded.

"You will go?" she asked softly.

Merlin nodded, not trusting herself to speak.

The Rememberer's eyes were filled with compassion. "I am sorry, but it must be this way. It would be best if you go now before the others wake. I will tell them as much as they need to know."

Merlin frowned. "Isn't that a lie?"

"A withholding," Marthe corrected gently. "Rememberers are trusted to withhold only what must remain unknown."

Merlin sighed. The Rememberer rose and touched Merlin's cheek.

"Life rewards those who do what they must with courage and conviction."

Merlin smiled wanly. "I find it hard to believe this is any kind of reward. I thought I would be able to stay, to make a home. It doesn't seem fair. Where will I go?"

Marthe pointed. "Travel that way. The land is wild and there are many creatures but no true humans."

Merlin took a deep breath and straightened her back. "Well, if I'm going I might as well go. Good-bye. Tell the others ..." Merlin looked down to where Ford lay sleeping. "Tell them I'm not like them. I'm an alien who doesn't belong. Tell them I'm sorry."

Marthe inclined her head, and Merlin left the camp-site quickly, not looking back.

She had been walking briskly, concentrating on the sweet, clean air and the warmth of the sunlight, when it occurred to her she had come away ill-prepared. She had no food, no water and nothing to protect herself with. She shrugged. Later in the day it would be hot, but for now she walked in the sun. She would have to organize food, clothing and a weapon of some description. Perhaps a stave like Era had carried. And then, she thought, I'll have to teach myself to use it.

She heard a rustling noise in the trees behind her and whirled, changing her mind about her priorities.

"You are still easy prey," Ford grinned, striding through the trees. He was panting slightly.

"What are you doing?" she demanded, angry because he had frightened her.

Ford smirked. "Following you."

"Really?" Merlin grated. "What I want to know is why you feel compelled to follow me?"

The scatterling laughed aloud, a merry sound that rang in the air. "I wanted to," he said. Merlin opened her mouth, but before she could utter a word, Ford leaned over and set down a great bag he had been carrying over one shoulder.

"What on earth . . .?" Merlin said.

He knelt and untied the edges of the bag to reveal knives and skins and food and tinder and boots. "I packed in a hurry," he said. "You didn't give me much choice."

"Much . . . I didn't ask you to come! I don't want you to come."

"Don't you?" Ford asked, sounding for all the world like the Rememberer.

"Don't do that," Merlin snapped.

Ford began to divide the cache. "I'm glad I finally caught up with you because you can take some of this. You can have this knife and this cloak. Oh, and you can carry . . ."

Merlin sighed in exasperation. "You're not coming with me," she said firmly.

"Haven't we gone through this before?" Ford asked, imperturbably continuing to divide his goods.

"You can't come," Merlin said. "Marthe . . ."

Ford smiled delightedly. "Oh, Marthe. Well, as a matter of fact, she sent me."

"What!"

"She did," Ford said. "She told me you had gone off and you had forgotten everything. What with one thing and another we thought I should come after you."

"Oh, you did, did you?" Merlin asked with asperity.

Ford smiled. "You see, she Remembered a little bit more. She Remembered that I was supposed to come with you, to keep you out of trouble. You wouldn't last a day on your own."

"I don't believe you."

"It's true, there are wild creatures and look how close I got before you heard me . . ."

"I don't mean that, I mean I don't believe Marthe Remembered any such thing."

"Clanfolk don't lie," Ford said.

Merlin opened her mouth, then closed it, realizing if Ford were telling a lie, he had already been affected by her, and if he weren't lying, Marthe really had Remembered something more.

"Good," Ford said. "Now that's settled, how about something to eat. I left without breakfast and I'm starving."

"I have been this way before, though it is forbidden. There are more of the old places that you call cities this way," Ford Sent.

Merlin looked at him with interest. *"Really? And they're all empty?"* She was enjoying her increasing mastery of talking mind to mind.

Ford shrugged. *"There are no clan tribes."*

Merlin looked forward with new interest. They had left the Region of Great Trees the previous day and now they walked over what seemed to be an endless grassy plain.

"How long does the grass go on for?" she asked aloud.

The scatterling youth frowned. "Rocky ground comes next, and then more trees. And beyond that are white hills of salt. At least I think it's salt. I've never been that far."

"Hills of . . . snow." Merlin's memory offered up pictures of frozen water falling as snowflakes.

"Snow . . ." Ford murmured. "What is snow?"

"Frozen water," Merlin said with a thrill of excitement.

"That Citizen who helped you escape," Ford said,

very casually, "Danna said he was sick and pale like a poisoned foxen."

Merlin looked at the scatterling curiously. "His name was William. He was dying. If he hadn't helped us, we would have been killed when the dome exploded."

Ford nodded. "Why do you think he helped you?"

Merlin thought of the cold tender kiss of the Citizen boy, and willed a rush of tears from her eyes. William's voice no longer intruded in her thoughts, but she could call it up as she chose, just as she could call up other knowledge bestowed on her by the computer. It was her legacy, and likely to be useful in whatever lay ahead of them.

Ford was watching her closely, waiting for an answer.

"I don't know why he did it," she lied.

"Did you feel the mating heat for him?" he demanded.

"I liked him," Merlin said. "I think this mating heat of yours is a bit more complicated than just liking somebody."

"What is complicated about it? You feel the hunger, you share body heat," Ford said.

Merlin repressed a smile. "It's more complicated than that for *me*."

"So," Ford said, his eyes avoiding hers. "What is your way?"

This time Merlin grinned openly. "We must know

one another as friends first. We must share eating and laughing and crying and many many words before anything else."

"Friends," Ford said dismissively. "*The clan way is better*," he Sent plaintively.

Merlin smiled broadly, then she laughed out loud. Ford looked at her, astonished.

"Why do you laugh?"

Merlin could not answer for laughing. He had sounded so put out! She watched her laugh and his astonishment made her laugh all the more.

Reluctantly, he smiled, and then he laughed too, finally caught up in her mirth. But when their laughter was spent, Ford gave Merlin a cunning sideways look.

"Well," he said slyly. "We have shared laughter. That's a good start."

"Oh, don't," Merlin begged, starting to laugh again.

They laughed harder still, until their bellies ached and tears squirted from their eyes. And their laughter echoed across the endless flat plain that lay before them, startling a bird that rose from its nest uttering a squawk of protest.